GLENN TRUST
TARGET DOWN

BOOKS

By Glenn Trust

Sole Justice

Sole Survivor

Road to Justice

Target Down

The Ghost

Dark Winter

Shadow Man

Vinci Books

vinci-books.com

Published by Vinci Books Ltd in 2025

1

Copyright © Glenn Trust 2020

The author has asserted their moral right to be identified as the author of this work in accordance with the Copyright, Designs and Patents Act 1988. This work is a work of fiction. Names, characters, places and incidents are the product of the author's imagination or are used fictitiously. Any resemblance to actual persons, living or dead, places and incidents is entirely coincidental.

All rights reserved. No part of this publication may be copied, reproduced, distributed, stored in any retrieval system, or transmitted in any form or by any means, including photocopying, recording, or other electronic or mechanical methods, nor used as a source for any form of machine learning including AI datasets, without the prior written permission of the publisher.

The publisher and the author have made every effort to obtain permissions for any third party material used in this book and to comply with copyright law. Any queries in this respect should be brought to the attention of the publisher and any omissions will be corrected in future editions.

A CIP catalogue record for this book is available from the British Library.

Paperback ISBN: 9781036704360

Printed and bound in Great Britain by Clays Ltd, Elcograf S.p.A.

PART I
Cat and Mouse

ONE

The Drill

He knew the drill. Actually, he invented it, part of it at least—the important part.

Dressed in a worn Army battle dress jacket from the Desert Storm Conflict era, he wandered aimlessly along city streets, muttering to himself or giving harsh looks to passersby. Sometimes he would stumble into a wall and lean there for support, appearing to rest and catch his breath.

It was all an act and the first part of the drill. That wasn't the part he invented, but he had learned to play the role of the homeless vet to perfection. That was the setup.

The aimless wandering came to an end when he rounded a corner, and his target was in sight. He had selected it earlier in the day, driving the neighborhood. Sometimes he drove for hours to find just the right spot. Today he had found it just minutes after arriving in the city.

It was a place along a curb across the street from a Detroit bar. The dealers worked as a team. One stood near the corner, taking cash from buyers. His partner stood at the other end of the block, near a public trash can. The theory was that if the cash-man got stopped and frisked by police, it was no big deal. There was no law about having a wad of money in his pockets, and he never had more than a thousand or so on him. When business was heavy, he would step inside a nearby door and hand off some of the cash to a third man working with them. Business was light today, and there was no third man.

After handing over the money, the customer made his or her way down the block where the second dealer would make a standard street pass, their hands touching briefly in the exchange. The buyer moved on to get high somewhere. The dealers set up for the next customer.

If the police approached the drug man, he tossed the drugs in the trash can and played innocent. Sometimes they caught on. Sometimes they didn't.

John Sole caught on. He had seen the technique operate before in Atlanta and spotted immediately what was going down on this seedy block, in a rundown Detroit neighborhood.

He approached the cash-man and stood swaying before him as he reached into his pocket.

"Hurry the fuck up, man. What you tryin' to do, bring heat on us?" The dealer put a hand under his shirt resting it on the butt of a nine-millimeter pistol tucked inside his Stone Island designer jeans. "And when you bring that hand outta your pocket, it better have cash in it and nothing else, or you one dead motherfucker."

"Naw, man," Sole swayed and slurred his words, looking up at the dealer as he pulled a wad of bills from the jacket pocket. "Naw … just cash … I'm good. Just wanna get high."

"Shit. You already high," cash-man said as Sole counted out three hundred dollars from a roll that contained several thousand.

Sole fumbled with the bills, slowly counting them out, giving cash-man plenty of time to salivate. Then he handed the money over.

"I need three."

"Three what?" The dealer snatched the bills from Sole's hand before he could answer.

"Grams … three grams."

"Shit, motherfucker, you light then. You tryin' to rip me off?"

"No … no." Sole shook his head. "No, I thought three hundred would cover it."

"Naw, man. Not tonight." The dealer grinned. "Tonight, that gonna be a grand."

"But …" Sole started then closed his mouth, playing the needy user who craved a hit. "Fuck."

He reached into his pocket for the wad of bills again and counted out another seven hundred.

"Fuck, man. Where you get that money? Must be ten thousand there." The dealer was transfixed by the crumpled wad of cash. "Who you rob?" He grinned. "That's it, ain't it. You robbed someone."

"Ain't sayin'." Sole shook his head and handed over the money.

"I bet you ain't." The dealer laughed and nodded down the street. "See the man at the end of the block." Then he pocketed the cash, lifted his hand to the flat-brimmed ball cap he wore, holding out three fingers.

It was the signal that the buyer wanted three grams. His partner made no signal in reply but turned to walk toward the trash can where they concealed the drugs.

Sole wobbled up the street. As he walked by, the dealer turned from the trash can and passed the three plastic bags. It was a clumsy pass because Sole made it clumsy, stumbling and bumping into the dealer.

"Shit, man. What the fuck's your problem. You fuckin' get me busted, and I'll find you and put a cap in your ass."

The dealer gave him a shove, and Sole moved away. He stood on the curb swaying as if he might fall over, looked across the street, and headed for the bar.

Inside, he found a single high-top table in a corner and sat. The bartender called out to him, "No sittin' unless you're drinkin'."

Sole looked up, his brow furrowed as if he was confused by the bartender's directive.

"I said, drink, or get the fuck out!" The bartender picked up a bat from behind the counter and moved to the end of the bar, ready to run the vagrant out.

Sole nodded. "Okay, okay. Gimme a Jack."

The bartender put the bat back in its hiding place and poured a shot of Jack Daniels. He called out, "No table service. Come get your drink."

Sole nodded and wobbled over to the bar. When he reached for the drink, the bartender put a beefy hand over the glass. "That'll be six-fifty ... cash ... now."

"Oh, right." Sole nodded. And fumble in his pocket for the roll of bills. He made the same show with it as he thumbed through the bills and pulled out a ten. "Here, keep it."

"I will." The bartender took the ten from his hand and turned away.

Sole returned to his table with the drink. He walked carefully, each step deliberate as if he were trying very hard not to fall over.

When he was seated again, he put the drink in front of him, and hunched over the tabletop, throwing a furtive glance around the bar. A few patrons noticed, said something to each other, and then returned to their drinks, pretending to ignore him, but nobody was ignoring him. The cash had everyone's attention.

When the eyes turned away from him, he pulled a plastic bag from his jacket pocket, looked around to make sure no one was watching, and poured some of the contents on the table, taking care to seal the bag again and stuff it back in his pocket. Then he pulled the roll of bills out once more and peeled off a twenty.

With the edge of the bill, he cut the white powder into two good-sized lines. Then he rolled the bill into a tight cylinder, hunched over, and snorted the powder, like a man desperate for it.

When he sat up straight, he shook his head as if to clear it and noticed a couple of patrons eying him. "What the fuck you looking at?"

The patrons looked away.

He didn't invent that either, snorting fake cocaine. Hollywood invented that. The white powder was actually Inositol, a B-complex vitamin, available at any health food store. Snorting it was harmless enough—at least as harmless as inhaling any powder into your lungs could be. Actors had been doing it for years to give the appearance of taking drugs on a movie set. It provided no high, although some claimed the vitamin B did give them an energy boost. Sole never noticed any boost.

Not long after he snorted the fake cocaine and returned the baggie to his pocket, the two dealers made their way across the street and entered the bar. They gave a surreptitious nod to the bartender who returned the gesture, unaware that the worn-out vet in the corner watched everything.

The dealers sat at the bar and ordered drinks. They spoke in low tones to the bartender. After a few minutes, they came over to Sole's table.

"Hey, man." It was cash-man. "You know I shorted you out there."

Sole looked up bleary-eyed. "Shorted me?"

"Yeah, I saw that roll of bills, and I got greedy … charged you a grand for that coke."

"Shorted me?" Sole repeated, trying to focus his eyes on them.

"Yeah, shorted. You fuckin' hard of hearin'?"

"No." Sole shook his head. "No, I hear good."

"Good, that's good," cash-man said. "Look here. I can see you a vet. You seen some shit, right?"

"Some shit." Sole smirked and nodded. "Yeah, I seen some shit." He reached for the empty shot glass and waved it at the bartender.

The bartender nodded, poured another shot of Jack.

This time he brought it to the table and walked away without asking for payment.

"So, like I say," cash-man continued. "We see you a vet. My uncle was a vet too. So, you see, we got that in common."

Sole nodded and reached for the shot glass without speaking, focused on getting the whiskey to his mouth without spilling any.

"Anyway, man, it got me feelin' guilty. We shouldn't a done you that way. We want to make it up to you ... you know bein' a vet and all."

"Make it up?" Sole turned his eyes from one to the other, as if trying to piece together a puzzle.

"Yeah, make it up. We got more shit ... better shit than the cheap-ass stuff we sold you. We want to even things up."

"Even things up?" Sole's said.

"Yeah, that's what I said. We gonna give you the good shit to make up for tryin' to rip you off."

Sole sat and stared at the table for a few seconds as if trying to make sense of everything cash-man had said.

"You want to even things up ... with some good shit?"

"That's right." The two dealers grinned, and cash-man nodded. "We gonna make it up to you."

"How much?"

"Like I said, we feel bad about cheatin' you. You already paid, so this is on the house. It's yours."

"Okay," Sole said and held his hand out. "Let me have the good shit."

The dealer laughed and looked around, pushing his hand back down on the table. "Not here, man. Never know who's listening." Cash-man nodded toward the bar. "Out back. We keep the good shit stashed behind a brick in the wall ... out in the alley.

"Okay." Sole stood and reached out for the table to steady himself. "Let's get the good shit."

"My man." Cash-man grinned and slapped him on the back.

The dealers led him behind the bar, through the kitchen, and out the back door. The bartender followed.

"It's just over here." Cash-man led the way to a point on the wall where the mortar around the bricks had crumbled with age.

They stood in front of him and turned together, pulling their pistols from their waistbands. The grins on their faces faded as they tried to bring the barrels up to fire.

With a barrel length of less than three and a half inches, the Walther PPK was almost invisible in his hand. Before they could raise their arms, he squeezed the trigger rapidly four times, sending two rounds each into their heads. At a distance of three feet, he couldn't miss. They dropped without ever knowing they were dead.

As they fell, he turned, the Walther held out in front. It happened so quickly that, at first, the bartender thought the dealers had done what they set out to do—shoot the coked-up vet so they could rob him.

The pistol pointed at his face, the bartender was outmatched, and he knew it. He held the bat up in front defensively, as if he could use it to swat away the bullets. He couldn't.

The .380 caliber Walther had four rounds left. Sole sent two through the bartender's forehead, then turned and walked from the alley.

The deaths of the dealers would send yet one more message to the *Los Salvajes* cartel. He was still out there. If they wanted to end his rampage, they would have to follow his trail, find him, and kill him if they could.

That was the part of the drill John Sole had invented. It was the part that kept him motivated. They would come for him, and he would be ready.

TWO

Find John Sole

No one sat. This was a council of war, and everyone stood before Alejandro Garza, like soldiers before their general, intent on every word he spoke.

"What information do you have on his location?" Garza looked from face to face waiting for an answer.

No one wanted to speak first. There was no news to give, not good news at any rate. The man they had been seeking for months had eluded them at every turn. A few times, they came close to laying hands on him, but not close enough. They closed in only to find him already gone, sometimes not more than an hour before their arrival.

Garza nodded at one of his senior lieutenants. "Speak Andres. I only want to hear the truth."

He was calm. Garza always remained calm. That was what worried his subordinates. They had no way to detect what might be boiling beneath the surface of his stone-like exterior. The one thing they all understood was that he did not tolerate failure, and the hunt to locate and capture John Sole had gone on for far too long.

Andres nodded. Appointed by Garza as the spokesman, he had no choice but to speak for the others.

"Our people spotted him in Colorado … in Denver," Andres began. "Our information is that he remained there for at least two days."

"Two days? And no one contacted us."

"He made contact with a low-level street dealer, not one high in our organization. It was only after the dealer met with his local boss that he saw the photo and recognized the man, Sole, as someone who bought cocaine from him earlier in the day. The next day the man, Sole, met with the dealer again to buy more cocaine."

"And?"

"And after that, he was gone. No more contact with him." Andres hesitated a moment, intent on every hint of expression passing across Garza's face then added, "Perhaps we should eliminate this dealer to send a message to the others … spread the word to the other cities that they cannot fail again."

Garza's brow slanted down in the way that they recognized as his only outward expression of displeasure. His voice remained calm.

"No. The dealer is not at fault here, but his supplier in Denver, his boss and our man, he should be held accountable."

"I'll see to it personally," Andres said, anxious to make up for the bad news he had delivered.

"Everyone is to be familiar with his picture. I thought I made that clear."

"You did, *jefe*. The photo from the newspaper was there. It seems our man simply failed to show it to this small dealer. Otherwise, he would have recognized Sole."

"Alright." Garza's dark eyes signaled it was time to move

on. A message would be sent. The other suppliers and dealers working for *Los Salvajes* would understand, if they did not already, that they would be held accountable for future failures to find Sole.

"After Denver, do we have any word of him?" Garza continued.

"Yes." Andres took a breath and prepared himself to deliver more bad news. There was no point in lying. The penalty for lying to Garza was the worst of all punishments. Those found guilty of deliberately hiding the truth had been known to linger for days, begging for death, before Garza would allow them to escape this world and their pain.

Andres, continued, "He stopped in Pueblo, another city in Colorado. It is one of our growing markets."

"And there he was recognized but not confronted."

"Yes, but he stayed only for a brief time … perhaps two hours, or less even. His behavior is strange, though."

"I'm listening," Garza snapped.

"Again, he bought cocaine from our dealer. The dealer did recognize him this time. He notified his supplier, who told him to follow the man. The dealer did and saw him go into a bar."

"A bar?"

"Yes. According to the bartender, he ordered one beer, drank it, and left within a few minutes." Andres shook his head. "They say it seemed he wanted to be recognized."

"And from there?" Garza's face showed no emotion, and Andres had no idea how he was processing the information he provided.

"The dealer followed him on foot to a parking garage. Sole got into his vehicle and left before our people could get to him. The whole incident lasted perhaps fifteen minutes, less even. It was not enough time for our people to get to him, and the dealer alone would not be equipped to confront a man like this."

"No, he would not," Garza agreed. "And after Pueblo?"

"No sign yet," Andres said frankly. "But he will show up somewhere. He always does."

"Alright. Nothing has changed. Find John Sole."

THREE

An Unfriendly Sort

At around ten thousand feet, he had to pull over. The low, high-altitude air pressure had the radiator coolant boiling and the pickup's engine overheating.

John Sole pulled onto the narrow shoulder, leaving the left two tires on the road. The right side of the truck almost touched the guard rail. Not the best place for engine trouble. He checked the rearview mirror as the truck came to a stop. There was no traffic in sight. In fact, he hadn't seen another vehicle for the last ten miles.

Pushing the door open, he stepped out into the road, raised his arms over his head in a luxurious stretch, and took a deep breath. In the valleys below, temperatures climbed into the nineties. At the top of the Sandia Mountains, the air blew fresh and crisp, carrying with it the scent of pine and cedar.

Sole went to the front of the truck and opened the hood. The engine popped and clicked metallically while the radiator coolant boiled over into the reservoir, bubbling as it cooled.

"Well, John-boy," he sighed. "Looks like you'll be here for a while."

He leaned against the truck, taking in the view. Beyond the guardrail, the mountain sloped away, revealing a spectacular vista across a valley to more mountains. She would like this, he thought.

"Which she?" the voice in his head asked. "Isabella or Shaye?"

"Both," he answered himself and laughed.

For a while, he had considered the possibility that he might be losing his mind. There were days when he carried on long conversations with himself. The more the miles piled up, separating him from the past, the more isolated he became. He didn't mind at first, but with the isolation came a nagging need to talk, to converse, to say something out loud, to remain human.

There was only one human in his life now. He'd learned that lesson the hard way. No friends, not even casual acquaintances, could be permitted to penetrate his shell. The dangers were too great for them and for him. It was better for everyone if he remained isolated from the world. That left him one person to talk to—himself.

Concern about his sanity faded in time. He was fine, he told himself. Conversing with the voice in his head was simply a defense mechanism. His brain used it to ward off the inevitable loss of reason that comes from complete isolation. It was the brain's way of saying, we're gonna keep you sharp and sane, John-boy, at least for a while, until things are done. That's the way he talked it over with the voice, and the voice agreed.

"Yes, they'd love this." He smiled and took another deep breath.

In the months since leaving Isabella in Georgia, the old pickup had taken him across thousands of miles of highway, back roads and, city streets. First, west through Missouri to Kansas City. Then north to Minneapolis, and from there, over to Chicago and Detroit. He considered crossing into Canada from Detroit but wondered if the *Los Salvajes* cartel would be able to follow him there. Probably, he thought, but he wasn't sure, and he needed them to follow. That was the point of everything he was doing.

He turned south and west again. Indianapolis, St. Louis, and finally Denver. In each city, he sought out the places where they might be searching for him.

The residents of the cities thought they were unique, somehow special. They gave themselves nicknames—America's Crossroads, Twin Cities, Motor City, Big D, Forest City, Mile High. He visited them all and found they weren't so special.

The same seedy underworld existed in all of them, lurking just out of sight of the people who thought their city was special. And that underworld was always the same, inhabited by the same demons, regardless of the city's nickname. Drugs changed hands. People killed for the price of a hit of meth or heroin. Women sold themselves to survive or to feed their drug habit. The same grinning faces laughed while others died.

These are the places John Sole found in each city. He made himself visible, bought drugs he didn't use, walked streets, sat in bars where his was the only strange face, just so they would take notice, recognize him, and pass the word —he's here, the one you are looking for we saw him here in Detroit, or Milwaukee or Denver. Then he moved on, leaving a trail for them to follow.

When it seemed the cartel may not be paying close

enough attention, he would leave a body behind. It was always someone tied to the cartel, whose misfortune was to be standing on a street corner while John Sole passed. He felt no guilt as long as he had their attention.

From Denver, he turned south. A newspaper there had said that Pueblo, Colorado had the highest per capita murder rate in the state, and attributed the murders and associated crimes to the local gang problem. Gangs in Pueblo. That meant drugs in Pueblo. It wasn't a place he would have considered visiting on his odyssey, but he decided he might as well leave no stone unturned and headed down the interstate toward Pueblo.

Once in the city, it didn't take long to identify the area he sought. He drove slowly, eyes scanning side to side. Two men in an alley passed each other, a word spoken, their hands briefly touching. The telltale signs of a drug buy.

A few minutes later, he found a city parking lot, left the pickup, and walked back to the alley. Heads turned. Eyes stared. Voices whispered.

Some figured he had to be a cop. Others said, "Naw, man. He just a stoner. Check out that doped up crazy look on the fucker's face."

A few simply shook their heads and said the white boy walking down the sidewalk was fucking crazy. Sole tended to agree with the latter.

Crazy or not, the dealer took his money in exchange for an eightball of cocaine. Sole walked away without speaking and entered a bar at the end of the alley. The chatter inside died out as he took a seat on a stool and ordered a beer.

"Five-O in the house," a voice called out.

"Fuckin' pig," another said.

The bartender stared into his face as he put the beer in front of him. Maybe he recognized him. Sole hoped he did, and sipped the beer slowly so the bartender had time to get a good look at him. With luck, he would report to the local cartel gangbangers that he'd seen the one they were looking for, the one in the newspaper picture.

His work completed, he finished the beer and left, walked to his truck, and headed out of town. That was how he ended up on the road over the crest of the Sandia Mountains. Albuquerque was the next big city on his route. He hadn't been there yet to leave his scent behind. After Albuquerque … well, he hadn't thought that far ahead. Just keep moving, always away from Isabella.

A car approached from the south. It was new, and the young couple inside were laughing as they passed without slowing. Good. He didn't want them to stop and offer help.

Another twenty minutes passed. The pickup engine had cooled now, the angry popping gone. Another vehicle came along, an old man in a pickup. He slowed and rolled the window down.

"Can I give you a hand?" He leaned toward Sole and smiled. "Looks like you overheated. Yeah, altitude will do that. Had the same trouble myself."

Sole closed the truck's hood. "No."

He got behind the wheel, cranked the engine, and drove away without another word. The man watched him leave, shaking his head as he scratched under his ball cap. "Well, he's a damned unfriendly sort."

"Remember," the voice reminded Sole. "Keep moving. No friends."

FOUR

Things Were Working Out

"There's one of my clients." Billy Siever put his glass of wine on the table and gave a small wave to a familiar face as she walked into the popular steakhouse in Gainesville, Georgia.

Isabella Palmeras stopped, uncertain for a moment, and then followed the hostess to a table, trailed by Sandy and Jacinta.

"Client?" His wife, Vera, turned her head in time to see Isabella give a smile and wave back as she was seated. "She's pretty."

"I suppose so," Billy said, retrieving his wine. "I hadn't noticed."

"Oh, come on," Vera laughed. "She's beautiful. How could you not notice? Hmm ... makes me think you have indeed noticed. Anything I should be aware of?" she teased.

"Stop, Vera. She's a client, nothing more."

"A client, huh?" Vera was having fun. "Exactly what kind of ... *work* ... are you doing for her?"

"You know me better than that," Billy said. "I'm too terrified of you to be unfaithful."

"I'll bet." Vera laughed. "Seriously, what are you doing for her, or is it classified?"

"Nope, not classified. I've been helping her with a name change."

"Name change? You need a lawyer for that?"

"No, not really, but she's new to the state and wasn't sure where to begin."

"That's it ... a name change."

"That and some domestic issues she's been having. That's what the name change is all about." He smiled at his wife and added, "In the interest of full disclosure, I should also advise you that she is renting one of our houses in Gainesville. Now, have I answered your interrogatory satisfactorily, counselor?"

"You have indeed, counselor." Vera nodded at the woman at the table across the dining room. "You should go talk to her. She keeps looking this way."

Billy turned his head and caught Isabella's nervous glance. "Maybe I should."

"And have them join us," Vera added. "I like to be acquainted with our tenants."

"Fair enough." Billy nodded and stood, taking his wine glass with him.

Isabella looked up as he stopped at their table. She glanced beyond him to see his wife smiling at them. Shit, she thought. She should have just gotten take out at McDonald's.

She gave Billy a wry smile. "Sorry. I didn't mean to interrupt your meal."

"Relax." Billy smiled. "You didn't. Just wanted to see if everything is alright. Is it?"

"Everything is fine. We're settling in pretty well."

"Good. So here's the thing." He lowered his voice. "Now's your chance to get into your new characters for real."

"New characters?" Isabella's brow furrowed. "Not sure I follow."

"Your new characters … your new identities. It's easy at home, but at some point, you need to begin interacting socially. You need to become the person on the IDs we got for you. Why don't you come over and join us for dinner?"

"Oh, I don't think I can do …" Isabella started to shake her head and saw Billy's wife smiling at her from across the room.

"Sure you can," Billy insisted. "Sit with us. Vera will want to hear your story, so this will be your chance to try it out in public and get comfortable with it in a friendly setting."

"Friendly?" Isabella cast a doubtful glance at Vera, who continued to watch and smile. She was aware that women's smiles were not always what they seemed, even if Billy Siever wasn't.

Billy caught the glance and laughed. "It's not a trick. I assure you. Vera doesn't have a deceptive bone in her body. She really would like to meet you. Besides, she always wants to meet our tenants, so this visit is overdue."

Isabella looked at Sandy and Jacinta, who had listened quietly to the entire exchange. Sandy nodded. "Let's do it, Mom. He's right. We can try out our cover stories and make sure they fly."

"If you think so, then okay." Isabella stood.

"Great," Billy beamed.

He waved over a server and explained they were joining his party. It took a minute to gather some additional chairs and get everyone seated. Billy waited and was the last to take a seat. He looked from their guests to his wife.

"Vera, I'd like to introduce Abigail Banks, her son Chris and his fiancé Margarita ..." He paused. "I'm sorry Margarita. I can be so forgetful. What was your last name again?"

Jacinta looked into Vera's eyes and smiled. "Flores ... Margarita Flores. I'm pleased to meet you, Mrs. Siever." Her English became more fluent as each day passed, with just the right hint of accent.

"Please Margarita, call me Vera." She looked around the table. "I think we should all be on first-name terms, don't you?"

"I do," Isabella agreed. "And please call me Abby. Abigail is so formal. My mother wanted a little girl to dress up like a doll and play house. She always hoped I'd be a little more feminine if she called me Abigail, thinking it would steer me in the desired direction." She laughed. "It didn't. I was more tomboy than girl, hated dolls, never played house, and I always preferred Abby."

There were laughs around the table, and the evening began.

On the run from the *Los Salvajes* cartel, John Sole turned to the only person he could trust. He contacted his boyhood friend, Billy Siever, and then left to lead the cartel away from the people he had endangered.

The next day, Billy attempted to make contact with Luis Acero, the CI—criminal informant—snitch Sole worked with during his police days in Atlanta. All Billy had to work from was a voice mailbox that Sole used to send and receive messages with those he trusted.

For three days, Billy called the number morning, noon, and night, leaving a message and his number. Not being familiar with the daily schedules and activities of drug dealers and snitches, he had no idea when Acero might return the call—or if he would return it at all.

On the morning of the fourth day, Billy's cell phone rang. The display simply said 'Wireless Caller.'

Usually, he would have let a call from an unknown source go to voice mail. This time he answered immediately.

"Don't hang up." Sole had warned Billy that Acero would be nervous about accepting the call.

"Who is this?" Luis said.

"A friend gave me your number, he told me to say to you … Esteban is napping."

It was a signal from Sole. Esteban Moya, an enforcer for the *Los Salvajes* cartel, had planned to kill Luis Acero. Sole prevented that from happening by putting a bullet through his brain.

There was silence on the phone. They needed his help, but Billy knew that Acero, a snitch and a drug dealer, would have a hard time trusting anyone. The seconds ticked by while he waited and hoped Acero would not hang up and disappear forever.

Finally, Luis whispered into the phone, "Only one man s'posed to say that to me."

Billy breathed a sigh of relief. "Yes. John Sole told me the words to say. He said it was the only way you would talk to me and help us."

"You know him?"

"Yes," Billy said. "We are friends … have been since we were boys."

"I got no idea 'bout that." Acero was hesitant, every word hanging in the air by itself as if he might end the call at any moment.

"John said you were a friend too."

Several more seconds of silence passed before Acero said, "I am."

"Good. Will you help John?"

"He knows I will if I can. Why he ain't talkin' to me hisself?"

"He's on the move, leading away the people who are looking for him … and for you. What he needs might take a little time to arrange, and he didn't have the time to do it. He asked me to help."

"Seems you know who I am and who Sole is. Who are you?"

"Like I said, we're friends. My name is Billy Siever. John and I grew up together. That's more than he wanted me to say to you, but I figure if we are going to help him, we need to trust each other."

"Trustin' someone you ain't never met is a hard thing."

"I understand," Billy said quietly. "I've never met you either."

"Alright. Let's meet."

"What?" Arranging things by phone was one thing. Meeting face to face with a known drug dealer and criminal informant was something else.

"We meet. You and me. Place where I say. Then I decide if this is legit and I can help you."

"Alright." Billy swallowed. He was about to take a step off the high dive, and he had no idea how deep the water was.

The meeting took place at a bar on the outskirts of Richmond, Virginia. Acero asked questions about Siever's relationship with Sole. Billy realized that he had taken the time to do some online research and came prepared to check Siever's story against the record. From old newspapers and court records, he had learned about Sole's arrest for car theft, his father who disappeared, the death of his mother, that there were no other siblings.

It took a while. They sipped beers, and Acero quizzed Siever the way a seasoned cop would. Now and again he threw in a falsehood to see if Siever would catch it.

Finally, Acero leaned back across the high-top table and stared at Billy, making a final assessment. He knew that anyone could have found the same information that he had online, but if Siever was a killer working for the cartel, it was the best damn disguise Acero had ever seen. He made up his mind.

"Alright, what does Sole want me to do?"

Billy explained the need for three new identities and provided Acero with all the information on Isabella, Sandy, and Jacinta. They had to be entirely off the record, common names to make any search so broad that it would be impossible to trace them through any state or federal database without getting a million hits on the same names.

Acero nodded. "I got someone. I'll be in touch."

It took three more weeks to fabricate the identification for each. Acero's contact was a professional, although he didn't have a business number listed, and customers could only contact him through a referral from another customer. It was worth the wait. The product he produced was indistinguishable from government-issued identification.

A high-quality fake ID that a college student might use to get into bars and buy alcohol runs about three hundred dollars. For that, they get a driver's license with the appropriate holograms and other security features embedded and laminated. The only way to determine they are a fake is to run the identifying license number through the corresponding state DMV system.

But Billy learned there was another tier of false identification, a level reserved for those with special needs and the money to pay for it. This level included not only false driver's licenses and other necessary IDs but also fabrication of entirely new identities, mirroring those in legitimate government databases.

For those who could afford it, this was the stratosphere of false identification. It would appear as valid in every state and federal system because it used an actual person's information as its basis and sometimes several persons' information just to muddy the waters.

Additional layers were added, new addresses, moves to other states, travel, and even credit card use, all verified, and based on real transactions and locations. Like money laundering, the more levels it runs through, the harder it is for authorities to trace its source and validity.

John Sole had emphasized that they should have the very best in false identification, and Billy saw that they got it. For the price of five thousand dollars each, they had new lives. Sole paid for it all from the cash he put away from the sale of his house in the Atlanta suburbs following the murders of his wife and children.

The evening passed pleasantly. The cover stories they had prepared while the new identities were cooked up worked flawlessly.

When the check came, Billy insisted on paying for everyone. Isabella stood and leaned over to give Vera a kiss on the cheek.

"It was so nice meeting you, Vera." She looked at Billy. "And thank you for dinner. Next time, you come to our place …" She laughed. "I mean the place we rent from you, and I'll fix some home cooking."

"Sounds wonderful," Billy beamed as they walked away.

"Such nice people," Vera said.

"Yes, they are."

Billy wished there was a way to let his friend know that things were working out.

FIVE

The Key

"I will be leaving for a while."

Alejandro Garza sat across from Bebé Elizondo in the hacienda office on a hillside that overlooked the Pacific. In the city below, the port of Lázaro Cárdenas was busy with activity.

Stevedores unloaded ships and reloaded them with cargo containers bound for ports around the world. Some containers held the precious cocaine that had made Elizondo a billionaire. The losses from the seizure of their cargo by the DEA and Coast Guard during a transfer to shrimp boats in the Atlantic had been more than offset by their ever-expanding business. There was no shortage of markets for the high-quality cocaine Elizondo imported from Columbia and shipped around the globe.

"I have sensed your restlessness." Elizondo looked up from the financial report his accountant had prepared. He nodded and smiled in the benevolent Buddha way that masked the ruthless killer beneath. "It's our elusive North American who has you on edge."

"It is." Garza nodded. "We must bring this matter to a close."

"That will happen eventually in any event, will it not?"

"It must happen under our terms, in a manner in which we can control the outcome and the future effects on our business."

"I wonder," Elizondo began, leaning back in his chair. He folded his hands together under his chin, and looked at the cartel enforcer over the top of his glasses. "I wonder if perhaps you have not become too preoccupied with this John Sole. Two years have passed since we took his family from him, and yet ..." Elizondo swung his arm in a gesture to include the office and the entire hillside estate. "Here we sit, and there is no sign of him ... no threats to us ... no interference with our business."

Garza was quiet for a moment. They had had this conversation before. Each time Elizondo was more anxious than before to put the matter to rest, forget about the American, and move on. Garza would have been willing to abide by his wishes, if not for one thing.

He was convinced he knew the heart of John Sole. They were alike, he believed, bound by loyalty and a code they lived by. The codes might be different, but the loyalty and dedication to seeing the mission through to completion were the same.

The difference was that Garza's code was brutal and ruthless, while Sole's remained tied to a morality, a concept of justice. Time and again that had been made clear.

His protection of the Mexican family trying to cross the river in Texas. His escape from Texas as he safeguarded the woman and her son. His reluctance to harm anyone other than the cartel drug dealers and men Garza sent after him.

For Garza, these were insights into his adversary's character—critical insights.

Sole lived by his code, and he would never stop planning for the moment when he would secure the justice it required. It was his reason for living. Garza understood this, even if Elizondo did not. He tried to explain.

"I understand your feelings on the matter." Garza spoke in his customary, emotionless monotone. "He has been playing a game with us these last months."

"How so?" Elizondo reached for a cigar from the humidor on his desk and lit up as he listened.

"He leads us on a chase, moving from city to city, always contacting our people, making his presence known, and then leaving before there is time to confront him."

"So, he is afraid of us, perhaps?" Elizondo interjected.

"No." Garza shook his head. "He is protecting someone, taking us away from them."

"Who?"

"I have no way of being certain … yet … but I believe it may be the woman who fled with him from the town in Texas."

"He leads us away from her; is that your belief?"

"Yes."

"And where is she?"

"I don't know. After leaving Texas, they disappeared. There was no trace of them until Sole began showing up to buy drugs from our dealers, always a different city, with no pattern to his movements. He moves randomly from one location to another. We never know where he will show up next until the report comes in that he has been spotted."

"You make him sound very clever."

"He is smart." Garza nodded. "There is no denying it, but protecting others is his weakness. That's why I must be gone for a time. Finding those he cares about is the key to finding him."

"I see." Elizondo puffed, sending a plume of blue-gray smoke into the air, considering Garza's explanation. "And how will you find these others, the ones he cares about?"

"I'm not sure," Garza replied honestly. "But I am certain that I cannot find them by remaining here."

They sat across from each other in silence for several minutes. Garza waited. If Elizondo said to let the matter drop, he would have no choice but to comply. Unlike John Sole, the code he lived by demanded complete loyalty to Elizondo.

"Alright," Elizondo said, breaking the silence, the stern eyes in his round face emphasizing his words. "Go on your hunt for the woman and for the American, but after ... whether you are successful in finding him or not ... it is over. We will get back to business and wait for him to come to us, if he ever does."

Garza had no doubt that Sole would come for them eventually, but he refrained from arguing the point with Elizondo. "Thank you."

SIX

Normal

___

"See you tomorrow." Isabella stopped in the door of the small office and smiled at the balding fifty-something man behind the desk. "Want me to lock up?"

Sam Goodwin looked up from his desk and nodded. "Yeah, you might as well. Won't be any walk-ins this late, and I've got to sit here and work on the quotes for that new tire shop in Hoschton. I'll be here a while."

"Anything I can do for you?" Isabella asked, knowing the answer.

"Nope. Not a thing. One man show." Goodwin lowered his head to his keyboard and entered a few numbers, then muttered, "Shit."

He hit delete and entered some different numbers and nodded.

"Okay, don't stay too late." Isabella turned and walked through the office to the front door.

"Uh, huh," Goodwin muttered, his eyes alternating between the keyboard and the monitor on his desk. "See you tomorrow, Abby."

The Goodwin Insurance Agency was small. Mostly it was just Sam Goodwin and a staff of two, Isabella and Courtney Smallwell, a young girl barely out of high school working as a receptionist and customer greeter. Courtney planned to attend Gainesville Junior College next year, but first, she wanted to save some money and take a cruise. She had made it clear she would not be working for Goodwin longer than it took to gather the necessary funds.

That was fine with Sam. An easy-going sort, he didn't mind and didn't feel taken advantage of. He recognized the job for what it was, busy work mostly with occasional moments of interaction with clients. The only real skill required was to be able to formulate a coherent sentence and answer the phone politely. Courtney qualified, and replacing her would not be difficult.

There were a couple of agents who used Sam as their broker and maintained desks in the open front office, but they didn't write much business, and most of the profit, or loss, the agency incurred rested squarely on Sam's shoulders. The real staff was Isabella, the office manager, and Sam, the broker-agent.

Isabella pulled the glass front door shut and threw the deadbolt with her key. She looked up and down the small strip shopping center where the office was located. Most of the businesses were closed except a pizza joint at one end and a drug store at the other. It was a nondescript place for a small business, like a hundred thousand others spread around the country. Its mundane normalcy suited her perfectly.

On a recommendation from Billy Siever, Sam had hired her not long after her new identity, Abigail Banks, had been established. It was on a trial basis at first, and she had much to learn about the insurance business, but it didn't take long for Sam to realize he'd discovered a golden nugget. Abby Banks turned out to be the hardest working employee he had ever hired.

The drive to the rental house took fifteen minutes. When she arrived, Sandy's pickup was already in the driveway.

He too had found work shortly after their arrival. Bearing the new identity of Chris Banks, he soon became one of the most valued mechanics at Brandeiss Trucking. The old-timers nodded and patted him on the back, amazed at how quickly he had picked up the basics of diesel engine repair and maintenance. Chris Banks possessed an attention to detail they found lacking in most young people his age.

Jacinta stepped onto the porch as Isabella crossed the yard from the driveway. "You look tired."

"I am tired." Isabella nodded. "It's been a busy day. How about you?"

"Not too bad. I worked this morning, but got home around noon." Jacinta smiled. "I made chili for dinner."

"Mmm, I'm starved."

"Good." Jacinta held the door open as Isabella came into the house.

She had also received a new identity—Margarita Flores, a common enough name that it would be difficult to verify which Margarita Flores she was if anyone ever checked. With the name and a forged Green Card and Social Security number, Jacinta had found work in the kitchen of a diner on Highway 53.

On the surface, they appeared to be an average family, at least for a single mother living with her nineteen-year-old son and his Mexican fiancée. Sometimes, Isabella worried about everything unraveling and exposing them. She kept the worries to herself. Sandy and Jacinta were adjusting to their new lives. In time, they really would be Chris and Magarita. In fact, the plans for their wedding were underway for them to become Chris and Magarita Banks.

The date was set for next month. It would be a small affair, just some friends from their jobs and Billy and Vera Siever.

Isabella hung her handbag on a hook by the front door and dropped into a chair. Sandy came from the kitchen with two brown longnecks in his hand.

"Hi, Mom. How about a beer?"

"You read my mind." Isabella reached up for the beer. "Did you get one for Jacinta?"

"Nope." Sandy grinned. "She's not drinking."

"No?" She looked past Sandy to see Jacinta grinning at her as well. "What …" Her eyes opened wide. "You mean …"

"Yes." Jacinta nodded and patted her belly.

"That's wonderful!" Isabella jumped from the chair to wrap her arms around them both.

She stood back and looked into their eyes. "I'm so happy."

Life in Gainesville, Georgia had just become a little more normal for her. They were a family, and a baby was on the way, and she was going to be a grandmother, like grandmothers everywhere. How much more normal could life be?

SEVEN

Fearsome Man

It was not his first trip to the States. Over the years he had made dozens of clandestine visits always on business for *Los Salvajes*. Typically, the business was to resolve some problem, which was a euphemism for eliminating the problem and burying the body where no one could find it.

Alejandro Garza's methods were invariably bloody. With every drop of blood, discipline and loyalty within the cartel ranks were solidified. Eventually, the number of problems decreased until, on Bebé Elizondo's advice, he had reduced the number and frequency of his visits. Then John Sole entered the picture.

He walked through the Atlanta airport, an anonymous face in the crowd. Invisibility was always a requisite for survival, and Alejandro Garza was a master of survival.

No excursion out of Mexico began without a new false identity. This was especially true for any trip to the States. In many places where *Los Salvajes* conducted its business, law enforcement maintained an often unscrupulous, if not entirely corrupt, relationship with the cartel. That was generally not the case in western nations, particularly the United States, a fact which significantly increased the risk of discovery.

While every enforcement agency knew of the *Los Salvajes* cartel, Alejandro Garza was a shadow figure. All knew of the existence of the cartel's chief enforcer. There had been too many dead bodies not to notice, but none had the slightest idea what he looked like or the name his mother had given him.

On the cartel organization charts posted on law enforcement bulletin boards around the country, Garza's name box was left blank. His image was represented by a dagger a DEA agent had drawn to represent the phantom-man they would all have loved to snare, but it was like trying to trap a ghost.

The truth was, he could have bought them drinks at their favorite bar, and they would have no idea that the tall, dignified man in the business suit, or Hawaiian shirt, or flip-flops and sunglasses, was the man they all sought. Garza, of course, would never knowingly do such a thing. He was much too cautious for that. He preferred to remain cloaked with anonymity behind the false identity he used on each visit.

On this trip, he arrived in Atlanta from Sao Paulo, Brazil, wearing heavy, dark-rimmed glasses, a gray mustache, and walking with the use of a cane. He waited patiently in the international arrivals line. When he was waved forward by the Immigration and Customs agent, he smiled and offered his Brazilian passport without waiting to be asked.

"Gabino Sousa," the agent read as he scanned the photograph, comparing it to the man standing before him.

"Yes." Garza nodded with a harmless smile.

"The reason for your visit to the United States?"

"To visit my niece … in Memphis." His voice held just the right amount of nervousness as would be expected from someone not familiar with international travel.

"How are you going to Memphis?"

"Oh … yes, there is another airplane I must take, somewhere here in Atlanta." He fumbled with the breast pocket of his threadbare sports jacket and pulled out a dog-eared ticket portfolio.

"May I see it?" the agent asked and gave a smile of his own.

"Certainly." Garza handed over the ticket and waited, leaning slightly on his cane for support.

The agent scanned the flight numbers and nodded. "Alright. Thank you, Mr. Sousa." He made a note on a piece of paper and handed it to Garza with the ticket. "This is your gate for the flight to Memphis. Just go through that door and follow the signs for the shuttle trains to Concourse D."

"Thank you." Garza fumbled with the ticket and passport, stuffing them into his breast pocket again in a clumsy fashion and nodded. "Sorry … Thank you again."

"Have a nice day, Mr. Sousa," the agent said as he motioned the next passenger forward.

Garza limped away on his cane, patting his pockets to make sure he had everything. The mannerism was clearly that of an infrequent traveler, making his way through unfamiliar territory. It was a persona that Garza maintained all the way to Memphis and to the car rental agency where he picked up a nondescript white SUV, thanked the attendant for helping him, after asking directions to a Latino neighborhood in the Berclair district.

He then drove away with a smile and a wave and disregarded the directions, heading east on I-40. An hour later, he stopped at a rest area, took a small duffel with him to the restroom and emerged a few minutes later, clean shaved, wearing sunglasses, and minus the cane.

It was five hours before he stopped again in Morristown, Tennessee, taking an exit that brought him into a modest residential neighborhood. As he pulled into the driveway, a man seated by a picture window in the front room folded a newspaper and came to the door.

His name was Hermilio, a fortyish man of slight build. Dressed in a white tee-shirt, blue jeans, and steel-toed boots, he was the image of a solid working-class man in a modest suburban community.

In fact, Hermilio worked for a local tool manufacturing company, but the tattoos on his arms and hands were evidence of his former life. Gang affiliations and a series of assaults had landed him in prison. As the time for parole approached, a church-sponsored outreach program put him in touch with the owner of a tool manufacturing company that decided to offer the man a second chance.

The church group gave him a glowing recommendation as an example of a rehabilitated felon who found a better life in Jesus. The parole board was impressed. They were also under pressure from the governor and legislature to reduce the crowded prison population.

After release, he quickly became one of the company's most valued employees, always willing to work late or come in early. At Christmas, the owner always stood him up at the annual company party and patted him on the back as a true

American success story and gave him a little extra in his bonus.

Hermilio was the owner's favorite mascot and pet project, and sound evidence of the businessman's Christian character. He often thought of Hermilio's success, and his hand in it, smiling benevolently as he sat in his church pew to hear the Sunday sermon.

"How was your trip?" Hermilio asked as he opened the door and stepped aside for Garza to enter.

Garza ignored the question. "You have what I requested?"

"Yes."

Hermilio's face remained expressionless. He had heard that this man was a serious one, not to be trifled with. Just provide what he requested and send him on his way.

"Show me," Garza said, his eyes moving around the small living room.

"This way."

Hermilio led him through the house and out the back door to a shed in the yard. A large ring of keys jingled in his hand. He thumbed through them and inserted one in the padlock securing the shed's door.

Inside, he crossed the narrow plywood floor to a trunk, also padlocked, and opened it, lifting the lid and taking a step back. Garza approached to examine the contents.

The weapons there glistened in the light from the single overhead bulb. Garza nodded. They were well maintained, oiled, and clean. He lifted several pistols, feeling the balance and checking the mechanisms.

"I'll take these." He placed three pistols, a Glock 19 and

two Walther PPKs in the duffel he carried with him. "And ammunition."

"Of course." Hermilio nodded and opened another trunk to reveal cases of pistol and rifle ammunition of various calibers from .380 to .30-06.

Garza selected several boxes and nodded. "What else?"

Hermilio understood and dragged over a third trunk. When the lid was lifted, rows of knife blades glittered under the light. Garza quickly selected a large combat style knife and two thinner piercing daggers. With everything secured in the duffel, he turned for the door.

"I ... I have other weapons for you to examine ... longer range, more firepower." Fearing that he may have overstepped his bounds, Hermilio added quickly, "I mean only if you would like to see them."

"I would not." Garza stopped, turned, and stared into Hermilio's eyes. The work he planned to do would be at close quarters. "These will do."

"Of course, of course." Hermilio nodded quickly.

Garza stepped from the shed into the afternoon light. Hermilio locked the door behind them and led the way back to the house.

A minute later, the fearsome man from the cartel was backing his car from the driveway. Hermilio breathed a sigh of relief.

EIGHT

Make a Happy Life

"Just like clockwork." Billy Siever smiled as Isabella walked into his office. "You know you don't have to do this."

"I do," she said, reaching into her bag for the envelope that held her monthly rent check. She laid it on the desk. "I need to pay my way."

"I know, I know." Billy placed the check on top of a stack of papers and motioned to a chair. "Got time for a visit?"

"I do." She sat in a chair across from his desk and laughed. "So, is this where all the murderers and mobsters sit when they come to consult with their mouthpiece?"

"More like, bankruptcies, and injury claims," he replied, smiling. "And no, I meet with clients in the conference room. Only friends visit in my office."

"That's disappointing." She grinned. "I was sure some well-known, criminal type ass previously occupied this chair."

"Nope. Just crotchety old mortgage bankers and shriveled up old matrons cutting their nephews out of the will." He smiled. "You seem happy today. It's good to see."

"I am happy." She shrugged. "Or reasonably so. Life hasn't worked out quite the way I planned." She stopped and threw her head back, laughing. "Who am I kidding? I never planned. I was just hiding out in that west Texas dust bowl, and then John came along. But all in all, life is good."

"I'm glad to hear it."

"It took a while," Isabella continued, settling into the chair as if she wanted to talk and get something off her chest. "Do you talk to John very often?"

"Not often. When he calls. He doesn't ever say where he is, but I know the plan is to continue doing what he's doing and make sure it doesn't involve any of the people he cares about, his friends."

"He's a good man." She nodded and looked up, her eyes moist. "I was hard on him ... too hard. It wasn't fair, the way I treated him."

"He understands," Billy said softly. "He never blames you, only asks how you are. I know he wishes things had worked out differently."

"I was angry at having to leave my life in Texas, but looking back, it was probably the only way I would have ever gotten away from the trap I was in. Without John, Jacinta would have been sold off or killed, and Sandy would be dead trying to save her. Whatever else happened, I know he didn't mean for us to be dragged into it. Sometimes ..." She shrugged. "It's trite, but sometimes a river of shit happens, and you just have to wade through it and get to the other side."

Billy laughed. "Shit definitely happens."

"Is there any way I could speak to him?" she asked.

"I can see what he says the next time he contacts me,

but …" Billy shook his head. "I think I know the answer. He will say no. Once John commits to something, he doesn't easily change his mind."

"Don't I know it," she said, a wry smile crossing her face.

"Seriously, though," Billy continued. "The rent is unnecessary, and besides, John takes care of it. I told him not to worry, but he insists."

"Well, we have that in common. I insist too. I can't continue to live off the good graces of others. Life goes on, and as this seems to be the place where I will make my life, I have to do it my own way." She paused, her tone becoming more serious. "That's one of the reasons I came by to see you, Billy."

"I'm listening."

It had taken her by surprise, although looking back she couldn't say why. She had been working side by side at the agency with Sam Goodwin for almost a year. Not once in all that time did he make any overtures or offer any hints that he had feelings for her outside of her competence as an employee.

But that was his nature. Sam was a quiet man, good-natured and affable, but not one to be demonstrative about his feelings. Then one Friday night, as she gathered her things to leave the office after a hectic week he asked her a simple enough question.

"Abby, do you have a second," he called from inside his office.

"Sure. What's up, Sam?"

Isabella poked her head around the corner and looked

through the door. He sat ramrod straight at his desk, his palms down flat on the surface in front of him, his face shining beet red.

"Are you feeling alright?" She took a step into the office.

"Am I …? Oh, yes, yes. I'm fine. I just wanted to ask you a question."

"Shoot."

"Would you have dinner with me?" he hesitated and added as if some clarification was required. "Tonight … dinner tonight?"

She hadn't been asked on a date since … well, not for a long time. She smiled and said, "Yes, I will have dinner with you."

It was a natural thing, and she thought at first that she should have seen it coming. In reality, neither of them saw it coming. Sam had been divorced for fifteen years. Since then, his business had been the primary focus of his life. Isabella had changed that for him.

As the months passed, she became more than an employee. She became a confidant and a friend. Sam had lots of good old boy buddies around Gainesville, but he didn't have anyone he could talk to the way he did with Abby. He began to anticipate her arrival at work each day and hated when the day ended, and she went home to her life. He wondered about that life and what it would be like to go home to a family instead of an empty house.

Isabella genuinely liked Sam. What was there not to like? Yes, he had a few more years on him, but not so many. He in his fifties and she in her forties, less than a decade separated them in age. She always thought of him as a happy soul with not an angry bone in his body.

It was true, he wasn't John. In fact, it would be difficult

to find two men more opposite in nature. The difference wasn't a bad thing.

Sam always had a joke, a smile, a self-deprecating grin about some little something he had done or neglected to do. With Sam, life could be a happy, calm place. She found it refreshing to be around him, and she liked that most of all.

She thought about that. Circumstances had ended what she had with John. There was no way to recover from it, but she could move on.

They began seeing more of each other after hours, always platonic and in public. Dinners, movies, a picnic at Lake Lanier, they did the mundane things that ordinary people do, and Isabella loved it. Over time, she began to love Sam in her own way.

Then one day, they had dinner at a cafe off the square in Gainesville. Afterward, they strolled, peering into shop windows, talking about nothing in particular. It was the sort of comfortable evening she had come to enjoy in his company. He went into a bakery and bought two enormous chocolate chip cookies. They were warm from the oven, the chocolate chips gooey and sweet.

"Let's sit and eat over there."

He led the way across the street, and they sat on one of the benches adjacent to the sidewalk. They nibbled the cookies in silence for a minute, and then Sam cleared his throat and spoke.

"How's the cookie?"

"Wonderful." She laughed. "How could it not be?"

"Good, good." He nodded, giving her the soft shy smile that she knew to be his fallback when he didn't know what to say, except this time he did have something to say. "So, I was wondering …" He paused, mouth open as if searching for a way to push out the words.

"Yes? Wondering what?" She turned to face him on the bench, puzzled at his hesitation.

"I was wondering if you would … if you could … consider marrying me."

It took her by surprise, although it shouldn't have. Maybe it was because she thought the question would come someday, just not that particular day.

"I would." Isabella nodded and looked into his hopeful eyes. "Consider it, that is, but can I have a little time to think it over … take it all in … I didn't expect it this evening."

"Sure, of course." Sam nodded emphatically. "It was probably not right of me to ask. I just …"

"Quiet," she ordered and leaned over to give him a kiss on the cheek. "I didn't say no. I only said I wanted to take it all in. You surprised me, that's all."

When he dropped her off at her house that night, she kissed him softly on the lips. "You are a very good man, Sam Goodwin."

She walked into the house. Sam floated back out to his car.

"So are you asking me a question or simply telling me the story," Billy said when she finished.

"Just getting things off my chest, I suppose." Isabella pursed her lips. "And asking you what you think."

"Sam Goodwin is a good man." Billy nodded and smiled. "The very best. He will do whatever he can to make you happy."

"I do believe that," Isabella said. "There's something else, though."

"John ... you still have feelings for him," Billy interjected.

"Yes."

"That's understandable. I know he cares deeply for you as well, although he won't talk much about it." He leaned across the desk to look into her eyes. "If you came here for some sort of absolution ... some release from him ... it is not necessary. Whatever he feels for you, John meant what he said when he left. You will not see him again. I know he would be happy for you and would say what I'm saying now. There's no need for guilt. You and Sam Goodwin should go make a happy life together."

"Thank you, Billy," she said, relief on her face. "Will you tell ... I mean, when you speak to him, can you ..."

"I'll let John know. He'll be happy that after all that has happened, you have a chance at a good life with a good man."

A load had been lifted. She almost danced from the office.

Billy watched her go, his feelings a mixture of happiness for her and sadness for his friend. What he told Isabella was true. John would want her to be happy, but he knew that was John's stalwart way, wishing happiness for others but never finding his own.

NINE

The Right Neighborhood

He descended from the Sandia Mountains in Tijeras, New Mexico and picked up old Route 66. Albuquerque was new for him, and he had no precise destination in mind, but he knew what he was looking for. Traffic on I-40 rushed into and out of the city to his right, but on the old U.S. highway the pace was slower, giving him a chance to take in the lay of the land, get his bearings, and gather information.

It was a game of cat and mouse. He was the mouse, enticing the cat to come after him, then darting away into a hole to reappear later somewhere else.

It was a dangerous sport. In his police days, he would have called the game reckless. John Sole had passed the threshold of recklessness long ago.

Leaving Tijeras, heading west toward the city, the landscape was rural at first. After a few miles, suburban housing developments began to dot the hillsides along the valley. Businesses catering to the suburbanites started to pop up—horse stables, shopping centers, and home improvement box stores. Industrial parks and large office complexes and then commercial districts replaced the housing developments along the highway.

Route 66 became Central Avenue, a main thoroughfare through Albuquerque. He was close now. All the signs were there.

Central took him under the I-25 overpass. A few blocks past it, he turned south toward the Barelas district and began cruising the neighborhoods. Older homes, some falling apart, and others painted in pastels, clinging to the memory of a past era, lined the streets. Many showed signs of neglect or outright abandonment. Residents with the ability to flee to other neighborhoods or other cities had done so.

Barelas had once been a pleasant Albuquerque neighborhood. Now older residents, trapped in their homes, living on pensions and social security, watched from their windows as the world changed around them.

More than a few houses were surrounded by chain-link fences, useless at keeping out intruders but perfect for keeping a dog on the property. The drug dealer's ubiquitous Pit Bull Terrier, or mixed breed mutts with Pit blood in them, patrolled and growled, or hunkered down in the bare dirt yards waiting for someone to make their day and enter their domain. There didn't seem to be much chance of that. Most of the residential streets were empty of pedestrians.

The business district was little better. Most businesses made an attempt at security by placing iron and steel bars on windows and padlocks on doors. Sole knew these would not be an effective deterrent against any determined burglar. Everywhere there were signs of the battle to retain some semblance of societal order and the decency of past decades. It was a losing battle.

Gangs had taken over. There were never enough police

to patrol the neighborhoods. Drugs were sold brazenly in the open. John Sole found what he sought and slowed.

He dropped the pickup's visor and adjusted his sunglasses. The western sun had lowered. A block ahead, it spotlighted two men on a corner, sending their long shadows down the street toward him.

The buy lasted only a few seconds. The dealer and buyer were not novices.

It looked safe enough as long as he left the area quickly afterward. He decided to circle the block, park away from the corner, and walk back to make a buy and continue the game of cat and mouse with the *Los Salvajes* cartel.

One day, when the time was right, he would do more, but there was time for that. For now, it was enough to ensure that they would never forget him.

He passed the dealer on the corner, made a turn at the next block, drove two blocks, and then another turn. Then, he slammed the brake pedal, the truck's tires squealing as it rocked to a halt.

A white van roared by, the passenger leaning out the window, pounding on the door. "Fuck you, *cabrón*!"

Sole watched the van without reaction. Gangbangers. He had definitely found the right neighborhood.

TEN

The Moment was Perfect

"So, I've been thinking." Isabella lifted the glass of beer, took a sip as if to clear her throat, and deliberately placed it on the table in precisely the same spot.

The great moment had arrived, and Sam Goodwin's brow wrinkled. There was only one topic that she had asked for time to think about. Concern, mingled with hope, flushed his face. He leaned forward, elbows planted on the table to anchor himself against the storm.

"Yes?" He managed to whisper, breathlessly

"You are a very good man Sam Goodwin." Isabella gave him a tender smile and reached up to touch the side of his face. "I would be very happy to marry you."

Relief flooded his face. He reached up to hold her hand, resting against his cheek. The position was awkward, but her touch held a tenderness unlike any he had ever experienced. A simple hand on his cheek, soft and warm and gentle, and he wanted it to linger right there forever. Somewhere inside, he knew he was acting like a lovesick schoolboy, but he didn't care.

"Thank you, Abby," he managed to choke out. "I promise to make you happy."

"You already have, Sam." She lifted the napkin, touched it to her moist eyes, and smiled. "You're going to make me ruin my makeup, and I worked so hard to put it on special for tonight."

"You two lovebirds certainly look happy." Ida Stokes, their regular server, stood over them, smiling. "Anything I should know about?"

Lacking any of the upscale pretension of Atlanta's spreading urban sprawl, the neighborhood bar and grill on the outskirts of Gainesville had become their favorite spot. The homey atmosphere, simple good food, and ice-cold beer offered them a relatively private spot to sit quietly together and talk, or laugh, or play music on the jukebox.

Sam had become a regular, known to the owners and most of the other patrons. He always got a welcoming wave from the bartender, servers, and those seated at the tables around the bar. Over the last several months, Isabella had also become one of the crowd, recognized when she walked in and made to feel at home.

"We are happy," Isabella said. "Sam and I are going to be married." Her brow wrinkled in concern for a second. "Oh, maybe I shouldn't have said that yet, Sam."

"Say it," he beamed. "Shout it to the world! Say it loud so you won't be able to take any of it back once you realize what you've done."

"I won't be taking it back, Sam. Not ever."

"Well, hell yeah! It's about time." Ida grinned. "This calls for something on the house ... champagne!"

"No." Isabella grinned and held up her glass. "I'm a beer-baby. I was drinking beer the night we decided to get married, and I don't want to do anything to change my good fortune. I'll take another just like this."

"Superstitious? I'm learning more about you as the seconds tick by." Sam never took his eyes from her face.

"Feel like backing out already?" Isabella said, teasing.

"Not a chance." The grin on Sam's face kept expanding until he looked like a cheery beaming sun. He nodded at Ida. "Beer, and a round for the house."

"You got it," Ida said and hurried off to the bar, as she called out to the other patrons. "Round for the house on Mr. Sam Goodwin!" She stopped in the middle of the room and pointed at Isabella and Sam. "They're getting married!"

Heads around the room nodded. Faces smiled. Glasses lifted in congratulatory toasts. Patrons stopped by their table to wish them well.

Isabella soaked everything in. The goodwill from so many was unlike anything she had experienced in her past life. Everyone, Sam's friends, acquaintances, and those he knew simply on nodding terms, was happy for them. The sentiments were genuine and sincere, and it became a time of joy they knew they would savor and remember in years to come, sitting on the porch or having coffee at the kitchen table or whispering in bed before falling asleep.

The congratulatory slaps on the shoulder and kisses on the cheek were completed, and the crowd returned to their tables. Isabella and Sam held hands across the table, silently looking into the other's eyes. Words were unnecessary. The moment was perfect.

ELEVEN

The Hunter - Closing In

He pulled the yellow, cracked newspaper from under the front seat and looked at the picture for the thousandth time. John Sole's anguished face covered nearly the entire top fold of the front page.

He stared at the image, looking for some sign of familiarity, something he might recognize in the face. The grainy picture held few clues about the man he hunted.

After the image, the story took up the rest of the front page. Detective John Sole's family had been murdered. The suspects were never identified, and despite the efforts of one of the best forensics teams in the country, no clues to their identity turned up at the scene of the crime. The article reported knowingly that the murders were probably related to a drug smuggling case Sole had been working with his partner. The man smirked as he read the article. It didn't take a genius to figure out that much.

He had spent countless hours studying the case over the last couple of years. Still, there might be something that he missed, some small piece of information that could guide him on his hunt.

The drug cartel came up with a plan to use shrimp boats to smuggle drugs into the country. Detective Sole and his partner were instrumental in breaking the case. Their work even implicated a sitting senator.

But there would be no accolades. The killers murdered his partner on the same night they slaughtered Sole's family at home. It appeared that Sole was the target, but he survived because he was away working with the DEA and Coast Guard on the case.

Without evidence or suspects, the police could do little but speculate, although they assured the public that they would not stop until the killers were brought to justice. That was more than two years ago. In that time, there had been no arrests and no suspects identified. While not officially a cold case, the investigation was as dead as if it had been placed in a deep freeze.

And John Sole disappeared.

The media clamored for more information about the detective, the only survivor of Atlanta's 'Night of Blood,' as they described the night of the murders. Sole was nowhere to be found. The department put out a brief media statement that left more questions unanswered than it answered.

"Detective Sole is understandably in seclusion, grieving the loss of his family and partner. We ask everyone to respect his privacy during this time of tragedy and mourning."

The truth was that he had resigned, and they had no idea where he had gone or what had become of him. He had no surviving relatives and no known friends outside the police department and his in-laws.

Speculation swirled around the department and in the media that perhaps the cartel finally found him and finished what they began on the day of the murders. It was only speculation because John Sole had not been seen or heard from since.

The hunter placed the newspaper on the seat beside a stack of others he had collected. Each held a link to the man he hunted. At least, that is what he believed.

He had spent months at the library, using public computers to scour the web. It was painstaking work, but he thought he knew the man he hunted and the kind of trail he would leave behind.

In the last year, a pattern began to emerge. A string of unsolved murders in a backwater Texas county along the border with Mexico caught his attention. Then the pace increased, and others began appearing.

The murders all remained unsolved. At first, he added any unsolved murder to the list. It was a very long list, but little by little, he narrowed it down.

Two drug dealers shot in a Detroit alley. There might be a link.

A mugging in New York. Sole wasn't a mugger.

A woman raped and murdered in Nashville. Sole wasn't a rapist.

A drive-by murder in Kansas City. A possibility.

Slowly, the list shortened. It took time to work through the cases, but he had time. It was a commodity that he had in abundance.

A drug dealer with links to a cartel found dead in Minneapolis. Another in Louisville. Then more in Charlotte, Memphis, Baton Rouge, New Orleans, Houston, Dallas.

The trail was clear, at least to the hunter. He couldn't yet tell where it would lead, but he knew he was closing in.

TWELVE

Find the Rat

The rat had disappeared. For some, that might have been a problem. They might have even given up and taken Bebé Elizondo's counsel to let the matter rest. Alejandro Garza was not one to give up. Instead, he changed tactics.

Where John Sole was at this moment was of little importance. The *Los Salvajes* cartel members might find him one day, but Garza doubted it. He intended to bring John Sole to him. To accomplish that task, he had to give Sole a reason to come, and Garza believed he had found the bait.

Chico Saludo forced himself not to look away and to keep his eyes focused on Garza's. Looking away might send the wrong signal, and sending the wrong signal to Garza could be a dangerous thing.

"How is business?" Garza asked before getting to the real purpose of his visit.

"Good, good." Chico bobbed his head up and down emphatically to demonstrate that his organization was meeting all of Bebé Elizondo's expectations in the sale and distribution of drugs around the southeast. "There are reports, back at my house, if you want to come see them," he offered, praying silently that Garza would not want to visit him in his home.

"Not on this visit," Garza said, his icy eyes fixed on Chico's. "I have other business just now."

"Yes, yes, of course. I understand completely," Chico said, not understanding at all but immensely relieved. "Can I offer you another drink?"

"No."

They sat in an upscale bar in Buckhead, sipping expensive tequila, and Chico toyed with the idea of ordering another for himself, but only for a moment. There would be plenty of time for drinking when Garza left. The most important thing now was to focus and to hurry Garza along on his journey and away from Chico as quickly as possible.

"How may I help you then?"

"I am looking for someone."

"Yes? That is easy enough. I will find him for you," Chico said, relieved. "Who?"

Garza took the photo of Sole from his breast pocket and placed it on the table between them.

"But this man … we all know that you seek him," Chico said, the worry creeping back into his mind, fearful that Garza might turn the task over to him. If Garza couldn't find him, how the hell did he expect Chico to locate the ex-cop? "You must believe me that my people are all on the lookout for him. If he comes to Atlanta, we will have him. I promise you."

"I am looking for someone who worked with him," Garza said, his eyes narrowing to indicate that Chico should pay close attention. "Before he left, before you inherited your position here, one of our people worked with him when he was still a detective."

Chico began to understand. He had been promoted to lead the *Los Salvajes* business in the southeast United States after his predecessor was murdered in his own taco shop. Chico had possession of the shop now and reported directly to Elizondo and Garza. The police never identified a suspect in the murder, but cartel members all knew that the detective, this John Sole, came into the shop and eliminated the drug lord, Esteban Moya.

"Yes, I see." Chico nodded. "As I recall, someone we suspected, but could never prove, was the rat. He was to be eliminated as a precaution, but then he disappeared after the murder of ..." His voice trailed off, thinking that it might be best not to speak of murders of drug lords since he was one himself now.

"Find him."

"Find him? But how? I don't ..." Chico's eyes widened, and then he nodded quickly. "Yes, of course. I will do my best to locate this rat for you."

"Not your best," Garza said. "Find out where he ran to. He had friends here, people he spoke with, family perhaps. Put the word out on the street that we want him. Is there a photo of him?"

"Possibly. There are boxes of photos in Esteban's ... I mean, my office. These were taken when we had people come in to meet or to discuss business. My predecessor was very careful about such things before he was murdered." He crossed himself reverently and touched his finger to his lips.

"Find the photo. Distribute it."

"Where?"

"Everywhere," Garza snapped. "Have your people look for his contacts here. Possibly someone heard from him or spotted him in a different city. A man like that, a street dealer, only knows one way to live, and he is no doubt doing what he did here somewhere else under a different name."

"Yes, of course." Chico nodded. "You are correct, of course. Stupid of me not to have come up with the idea myself."

Garza was silent for several seconds, staring at Chico. "I expect daily reports until you provide me with the information I seek."

Chico nodded. "Yes, of course … every day."

"We are done now. Go."

Without another word, Chico scurried from the table, leaving a half-full glass of tequila. He almost ran out to the street, muttering, "Thank you, Jesus, for not letting him kill me today. Now please help me find the son of a bitch rat."

PART II
War and Peace

THIRTEEN

Latest News

In New York, the store might have been called a bodega. In Atlanta, a quick-mart. In Montreal, a *dépanneur*. Depending on the region, stores like this one—superettes, corner markets, dairies, milk bars, corner shops, convenience stores, *tiendas*—exist in virtually every corner of the world in some fashion or another.

This one was known simply as Dupart's to the locals, taking its name from the owner, Edgar Dupart. Located on a side street in southwest Albuquerque, it was a purveyor of various necessaries for its customers. Candy bars for youngsters and grownups with a sweet tooth. Beer and wine for those with more adult tastes and the requisite ID. Dupart's had a little of everything, including gossip.

Edgar himself served as the community bulletin board. His brain was a repository of information, important and trivial. Edgar didn't sort it by value. That was up to the listener.

Bits of gossip, family news, births, deaths, tragedies, and joys were all dutifully reported to him by the locals to be passed on to other members of the community. Customers visiting Dupart's always found the owner engaged in conversation with any and every other customer in the store, discussing various bits of neighborhood news. Soon they would be drawn into the conversation and brought up to speed while passing on their own tidbits of news for Edgar to remember and share with the next visitor.

A conversation about the weather that began over coffee with the early comers who wanted their morning paper would morph into a discussion of neighborhood real estate prices and the difficulty old-timers faced when they attempted to sell out and move. This would shift to a detailed summary of the local high school football record, then to the news of a layoff at a business that had hired two hundred workers only six months earlier. The news of old Mr. Santiago's passing and the birth of a little girl to the young couple at the end of the street, the Clarks… or Clarksons… or Cleery. No one could quite remember the young couple's name, but Mrs. Alvarez assured Edgar that the baby was beautiful.

The conversation never ended, flowing smoothly from one customer to the next. Edgar heard it all and passed everything on. While the rest of the world distanced itself from personal interaction, relying on digital communication whenever possible, Edgar and his customers clung to the old fashioned method of communication. They talked.

In the process of this communication, Edgar became a sort of glue, binding the neighborhood together amid a raging storm. Crime rates soared. Drugs were sold on corners. People were assaulted in the streets. Gangs raged and fought and took the lives of the young. But in this tiny corner of Albuquerque, the locals clung to the lives they had always lived, and Edgar helped them do that.

Target Down

A Louisiana boy of Creole descent, Edgar Dupart had returned from the jungles and rice paddies of Vietnam and his service with the air cavalry. With nothing better to do, he went with a friend to see the Mardi Gras festivities in the French Quarter.

Louisa Lopez was also there, visiting for Mardi Gras with friends from Albuquerque. They met by chance on a sultry morning in a patisserie off Chartres Street, each searching for something they might manage to hold down in their stomachs after a night of partying. Edgar helped her read the menu, and his life changed.

Beignets led to lunch, led to dinner, led to a long walk hand in hand along the Mississippi. By the end of the day, he had proposed marriage to her. She accepted on one condition. She could not leave her family in Albuquerque. Edgar began packing the next day.

Young, impetuous, and full of love, with a good portion of lust mixed in, they were married a month later. He took a job at a refinery near the rail yards, working long hours. Within a month, they were expecting their first child. Life stretched before them, seemingly without end, as it always does for young people, full of hope and anticipation. What more could they ask?

Louisa gave birth to a boy less than a year from the day she met Edgar at the patisserie shop. They named him Jean Paul for Edgar's father, who had passed away while he was fighting the Viet Cong. It should have been a day of rejoicing. Instead, it broke Edgar's heart.

The doctor listed the cause of death as left ventricular outflow stenosis, brought on by a previously undetected congenital condition. The words didn't mean anything to Edgar. Louisa was dead. His life changed again.

The years passed, raising Jean Paul. He remained close to Louisa's parents until they passed within a year of each other. They never recovered from their daughter's death, living in mourning in a darkened house until the day they ceased mourning and joined Louisa.

Edgar had to find a way to support his son and provide a home. He bought the old store using money he had saved while in Vietnam plus a small inheritance his father had left him. It was enough for a down payment and convinced a bank to lend him the rest. Dupart's Market was born.

In time, Jean Paul grew and followed his father's steps, joining the army. Unlike his father, he did not return. He died in a minor fight at a place that had no name in the barrens of Afghanistan.

Jean Paul left a wife and small son behind, and Edgar welcomed them into his home. They were all that remained of the family he and Louisa had begun.

"*Hola*, Edgar." Salvadore Estevez walked in for his newspaper and cup of coffee.

Edgar always joked that you could set a clock by Salvadore's visits. Newspaper, coffee, precisely one-half hour of conversation to catch up on the local news, and then off again to complete his circuit of the neighborhood. Edgar worried about him. Sometimes Salvadore wandered into places where the gang presence was heavy, but Salvadore shrugged off the concern and flashed a wide, toothy grin.

"See this smile," he would say.

"I see it," Edgar would reply, knowing the routine by heart.

"Who would hurt this smile?" He would chuckle and touch his fingertips to his forehead in salute as he went out to the street. "Until tomorrow, *mi amigo.*"

"Tomorrow, *mon ami,*" Edgar would call after him with a smile of his own as he helped the next customer and passed on the latest news.

FOURTEEN

Knockout

The van had been stolen an hour earlier, chosen solely for this occasion. An hour from now, it would sit abandoned in some vacant lot engulfed in flames.

There was nothing remarkable about it. No special paint job, no company logos, or phone numbers, not even any gang graffiti spray-painted on the inviting plain white surface, a common occurrence in this part of town. It was one of thousands of similar fleet vehicles, unidentifiable on the surface. The only alteration was the license plate, swapped for a different one, also stolen.

It cruised slowly along Central Avenue in Albuquerque. At Third Street, it turned south, still moving below the speed limit, the occupants leaning forward in their seats peering out at the passing shops and pedestrians.

"There." One of the young men in the back seat pointed off to the right down a side street. "That one."

"Yeah."

The driver nodded and spun the wheel, making the turn and accelerating rapidly to the end of the next block.

Braking hard, he turned at the next corner and pulled to the curb.

The driver turned in his seat to stare at the young man wedged in between two other members of the gang known as *Demonios de la Muerte*—Death Devils, or DM for short. His name was Jose 'Joey' Gonzales, but the others had taken to calling their newest gang member Keet, short for parakeet, because of his habit of repeating back whatever anyone said to him.

"Do it," the driver said.

His gang name was Slice, and no one asked how he had earned the sobriquet. The others in the van, all gang members, included Poco in the passenger seat and Cheech and Ape, both large men whose bulk held Keet firmly in place. It was his initiation day, and no one knew how he would react.

"Do it?" Keet stammered, barely able to make eye contact with Slice.

"Yeah. Do it," Slice growled. "And don't say it back to me again. Just get your ass out and do it."

"Right." Keet nodded. "Do it." His eyes darted to Slice. "Sorry, man. I mean, yeah. Let me out so I can handle it."

Ape slid the rear door open and stepped out. Keet followed, and Cheech slid across the seat to stand on the sidewalk with them. All eyes were on Keet. It was his show. He could pass through his initiation or—what? He wasn't sure what would happen if he backed out now, and he didn't want to find out.

No one spoke, giving him nothing to repeat back, so he said. "Okay, let's go."

Sandwiched between Ape and Cheech, he walked to the corner and turned down the street the van had driven a minute earlier. Slice watched in the mirror as they disappeared from sight.

Less than two minutes elapsed before the three came running at full speed around the corner and climbed into the van.

Salvadore Estevez had lived in the Barelas district of Albuquerque for thirty years. He'd come there after gaining his U.S. citizenship and securing a job with the railroad. In those years, he and his wife, Carmen, had raised a family and seen their children go off into the world. They remained behind in Barelas, partly out of reluctance to leave their home of thirty years, but also because depressed property values in the neighborhood made selling and moving nearly impossible for those on fixed incomes.

As on most days, he stopped by the shop of his friend Edgar Dupart and picked up a copy of the Albuquerque Journal. Edgar poured him a cup of coffee from the pot he kept brewing behind the counter, and they chatted for half an hour. Then, newspaper tucked under his arm, Salvadore left to continue his walk.

"If someone stops you," Carmen always reminded him when he left for his walks. "Give them what they want. Hand them your wallet. Don't make trouble or fight. They will only hurt you if you try." Then she would pat his arm, kiss his cheek, and send him on his way.

The counsel from his wife was unnecessary, but Salvadore listened every day and nodded sincerely that he would comply with her wishes. In reality, he had no intention of resisting. Salvadore had always been a peaceful man, a pacifist in the truest sense of the word. He considered all confrontation, unnecessary, and a waste of the little time that God had given him on the earth. In his long life, he had never been in a real fight, only a small school tussle or two over a girl when he was a teenager, and that was driven mostly by hormones and not any genuine desire to fight.

Some mistook him for a coward. He was not. He would defend his wife or his children or a friend if the occasion required such action. But as far as protecting his property, there was nothing he valued so much that he wanted to fight over it. Take what you want, and let me go in peace. That philosophy had served him well as the Barelas district transformed into one of the highest crime areas of the city.

He had only gone fifty feet from Dupart's door when the three young men turned the corner, walking briskly toward him. Young men wandering the streets like that made him nervous, so he did what he always did to relieve the tensions. He tried to make eye contact with them and smile.

The young men ignored him and passed to either side, one to his right and two to his left. He breathed a sigh of relief as their footsteps receded down the pavement.

Then there was a shuffling sound behind him. The footsteps were returning, louder, moving faster.

They were on him now. He started to turn and smile, but not in time to see the gloved fist flying in an arc toward him. It caught him in the side of the head, and the world went dark for Salvadore. He fell to the sidewalk, his head smacking into the concrete.

By the time Edgar Dupart, ran from behind his counter to aid his friend, the three young men were turning the corner they had rounded a minute earlier. He knelt by

Salvadore. Blood pooled on the sidewalk from a gash in his friend's head. Edgar pulled out his cell phone and dialed 911. As he spoke to the operator, the sound of tires squealing and an engine roaring reverberated down the street from around the corner.

Keet panted heavily and grinned broadly as he followed Ape and Cheech into the back seat. Slice put the van in gear and pulled to the end of the block, turning down another side street that would take them away from the area.

"I did it, man!" Keet was jubilant, flushed with the thrill and exhilaration of the moment. "That motherfucker hit the ground hard. Shit, he might be dead." He put an arm out the window, his fist pounding on the door.

Slice cast a doubtful eye to the mirror and looked at Ape.

"He did it." Ape nodded. "Don't know if he'll die, but he did it."

"Shit. You see how hard the motherfucker went down." Keet bubbled. "Shit, if he ain't dead, he gonna wish he was."

Slice accelerated to the next corner and ran the stop sign, nearly hitting a pickup turning in front of them. John Sole, turned his head and stared stone-faced through his sun glasses at the men in the van.

"Fuck you, *cabrón*!" Keet shouted, out the window at the pickup man, feeling powerful and invincible, surrounded by his gang brothers.

The others nodded and smiled. They understood. The van roared away from the area.

It was the gang's right of initiation—the knockout game. The rules were simple, find some unsuspecting person, and deliver a blow to the head to send them to the ground unconscious. If they died, even better.

They allowed the prospective DM one punch. If that blow did not render the victim unconscious, he failed the initiation and had to ask for another chance to select another victim and repeat the process until he got it right. It was a badge of honor to succeed on the first attempt, and a deep disgrace to fail.

The choice of victims was critical. Generally, women were considered off-limits for the knockout initiation, although they were fair game for other activities. Old men, however, were definitely allowed, even preferred, because they were frailer and less able to defend themselves. The gang's *machismo* bravado had its limits. Besides, the proper choice of victims made for successful initiations, especially for newcomers participating in the game for the first time.

"Goddamn, that felt good." Keet pounded his gloved fist into the other bare hand. "Let's do another."

"You done good, *cholo*," Slice said, smiling at the new member's exuberance. "But first, we dump this ride and move out of the area."

He steered the van south on William Street alongside the rail yards. A turn to the right took them across the tracks and onto a dirt trail that led down to a secluded spot near the banks of the Rio Grande. The van rocked to a stop, and everyone piled out. Ape and Cheech took two five-gallon gas cans from the back and doused the inside of the vehicle.

Slice handed a lighter to Keet. "Your day, bro. You do the honors."

Keet reached out, grinning and thumbed the lighter, tossing it into the van. The gasoline flamed up, and they all stepped back

"Time to go." Slice led them to another vehicle they had positioned there earlier in the day.

Before they had gone a half mile, headed north on William Street, the van was engulfed in flames. Thick black smoke billowed into the sky. A pilot in an airliner on approach to the airport a mile away reported seeing a fire and suggested they call the fire department.

Slice retraced their route back to Central Avenue. As they passed the side street, they could see an ambulance pulling to the curb. The siren of a police cruiser wailed down the block. The van continued on without being noticed. The old man lay motionless on the sidewalk. A small crowd had gathered around his prostrate form. Two people knelt beside him.

"Told you." Keet grinned. "Knocked that motherfucker out!"

FIFTEEN

Sidetracked

"Fuck you, *cabrón!*"

The white van sped away. Gangbangers. Sole had, indeed, found the right neighborhood.

He lifted his foot off the brake, and the pickup began to roll forward when he noticed the crowd gathered around a man lying on the pavement half a block down a side street. He pulled to the curb and stopped.

Stepping from the pickup, he reached under the seat to retrieve his .45 auto, tucking it securely under his waistband. He began walking down the block.

"What are you doing?" the voice inside called out to him.

Just going to see if there's anything I can do. Then I'll move on. No delays. No entanglements. Looks like those gangbangers might have hurt someone.

The voice inside sighed, but did not try to convince him to walk away.

He pushed forward to kneel beside the old man lying on the sidewalk. Another man knelt beside him, a cell phone in one hand as he cradled the old man's head in his lap, rocking him back and forth to comfort him. A pool of blood spread around the man's head where it had struck the curb and opened a gash in his temple.

"They hit him," Edgar Dupart said to the stranger who knelt beside him. "They just came up and knocked him down."

Sole realized the gangbangers in the van must have been fleeing the scene after attacking the old man. He recognized the signs of the knockout game and a gang initiation. Better than shooting the old man, he thought, but not by much.

"He may have a neck or spinal injury." Sole leaned forward to take the man's head between his hands. "We should lay his head flat and keep his neck straight."

"Okay." Dupart nodded. The stranger seemed to know what to do for his friend.

Sole eased the old man's head back onto the pavement, keeping his neck aligned, then lifted his eyelids one at a time. His years in the Marine Corps and law enforcement had taught him to recognize mydriasis, extreme dilation of the pupils, a typical result of brain trauma, especially in the elderly.

"That's bad, isn't it, his eye like that?" Edgar Dupart looked at Sole.

"It means he's had a brain injury. Do you know him?"

"Yes. Salvadore Estevez." Dupart's eyes watered. "He's my friend."

"Is that 911 on the line?"

"Yes."

"Can I speak with them?"

Dupart handed the phone to Sole. He began speaking, briefing the dispatcher on what the paramedics would find on arrival.

"Elderly male, appears to have a traumatic brain injury, mydriasis present. Some bleeding present but no apparent arterial blood loss."

He waited a moment while the dispatcher relayed the information to the responding EMTs, and then added, "I have a possible lookout on the suspects."

"Go ahead with the lookout," the dispatcher said, typing rapidly as he spoke.

"White van, no marking of any type. Two males in the front. Two or three passengers in the rear, also appeared to be male. Last seen southbound on…" He looked around, not sure of where he was exactly. "Southbound on the adjacent street a block to the east from this location."

"10-4," the dispatcher said, and then muted the line to relay the information. A minute later, she was back. "The EMTs and responding officers will be with you in a minute."

"Right." Sole restrained himself from using the usual 10-4 response that came naturally to him.

They heard the sirens, and a few seconds later the ambulance pulled up to the curb. Two EMTs jumped out and began examining Salvadore Estevez.

A police unit arrived right behind them. The officer stepped out, saw the phone in Sole's hand, and took him aside.

"You law enforcement?" the officer asked. "Dispatcher said it sounded like it."

"Marine Corps," Sole replied, leaving out his police experience.

"Well, she said you definitely had your shit together."

"He helped us." Edgar Dupart joined them as the EMTs worked on his friend. "I could hardly speak. I couldn't think of anything except to call the 911." He shook his head. "Salvadore just left me in the store. Hadn't been gone five minutes."

"You did right, sir," the officer said. "We're looking for the van and people who did this right now, and the EMTs will get your friend to the hospital." He turned to Sole, his clipboard in hand, ready to complete the necessary report. "Your name?"

Sole reached in his pocket and pulled out a wallet, careful to keep the .45 concealed. "Myers … Bill Myers."

"And you?" The officer turned to Edgar Dupart.

"That's me." Dupart pointed at the storefront a few doors away. "Edgar Dupart."

The officer spent a few more minutes gathering information. When he was done, the EMTs had Salvadore Estevez on a backboard, his neck stabilized with straps. They loaded him in the ambulance and left, driving carefully to avoid any unnecessary jostling of their patient. A minute later, the officer departed.

"Well, I suppose I'll be heading out too." Sole put out a hand to Edgar. "It was good meeting you, Mr. Dupart. Sorry it had to be under these circumstances."

"Call me Edgar." He shook Sole's hand and held it. "I can't thank you enough for helping me … helping Salvadore."

"It was nothing. Glad to help." Sole extricated his hand from Edgar's grasp. "I should be going now."

"Do you have to?" Edgar hesitated. "There's something I could use your help with."

"What's that?"

"I need to tell Salvadore's wife what happened. I …" He shook his head. "I've known him for thirty years, but I don't know what to say. Carmen will be very upset, and I don't know how to tell her. You have a calm way of saying things, like you did to the police and 911. Please, I could use your help."

"Sidetracked again," the voice inside whispered. "What happened to no entanglements?"

Sole nodded. "Alright. I'll go with you."

SIXTEEN

When Was He Going to Learn?

"Carmen, are you there?" Edgar Dupart knocked softly on the screen door.

John Sole stood at his side, hands folded respectfully in front of him. It wasn't his city or his fight, but Edgar asked for help, and he couldn't look the old man in the eye and deny him.

Apparently, he still had a conscience. That surprised him, and he wondered if that was a good thing.

The old man, Salvadore Estevez, was still alive, at least he was when they loaded him in the ambulance, but this had the feel of a death notification. He'd done more of those during his police years than he cared to remember. They were never easy, and the reality was there was nothing to do but say what you had to say, get out of the way and let the family begin to grieve.

Sometimes they thanked you for coming by, but Sole always knew it was a lie. How could you really thank someone for stopping by to tell you your son or daughter, father or mother were dead? They were just the words people say when they don't know what else to say.

He shifted uncomfortably from one foot to the other. Edgar Dupart leaned over, peering through the screen into the dim interior. Just do this and get back on the road, he reminded himself.

He caught a glimpse of an old woman shuffling through the small living room, unaware of their presence, muttering to herself. Her movements seemed erratic and confused. They watched her pick up a handbag from a table, then put it down and go to a closet to get a pair of shoes. She sat in a chair to put on the shoes, but stood up again and rushed to the back of the house barefoot.

"The stove," she said. "I left the burner on."

A few seconds later, she rushed back into view, muttering. "I told you, Salvadore to be careful when you are out. Give them what they want. I told you, you're no fighter." She put a weathered hand to her forehead, shaking her head to clear away the fog. "I have to go …. that's it I have to go."

She disappeared out of sight down a hallway.

Edgar knocked again and gave the screen a tug. It rattled in its frame but did not open. The old fashioned safety hook was dropped down in the eye screw.

Sole glanced up and down the street and wondered at the innocence of an elderly couple, sitting in their home in one of the highest crime areas in a major city with nothing more than a safety hook on a screen door to provide security. It would not have deterred even the most incompetent burglar, yet, Salvadore and Carmen Estevez sat comfortably behind their screen door, secure in the knowledge that they had done what they could to keep the devil away. He envied their innocence.

"She doesn't hear too good," Edgar said to Sole then called again as Carmen shuffled from the hallway into the living room. "Carmen! Over here, at the door!" He waved a hand.

It was the wave that caught her attention. She hurried to the door and pushed the safety hook out of the eye screw. Edgar pulled the door open. Carmen rushed into his arms, her wrinkled face wet with tears.

"Edgar, they hurt my Salvadore," she sobbed. "Someone called … they said I should come." She looked up into his eyes. "But I don't know where to go! Where do I go, Edgar?"

"That's why we came, Carmen. We wanted to tell you before the hospital called." Edgar patted her shoulder.

"What happened, Edgar?" Carmen wiped the tears away with the palm of her hand.

"He was attacked."

"My God! Who would attack my Salvadore!" She cried, and in the next breath added, "I told him to be careful, to just give them what they want and not fight." She shook her head. "He's no fighter, my Salvadore.

"He didn't fight. Listen to me." Edgar put his hands on her shoulders, holding her so she would look him in the eyes. "He was attacked by some young people."

A few more minutes to be polite, and then leave, Sole reminded himself. There was nothing he could do for these people that the hospital and police weren't already doing.

"Who would do that?" Carmen asked.

"This man saw it. He can tell you better than me." Edgar turned to Sole.

So much for leaving. Sole fought back the urge to sigh.

Carmen looked at him, puzzled, acknowledging his presence for the first time. "You saw what happened?"

"Part of it." Sole nodded. "A van with the people who did it inside almost ran into me."

"But who was it?"

"I don't know. Gang members maybe. No one I know." He tried a smile to put her at ease. "I told the police everything. I'm sure they will find the ones who did it."

"Bah!" Carmen threw her hands in the air. "The police. They aren't any use around here. This used to be a nice place to live. Now ..." She nodded at the screen door and its sad little safety hook. "You have to keep the doors locked in the middle of the day."

"Well, I'm sure they will try to find out who is responsible, and ..." He fumbled for something to say. "I'm sure he is getting the best treatment at the hospital."

"The hospital!" Her eyes opened wide, remembering what she had been doing when they arrived. "I have to get to the hospital to see about Salvadore." She shook her head. "But I don't have any way to get there." She looked from Sole to Edgar. "Can you take me?"

"Yes, of course," Edgar said. He looked at Sole. "Is that alright, I mean?"

They had come in Sole's pickup. It seemed like a good idea at the time. He could help break the news to Carmen Estevez and then take his leave without having to rely on Edgar to get him back.

"Sure. We'll go together."

They waited while Carmen put on her shoes. Edgar reminded her to take her handbag.

The University of New Mexico Hospital Emergency Room was ten minutes away. Edgar sat in the back crew cab seat, silent, the worry about his friend plain on his face. Carmen sobbed and muttered softly to herself. John Sole asked himself what he was doing.

He shook his head. When was he going to learn?

SEVENTEEN

I'll Stay

He hated hospitals. Nothing good happened in hospitals.

Bobby and Samantha were born in a hospital, he reminded himself. That was a good thing, the best thing that had ever happened to him, for him, in spite of him, thanks to Shaye. Alright, some good things happened in hospitals, he admitted, but not this.

John Sole looked around the waiting room. A television mounted in the corner, seven feet up a wall, displayed a fuzzy image of a pride of lions with their heads buried in what looked like the carcass of a zebra. The volume was turned down, making the narration inaudible. It didn't matter. No one was watching.

A dozen others sat on plastic chairs outside the UNM Hospital emergency room. A few had their heads back, dozing. Some were whispering among themselves. One man had a blood-soaked towel wrapped around his forearm, and another woman held a rag to her swollen cheek. Apparently, neither was injured severely enough to be granted immediate access to a treatment room.

Edgar Dupart had disappeared down the hallway with Carmen Estevez thirty minutes earlier. Sole sat on a plastic chair, waiting, annoyed with himself, anxious to be away and back to his game of cat and mouse with the cartel.

Another fifteen minutes passed before Edgar emerged through the double doors into the waiting area. Sole rose to meet him, ready to take him home and move on.

"How is she?" he asked.

"Alright, I suppose," Edgar replied and shook his head. "She was shocked when she saw Salvadore … almost fainted. He doesn't look good."

"That's understandable. Any prognosis from the doctor?"

"Not really. They gave him some medication, a diuretic to reduce fluid pressure on the brain. If that doesn't work, the doctor said it would take surgery … can't remember what he called it, but it is supposed to relieve pressure if the drugs don't work."

"Decompressive craniectomy," Sole said. "Friend of mine in the Corps had it done after he was thrown into a block wall by an incoming mortar round."

"Right. That's it." Edgar nodded. "Did your friend survive?"

"He did," Sole said, without adding that his friend also, spoke with a slur from that time forward and was partially paralyzed on his left side.

They stood without speaking, Edgar staring at the wall beyond Sole's shoulder, worry etched into his face. They might have remained like that all night if Sole had not cleared his throat and said, "I suppose I should take you home now."

"Oh." Edgar nodded. "Right … home. Sorry. I guess my mind is a little preoccupied."

"That's understandable." Sole waited, ready to go but not wanting to rush the old man

"Well." Edgar turned toward the exit. "Yes, I suppose we should go. I can come back tomorrow and check on Salvadore."

They walked side by side under the yellow glow of the parking lot's sodium lamps. Sole unlocked the pickup door for Edgar then went around to the driver's side. As he climbed behind the wheel, he noticed Edgar watching him with a disquieting intensity. He ignored the stare, determined to take the man home, wish him well, and get the hell out of Albuquerque.

Sole pulled from the parking lot. Traffic was light around the hospital at this time of night. Edgar's eyes continued to bore into him. Sole continued to ignore the stare.

They almost made it to the place where they met, the sidewalk in front of Dupart's Market, when Edgar finally spoke.

"There is something I wanted to talk to you about." He hesitated and added, "I mean, we barely met, and you've already done more than enough, but ..."

Here it comes, he thought. Be strong, John-boy. Life is hard for everyone, but you can't change the world. You've got business elsewhere.

"I could use your help with something ... with someone."

Sole remained silent. Should he just say no now, or let the old man finish and then decline?

After several seconds, Edgar nodded. "I don't have any right to ask ... to impose on you ... it's just ..."

Sole sighed. "What?"

"It's my grandson, Benjamin ... Ben his friends call him."

"What about him?"

"These gang people ... the ones who hurt Salvadore ... they have their eyes on him, always watching, tempting him to join them, like wolves ready to bring them into their pack." He shrugged. "I don't know how else to say it."

"Wolves." Sole nodded. "Good a description as any. You think he is really interested in joining a gang?"

"It's not a matter of interest. For some young men, the gang means survival, a way to find their place in the world." Edgar said, shaking his head. "But it is a bad place, an evil one that changes these young boys. I have seen it happen too many times."

"What is it you want me to do?"

"I don't know. I'm not sure there is anything that can be done, but I have to try something, anything, and you ..." He shrugged. "There's a strength in the way you handle yourself. I think he might respect that."

"Sounds like something his father should be doing," Sole countered, searching for a polite way to say, no, find someone else.

"His father is dead."

"Oh." John-boy, you are an ass, he thought. "Sorry, Edgar. I didn't mean ..."

Edgar held up a hand. "No, no. You didn't know. Besides, he has been dead for many years now, not long after my grandson was born."

"Still, I'm sorry," Sole said. "But I don't think I'm ...."

"His mother, Magdalena, and I raised him," Edgar interrupted and continued. "He was always a good boy, and then we started to see him being pulled from us." He shook his head. "I want to save my grandson. I thought maybe another man, someone like his father, might be able to show him another way to live. Someone like you."

"But I'm not his father," Sole said shaking his head. "I wouldn't be comfortable …"

Once again, Edgar interrupted.

"You are even about the same age as his father, Jean Paul, would be." Edgar spoke rapidly now, trying to get it all out before this man said no. "We have room for you. You could stay. There would be no charge, and it would be a blessing for us."

"Do you mind if I ask how his father died?"

"In the war … Afghanistan. He said he would be gone for a year" Edgar shrugged, his face a wrinkled mask of sorrow. "He went into the army. I did the same at his age." Edgar gave a shrug and looked down. "I came home, but he did not."

Sole sighed again. Seventeen years of war and the casualties kept mounting, on the battlefield and at home. He nodded.

"I'll stay."

EIGHTEEN

Blooded

"That's some classic shit!" Slice bobbed his head in rhythm to the beat coming from an MP3 player pumping out *Scarface* by the Geto Boys.

"Classic!" Cheech laughed. "That's just old shit, man."

"Naw." Slice smiled benevolently and took a pull off the oversized joint dangling between his fingertips. "I'm tellin' you, that's classic. That's where we come from, bro."

"Hey, Keet," Sliced shouted across the empty warehouse they used as a gang meeting place. "What do you say? This shit classic or what?"

"Classic, bro." Keet nodded and grinned, his head bobbing in time with Slice's.

"Whatever, man." Cheech shook his head and ambled away, muttering. "That's the shit my daddy was listenin' to in the day."

Slice leaned back in the lawn chair that served as his throne and surveyed his domain. *Demonios de la Muerte* gang members were sprawled in various positions around the room. A few were in the dark corners where girls who hung with the gang were giving blow jobs.

They took turns with the girls. In exchange, the girls received protection from the gang and had access to the meth, cocaine, and weed the DMs dealt on street corners around Albuquerque. Most importantly, they had status in the community. No one fucked with DM's women.

It was time to call the group to order. There was business to conduct.

"Yo!" Slice shouted.

Heads turned around the warehouse. A couple of DM members stumbled from the corners zipping up their pants. Ape moved to stand beside Slice, acting as the sergeant at arms.

"We got a new man today," Slice called out.

Heads bobbed and nodded. A few reached over to clap Keet on the back. "Yeah, a new man," they chimed in. "New blood!"

"That's right, new blood." Slice nodded. "And tonight, he got to *be blooded*."

Keet paled. He knew it was coming, but after his success in the knockout game, somewhere in his cocaine-jacked brain, he had hoped this might be forgotten. He was learning that Slice never forgot anything.

"Stand up!" The DM leader ordered. "Stand in the center."

Keet rose from the stack of pallets he sat on to stand in the middle of the room.

"You know what gonna happen?"

Keet nodded, his eyes wide, but determined to see it through. Knocking out the old man was only the initiation that gave him the right to receive the ritual that would make him a full-blooded DM. He was close now to being one of them. Soon, he could sit in this room, not just as the new blood, but respected by the others and feared by those outside the gang.

The first blow was landed by Ape, universally respected as the strongest gang member, and whose personality rivaled even Slice's viciousness. Keet staggered and went to his knees. The DMs watched. The circle tightened around him. They waited. If he rose to face them, the beating would continue until every DM had a chance to use his fists or feet on him. When it ended, he could stand there, bloodied and battered, but one of them

If at any point, he remained down, the beating would still continue, with even more ferocity, but when it ended, they would drag him from the room, load him in a van and dump him unceremoniously in a ditch somewhere. He might survive the beating, but he would never be a blooded member of the gang.

Keet rose to his feet and turned his now bruised and lopsided face to Ape. Ape nodded and stepped aside. Cheech was next, followed by Poco, then by all the gang members. The last was Slice, who did a flamboyant Bruce Lee imitation that had the others shouting approval and ended with a roundhouse kick to the gut.

Keet doubled over, bleeding from his mouth and nose, his face bruised and ears red from the blows they had dealt out to him. Slowly, he stood up straight. It was over.

Slice stepped forward, took his head between his hands, and looked into his eyes. "You one of us, now, for real. What they do to you, they do to us all. What someone does to one of ours they do to you. Right?"

Keet nodded and managed to whisper through swollen lips, "Right."

NINETEEN

A Good Start

"Come in." Edgar pushed the door to the upstairs apartment open and stepped aside.

Sole smiled and stepped over the threshold into a world filled with the aromas of something he couldn't quite put his finger or nose on. Edgar followed him in and closed the door behind, hanging the keys to the store downstairs on a hook mounted on the wall beside the door.

"It's not much, but we live comfortably here over the store," Edgar said, leading Sole down the short hallway into the living room. "And this is our world."

He laughed and spread his arms out, motioning around the room. The walls were covered with an odd mix of art, some of it clearly from south of the border, mixed with images and landscapes that reminded Sole of the south, but he couldn't quite put his finger on why.

A woman came from the kitchen, wiping her hands on a dishtowel. Her hair was black, her eyes brown, and her smile as broad as Edgar's.

"You must be Bill Myers, the one Edgar phoned to tell

me about." She extended a hand to Sole. "I am Magdalena, but call me Maggie."

"Alright, Maggie." Sole returned her smile and the handshake. "Nice to meet you."

He turned to Edgar. "You phoned?"

"Yes. While I was with Carmen at the hospital." Edgar shrugged, a sheepish smile on his face. "I had to check with her first before I spoke to you. She is Ben's mother after all."

You were set up John-boy, he thought. They set an ambush and you fell right into it.

He shook his head and looked around. The apartment was homey and comfortable with an old-world air about it. Edgar and Maggie were clearly happy to have him as their guest. He was instantly at ease.

"Nice home you have here," he said, taking in the room. "Wouldn't expect all this up here over the store."

"Ah," Edgar laughed. "Yes, our small oasis in the midst of the barren desert. Magdalena makes it a home for us."

"Papa, show Mr. Myers his room so he can put his things away, and then we'll have a drink and eat."

"Yes, madam," Edgar said with a nod. "This way, Bill."

They walked down a small hallway to the rear of the apartment. Edgar pushed a door open and stepped aside. "Here you go. Your home away from home."

Sole entered and found a room lined with books. A desk had been pushed to one side and a folding, roll-out bed positioned in the center of the room.

"It's not much. I use the room as a den mostly, but the bed is fairly comfortable," Edgar said and laughed. "I should know. I slept on it for years after Louisa died. We never had time or money to buy real furniture. We were saving for it, and then the baby came, and we put every extra penny into making a room for Jean Paul." He shrugged. "After she passed, I lost the desire to worry about beds and furnishings. It was a dark time for me. If not for Jean Paul and the need to care for him ..."

His voice cracked, and he swallowed and said no more.

"This is perfect," Sole said. "Couldn't ask for a nicer place to stay."

"Yes, well, make yourself at home. There is a bathroom across the hall and three other rooms. Bedrooms for Magdalena, Benjamin, and me. You'll find you have lots of privacy. Nobody will disturb you."

"Thank you, Edgar." Sole placed the duffel he carried on the bed. "Feels like home already."

Edgar smiled. "Good, good ... and no thanks are needed. I owe you thanks for agreeing to stay for a while to try and help my grandson."

It was an uncomfortable reminder of why he was standing in this apartment with a man he hadn't known until today. Sole wasn't sure what help he could be but found it impossible to say so to Edgar and dash his hopes of salvation for his grandson.

"And Benjamin, when will I meet him?" he asked.

"Oh, we never know." Edgar shook his head. "He comes and goes, but at some point he has to come home if only to eat. Then you'll meet him."

"Fair enough." Sole nodded.

"Dinner is ready," Magdalena called from the kitchen.

"Good. I'm famished," Edgar said, patting his stomach.

They sat around an old-style kitchen table, chrome-plated steel with a pink formica top. There were four places set, but only three were needed. Maggie placed a large pot on a trivet in the center of the table.

"Hope you like jambalaya," she said. "Please help yourself, Mr. Myers."

"That's what I smelled," Sole nodded, grinning. "Couldn't put my finger on that aroma."

He lifted the ladle and filled his bowl, then held it out for Maggie. She shook her head.

"Nope. Guests first, then the others at the table. The cook always goes last." A mischievous look twinkling in her eyes, she added, "The cook knows what's in the pot."

Edgar laughed, slapping the table with his palm. "That's a good one!"

Sole grinned and filled his mouth with jambalaya.

The conversation was mostly about Salvadore Estevez's condition and how Carmen was handling things. Edgar filled in the blank spots for Maggie. She had stayed behind to mind the store after they left to get Carmen and go to the hospital. Occasionally, she would shake her head and mutter, "*Animales.*" Animals.

"Yes," Edgar would agree and nod.

Sole said little, keenly aware of their concern that Benjamin was on track to become an animal like the ones who had attacked Salvadore Estevez. They were hoping for a miracle from him. He felt all out of miracles.

After dinner, Sole helped them clear up and sat with them in the living room. Edgar poured absinthe into small glasses and passed them around. He held a glass up to the light and smiled as the emerald substance shimmered in his hand.

"From my French Creole heritage," he said. "A habit I acquired from my father." Edgar lifted the glass higher, looking into Sole's eyes. "To new friends."

"To new friends." Sole nodded and sipped the absinthe. The flavor was complex, anise with hints of fruits and bitters. He nodded, pleasantly surprised, and sipped again.

They finished their drinks in silence, and then Edgar

placed his glass on a side table and turned to Sole. "You must have many questions. Perhaps you should ask them so you know we are hiding nothing from you."

"I'll probably have plenty of questions later," Sole replied. It was time to be honest. "But truthfully, I am not sure what I can do to help. I'm a stranger. Seems like Ben is as likely to resent me and anything I have to say, than to listen."

"This is true." Edgar nodded. He looked at Maggie. "Explain. You say things better than me."

"I understand my boy," she began. "He is not bad. I can't speak for the others ... these gang boys ... but my son is not bad, but there is something missing." She looked into Sole's eyes. "He lacks a father. We try our best, but he needs more than a grandfather and a mother. He needs a man to help him see what a man is and how to become one."

Sole knew most gang members came from broken homes, single-parent families, or families where parents turned their children over to the streets to be educated. A common denominator was the lack of a male figure in the home.

"Just be who you are," Maggie continued. "Let him see what a man is. It's that simple."

It didn't sound simple, and Sole was more than a little uncomfortable under her intense gaze. Maggie read it on his face and laughed.

"Don't worry, Bill Myers. I am not looking for a man in my life, only one in my son's life." She turned to a picture on the wall over Edgar's chair. It was a soldier, wearing desert utilities, an M-16 rifle cradled in his arms as he smiled into the camera. "There will only ever be one man in my life."

The front door crashed open and slammed shut. Heavy

footsteps tromped down the hallway. A young man came in wearing baggie jeans, the ubiquitous, flat-brimmed ball cap, sneakers, and a tee-shirt. He was tall like his grandfather, dark-haired and brown-eyed like his mother.

Benjamin Dupart stopped as he entered the living room, stared at Sole, and scowled. "Who the fuck is this?"

Maggie was about to reprimand him for his rudeness. Sole shook his head, rose, and stepped across the room to stand directly in front of the boy. He put out his hand.

"Bill Myers." He smiled. "You must be Benjamin."

The boy made no effort to accept the handshake.

"His friends call him Ben," Maggie said to break the uncomfortable silence.

"Alright ... Ben," Sole said. "Good to meet you."

The boy eyed the newcomer in silence, his chin lifted, jaw clenched, eyebrows raised in the typical gang challenge posture. They remained like that, Sole smiling, Benjamin glaring back, for several seconds before the boy turned and stomped down the hall to his bedroom without speaking a word. The door slammed behind him.

"Well, that didn't go so well," Sole said, returning to his chair.

"You are wrong," Edgar said, smiling. "He said nothing. I think it is a good start."

A good start? Sole wondered what a bad start would have been. The little voice inside his head was laughing.

"Told you to keep moving. You never listen, do you, John-boy?"

TWENTY

News

The chorus of an old Hank Williams song began playing in his pocket. It was Billy Siever's ringtone for calls from unknown numbers.

John Sole called infrequently and never from the same number, preferring to use disposable, burners. Billy accepted the minor inconvenience. It meant he ended up answering the occasional robocall or survey-taker or salesperson trying to convince him about the best deal on a mortgage or insurance, but he reckoned he owed at least that much to his friend.

Hank's mournful voice sang out, "I'm so lonesome I could cry …"

Billy answered the call. "Yes?"

"Semper Fi."

Hearing John always made Billy smile

"How are you?" he asked, careful not to inquire about John's whereabouts, information he would not have provided in any event.

"Wandering as usual. How about you?"

"No changes in Happy Valley."

It was the signal they used. Isabella, Sandy, and Jacinta were safe and well. Sole nodded, satisfied.

"Good." He sat on the rollaway bed in Edgar Dupart's den and spoke in a low voice. "Anything out of the ordinary going on? People nosing around, asking questions?"

"No. Not that I'm aware of. Why? Is there a problem?"

"No problem. Just wanted to be sure. I'm thinking of staying put where I'm at right now, at least for a little while. Maybe a few weeks. Kind of up in the air, but I wanted to be sure everything was okay in Happy Valley."

Billy understood. Wherever John was, he wanted to stay for a while and postpone his game of chase with the cartel.

"Everything is fine here," Billy said, reassuring him.

"Good. Then you may not hear from me for a while. I don't want to spend much time on the phone as long as I'm in one place, using the same number."

"Understood." Billy didn't hear from him much now and wondered how long 'a while' might be in John's estimation.

"Alright, then." Sole was about to end the call.

"There's some news you need to hear."

Billy hesitated, reluctant to mention the information Isabella had shared with him, but he knew he had to. It was only fair.

"Okay." Sole listened, curious. Billy was not given to drama.

"Well, first of all, Sandy and Jacinta …"

"No names," Sole interrupted.

"Right, sorry," Billy continued. "They are having a baby … the young ones. Looks like you are going to be …" Billy paused. "An uncle, I guess."

"That's wonderful! You're right I needed to hear that."

Billy could almost see John grinning through the phone. He worried that the next piece of information would not be so welcome but pressed forward.

"There's something else." Billy hesitated considering how to say it without mentioning names. "She met someone."

"She?" John understood immediately who 'she' was, but he hesitated anyway, working hard to push his lingering feelings for her deep down inside. "Oh. That's ... that's good too." His tone was soft and distant but became firmer as he spoke. "That's very good."

Billy had one more piece of information, and he felt like an ass saying it, but John had a right to hear it. "They are planning to be married."

John was silent for several seconds, then his voice was back, firmer and in control. Billy knew that the grin had faded, replaced by grim acceptance. John would feel duty-bound to say the right thing.

"Of course," John said. "It's what she should do. It's time. She should be happy. Tell her I said so, and give her my best."

"I will."

"Anything else?" John asked, businesslike and abrupt.

"No. That's about all ... enough I suppose."

"Alright. Like I said, you won't hear from me for a while. I'll contact you when I am on the move again."

The call ended quickly after that. One minute they were talking, the next the line went dead.

Billy's conscience nagged at him. He second guessed himself and wondered if he should have given John the news about Isabella. What would it matter of he hadn't? John Sole was alone. Why make him feel even lonelier?

Because John never lied to him, and he deserved to hear the truth. It was a shitty situation, but it was the only one they had.

TWENTY-ONE

See How It Is?

Ben Dupart ran the gauntlet every day. At least, he did any day he went to school.

As in many inner-city communities, the gangs were the real power on the streets, controlling blocks of territory like feudal lords. If you were known as a local by the controlling gang, it was usually safe enough to move about, but as soon as you left your neighborhood you became a potential target.

Gang eyes were everywhere, and an unwary pedestrian ran the risk of being spotted by a local gang member from a different neighborhood. Simply crossing from one corner to the next always carried with it an element of risk. Harassment by groups of gang thugs was common. Tolls were often required to pass safely through the gang's turf, and once the offending outsider paid up, there still was no guarantee he wouldn't be waylaid in an alley as soon as he turned the corner.

Robbery, random assaults, and murder were all part of life in gangland. Victims were usually those the gang did not accept as one of theirs but could be anyone, often determined by the quantity of meth, cocaine or pot the gang members had consumed that day.

Ben Dupart's walk to and from school stretched a half-mile. Too close to qualify for school bus service, in that painfully long half-mile he passed through the turf of three separate gangs. It would have been infinitely safer if the entire area had been controlled by the *Demonios de la Muerte* —DMs—the gang that controlled the street where he lived over the store with his mother and grandfather. The school board, however, drew the district boundaries without consideration of the turf staked out by the gangs.

After passing unscathed through DM turf, Ben faced the three-block stretch claimed by the Death Bombers—DBs. The final four blocks, with the high school in sight at the t-intersection ahead, belonged to the Central Avenue Killers —Cent Killers, or just Cents.

He maintained his usual brisk pace, eyes focused ahead, not making eye contact with anyone. His senses tingled, searching for signs of approaching danger. Seven minutes had elapsed since he left the store, ignoring his mother's goodbye. In that time, he had covered three-quarters of the distance to the high school. Ben began to breathe easy.

"What you doin' here, boy?"

He tensed, his muscles twitching involuntarily, his fight-or-flight reflex taking over with flight dominating. He wanted to run as quickly as possible to the relative safety of the school. He had to force himself to hold his ground. *Don't run. Running will make things .worse, maybe get you killed. Take the beating if you have to, but survive another day.*

He turned to face the two Cent Killers dressed in the gang's blue and gold colors. His eyes met theirs but he remained silent. There wasn't anything he could say that would change the outcome. This was about maintaining a certain amount of street credibility—cred—by showing that he wouldn't run. Unflinching silence in the face of the danger—fearless indifference to the threat—these were his only real defense. An air of passive defiance might make them go easier on him. It didn't always work out that way, but resisting or fleeing would only make it worse.

The speaker was short and stocky. A long scar across his cheek proved that he was a blooded member of the gang, knifed in some fight with a rival gang or one of his own gang members. His mother named him Carlos. The Cent Killers simply called him *Cicatriz*—Scar—or Triz for short.

The second was taller and although his face bore no scars the three red tattoos on his neck in the shape of drops of blood were evidence that he had assaulted others and drawn blood, possibly killing them. No one knew for sure, but he was known on the streets as Rip, short for Jack the Ripper.

Ben recognized both, had passed them before on the street without incident. Today fate had turned against him. For whatever reason, they decided that this was the day to fuck with the interloper onto their turf.

"I said what you doin' here, boy?"

The gangbangers closed in. The speaker pushed his face to within three inches of Ben's, his chin held up in the gang challenge posture. His partner moved in close enough for his chest to touch Ben's shoulder.

Ben let his eyes move in a lazy unconcerned way up the street to the school and then back to the speaker. The next few seconds were critical. They would either respect his fearless indifference or beat the shit out of him.

"School?" Triz sneered and looked at his taller partner.

"This pussy thinks he can just walk up our street 'cause he goes to school."

"Fuck him," Rip growled back.

He was almost leaning against Ben now, and the speaker had his face so close their chins nearly touched. The blatant violation of his personal space sent a message. They had no fear of him and dared him to resist or fight.

Mentally, Ben resigned himself to the inevitable. He knew they had already made their decision. All he could do was try to survive the inevitable beat-down that was only seconds away.

"Hey, Benny!"

The SUV pulled along the curb before the two Cent Killers could turn. Slice sat behind the wheel, Ape in the passenger seat, Cheech and Keet in the rear.

The Cent Killers backed away an inch so that they could turn and face the newcomers. Ben remained motionless, only his eyes moving toward the SUV. He gave a nod to acknowledge their presence.

"*¿Qué está pasando aquí, pendejos?*" What's going on here, assholes?

The Cent Killers moved another couple of inches away from Ben.

Keet leaned out the rear window, grinning. "Hey, Benny. We been lookin' for you. Climb in."

Triz decided it was time to meet this overt challenge to their control of the situation. "You in the wrong place DM. You best get your ass off our street."

"Don't think you're in any position to be talkin' so tough." Slice grinned and held the pistol up, pointing it at Scar's face.

The Cent Killers were not novices and had their own

street cred to consider. A pistol pointed at them from a car would not be enough to scare them away.

"You thinkin' about startin' a war here on our turf." Triz laughed. "You fuckin' outta your mind. We'll kill you and your mother and your dog. Hell, I'll even kill your sister after I fuck her."

"Our friend Benny is comin' with us." Slice turned his head to the others in the car. "Ain't that right."

"Yeah, that's right." Keet lifted a pistol and leaned out the window toward Rip. Ape opened the front passenger door and stepped out, leveling a short-barreled shotgun at Triz.

Ben began to think he might survive the encounter without the beatdown. The trick now was to extricate himself from between the two Cent Killers and get into the SUV before the bullets started flying.

He turned his body sideways and stepped toward the curb, trying not to brush against either of his captors. Still holding the pistol on Rip, Keet pushed the door open and stepped out so that Ben could climb into the middle. When he was seated, Keet reentered the SUV as did Ape. The only gun visible now was Slice's, still pointing at the Cent Killers from the window.

"We'll be goin' now." He grinned and put the car in gear, squealing the tires as he roared away.

"*Eres pendejos muertos!*" You're dead assholes, Triz shouted after them.

"Not today, motherfucker," Keet shouted back.

Slice roared past the high school at the end of the block.

"I need to get out here," Ben said. "Exams today."

"No school today." Slice watched him in the rearview mirror.

"It's all good, bro." Keet clapped him on the back. "You gonna see."

Slice drove them through the city on a sort of tour. Here and there he would slow and point out a corner where another gang sold drugs, or had a safe house, or where there had been a drive-by shooting the previous week, or where the DMs had found another gangbanger trespassing on their turf and had sent him away with a beating or worse.

Sometime during the drive, Keet passed him a joint, then another. He mellowed out, sitting back and taking in Slice's orientation tour.

They ended up at an old warehouse. A bay door opened in the rear and Slice drove the SUV inside.

As they climbed out of the car, Ben saw a group huddled around a bloodied young man hunched over under a fluorescent light on the other side of the room. Slice led the way to the group and paused in front of them to stare down at the young man on the floor. His face swollen and bloody from the beating they had given him, he looked up with pleading eyes.

Slice turned to the apparent leader of the group. Tall and impossibly skinny, his long narrow head swiveled on a pencil neck. An uneven three-day growth of whiskers covered his scruffy cheeks and a missing front tooth made it hard not to stare at his mouth. Like many gang members, he earned his gang name from his dominant physical attribute.

"What's up, Thin?"

"He short." Thin turned to Slice. "Went out with ten

eights and come back with a grand. Shoulda been almost two grand."

Growing up in the neighborhood, Ben knew enough about the drug culture to understand that the young man on the floor was one of their dealers who had been sent out to sell ten eightballs of cocaine. Thin said he only brought back a thousand dollars, when the price should have been almost two thousand.

Slice looked down at the young man, not more than sixteen years old, shifting his feet nervously as if he might try to get up and run. "Why you shortin' us Edgy?"

"I was gonna pay it back, Slice. I swear."

"You steal from your brothers, you know what happens."

Edgy began sobbing. "You know, I know. You think I would steal from my brothers?" He shook his head, and tears flew from the sides of his red cheeks. "Never. I swear. I only needed a loan ... that's all just a loan. I woulda paid it back from my cut when I got it. You got to believe me."

"A loan?" Slice's eyebrows crinkled like he was examining a curious insect on the sidewalk before stepping on it. "What the fuck that mean?"

"My sister ... she's sick. My mother took her to the clinic. They gave her a prescription, but we needed money to pay for the medicine." He looked up, his eyes begging Slice to believe him. "I took some money for the medicine and the doctor, but I was gonna pay it back. I swear it on my mother's life ... on my sister's life!"

Slice was silent for several seconds before looking around at the group. "Alright. Edgy's sister is bad sick. Throw in what you can to help out."

Rolls of bills came from pockets. Ape walked around collecting the cash and handed it to Slice who thumbed through the wad of bills, counting. "Looks like about a grand here." He held it out to Edgy. "Take it … from your brothers."

Hand trembling, Edgy reached up to receive the roll of bills. "Thank you, Slice … I mean thank you all … I didn't know what …"

"Stand on your feet," Slice ordered.

Edgy rose from the floor, wiping the tears from his eyes. They stood face to face, eyes locked for several seconds before Slice spoke.

"You need something, you come to us. You understand?"

Edgy nodded without speaking.

"You take from us again … from your brothers … and you die. You understand that too?"

Edgy nodded again.

"When someone takes from *Demonios de la Muerte*, there has to be blood."

The knife came out of Slice's pocket in one smooth movement. The blade passed across Edgy's cheek before he had time to realize what had happened. His hand reached up to hold the gash closed, but he did not cry out.

Slice nodded his approval and turned to the others. "We got our blood. Bandage him up and give him a shot of tequila." Then he laughed and added, "Fuck! Give everyone a shot."

Thin led Edgy away to bandage his face. Afterward, they sat together on a stack of old pallets, passing a joint back and forth in between shots of tequila.

Ben watched the entire scene, standing beside Keet, his eyes riveted on Slice and Edgy, moving from face to face as the drama played out. There was a sort of justice here, hard but also fair in a perverted sort of way.

This was his school now. The things he could learn here would help him survive on the streets. The building he had set off walking to that morning to appease his mother and grandfather had little to offer. The rules here might be harsh but they were clear and easy to understand. Break the rules and pay the price.

And there was brotherhood here too. Slice had shown mercy to Edgy because he was a brother. The forgiveness from the group had been immediate. It was an intoxicating concept for a fatherless young man, looking for his place in the world.

"You see how it is, Benny?" Keet said.

"I see how it is." Ben nodded.

TWENTY-TWO

The Man in the Alley

He was feeling unnecessary. Worse, he was failing.

Ben embraced his gang friends more closely and became more distant from his family as the days passed. It was only a matter of time before the *Demonios de la Muerte* dragged him in as a full member.

Sole knew Ben was not alone. Gang life could seduce young men like a backstreet whore. Lost in a world they did not make, mostly without fathers, the brotherhood and respect of the gang became their reason for living, and sometimes dying.

He needed a better plan. Waiting for the chance to strike up a conversation with Ben was not a plan. Over dinner the previous evening, he had explained his feelings of inadequacy to Edgar and Maggie.

"I don't see that I'm doing much good here. Maybe I should move on."

Maggie stared down at her plate without speaking.

"Things take time," Edgar replied, looking into Sole's eyes.

Maggie remained silent.

"True." Sole nodded. "Some things do take time, but ..."

He hesitated. The truth was that Benjamin might already be lost, one more wasted life in a generation of wasted lives.

"Please don't give up." Maggie looked up, her eyes pleading with him.

"Bill has a life to live, Magdalena ... someplace else to go." Edgar patted her hand and turned to Sole. "I see it in you. There's something you must do and you are only here because we pressured you, and you are a good man who could not refuse a widow and an old man who begged for your help."

"It's not that. It's just ..."

"Of course, it is." Edgar held up his hand. "No explanation is necessary. You have every right to want to move on to your business elsewhere."

"I want to help," Sole said. "I'm just having a hard time finding a way to make a connection with Ben." He shook his head. "I want to help. I'm just not sure how."

"Stay a little while longer... a few more days even ... then leave and take care of your business," Edgar said. "I know we are not being fair to you. We have no choice. If you could spare us a few more days, we would be grateful ... my dead son, Ben's father, would be grateful."

Their eyes locked together. Neither spoke. If Sole felt any resentment at the pressure Edgar placed on him, he didn't show it.

The truth was Edgar had struck a chord in his heart. Do

it for the boy's dead father, a comrade in arms. It was settled. For once, the voice in his head didn't argue.

"Alright, let's talk tactics."

The morning rush at Dupart's Market wasn't really a rush. It was a procession of older residents of the neighborhood, mixed in with a few younger patrons, mothers or fathers mostly, running in for a gallon of milk, or cereal, bread, and eggs. The older residents mostly just wanted a good cup of coffee, the morning paper, and a chat with Edgar about the latest neighborhood news.

Above, in the second-floor apartment, Sole sat at the kitchen table with Maggie, sipping coffee and waiting. Bumps and thumps coming through the walls signaled that Ben was stirring. He'd come in late the night before and to this point, his only interaction with the Sole had been to throw a snarl in his direction as he stomped by.

Sole stood up from the table. Maggie watched him, coffee cup in hand.

"Be careful. The boys he is with … the gang boys … they are dangerous, vicious like wild dogs in the alley when I take out the garbage at night."

"I'll be careful." Sole nodded and left the apartment.

Descending the stairs, he glanced into the store as he passed. Inside, Edgar leaned over the counter chatting with an old woman. Bundled in a frayed sweater, she folded her arms across her body against the chill of advanced age. Edgar nodded at Sole, then turned back to the woman who passed on some bit of news he would repeat later to others who came in.

Sole went into the alley and sat in his pickup. Ben was missing school, which meant he had found somewhere else to be during the day. No doubt, he was spending time with the DM gangbangers, but Sole needed more information. Where were they? What were they doing? What was Ben doing?

With those pieces of the puzzle, he might find a way to help, or at least stop something bad from happening to the boy. It was now an intelligence gathering mission. Those were the tactics he had discussed with Edgar and Maggie the night before.

In the apartment above, Ben's bedroom door opened and slammed shut. He appeared, walked through the living room, and ignored his mother.

"Where are you headed today?" Maggie called from the kitchen.

"Out," Ben snarled in a surly, don't-fuck-with-me tone.

"Out where? I know you aren't going to school."

Ben paused and looked into the kitchen. "You spying on me?"

Future gangbanger or not, he used the usual juvenile misdirection many teens employ when confronted by their parents. He turned the question back on her as if the real issue was whether she had been watching her own son.

"No." She shook her head and put down the coffee cup. "I don't have to. The school called and asked me how long you would be out. They said you missed the end of quarter exams, and you might have to repeat the year if you don't make them up."

"I don't need fucking school," he sneered and tramped out, leaving the front door open.

She wanted to jump to her feet and throw her arms

around her son, begging him to stay with her. Instead, she took a breath and trusted her son's fate to the man waiting in the alley.

TWENTY-THREE

The Hunter - The More Things Change

He was close now. Sights he had not seen, had forgotten or tried to, for almost fifty years, reappeared.

The more things change, the more they stay the same. That was what his grandmother always told him. Driving through the green Tennessee landscape, he understood the truth of it.

For almost fifty years, he had lived in the deserts of the far west. He really didn't remember why he had gone there in the first place, except to escape the secret bottled up inside.

He only knew that he began wandering and one day looked up to see—nothing. All the way to the horizon, there was nothing. He learned over time that nothingness was the great deception of the desert. There was a great deal hidden in the barrenness. You just had to know where to look for it.

But when he first arrived there, he saw nothing, and it

suited him, so he stayed in the desert. If he focused on the nothing, maybe the secrets bottled up inside wouldn't find him and haunt him. That was the thing. Focus on the nothing. Remember nothing.

They were always there—the secrets. They hovered somewhere out there in the desert, just over the empty horizon, but the emptiness held them back.

He worked odd jobs, to survive, sleeping on the ground or in the old pickup he had driven from his home in the east, he moved from place to place. He embraced the emptiness of the desert, making it part of him.

One day he found a garage along Highway 93 in the barrens between Las Vegas and Kingman, Arizona. He stopped, spent his last ten dollars on gas and a bag of potato chips, and wondered what to do next. When he paid for the chips, he saw the help wanted sign.

He picked the sign up and held it out to the man behind the register without saying a word. The name stitched on the man's shirt said "Roger."

"What's up?" Roger asked.

He continued holding the sign without speaking.

"You don't talk much." Roger leaned forward to peer into his eyes. "Or can you talk?"

He realized the man was waiting for him to say something, so he said, "Job."

"Good. You can talk. That will make things easier." Roger crossed his burly arms over the blue striped shirt stained by grease and oil from the cars and trucks he repaired. He studied the man for a moment and asked, "What can you do?"

He hadn't spoken more than a few words at a time in months. Now, this man was giving him a job interview. He almost walked out, until he realized he still needed money before he continued wandering. He nodded at Roger's shirt.

"Cars. I fix cars."

"So you're a mechanic, that what you're saying?"

He shrugged. He wasn't really a mechanic, but he could change oil and lube most vehicles and do an occasional brake job. He figured it would be worth something.

"Where you from?" Roger asked.

Was this demand for information ever going to end? "East," he said simply.

"Hmm. Wanted by the law?"

He shook his head.

"Anybody trying to kill you? You on the run from the law?"

Another shake of the head. He wasn't running from the law or anyone else. Things would have been much simpler if he were.

"Just a drifter, huh? That it? Just drifting about, like the tumbleweeds."

He nodded.

Roger eyed him for another full minute before he shrugged and said, "Alright. I'll give you a try." He pointed to the garage bay. "Got a pickup from the Calhoun Ranch on the lift ready for an oil change. You take care of it, and we'll see how you do."

The oil change was no problem for him. By the end of the day, he had done two more and helped Roger replace a carburetor. He was hired.

He figured he would work for a week, accumulate some more cash, and move on. On the third day, Roger found him sleeping in his pickup behind the garage.

Roger tapped on the window to wake him. "Hell, I been wondering how you get here before me every day."

He sat up in the seat and looked back through the spotted glass. He thought about cranking up the engine and calling it quits right then.

"No place to stay?"

He shook his head.

"I got a place you can use if you want."

He almost shook his head and was going to turn the key to start the pickup, when Roger added, "It's private, in the middle of nowhere. Might suit your tastes until you decide to move on."

He hesitated. Roger spoke again.

"Come on. We'll open late today. Nothing coming in anyway. Follow me. I'll take you there and you can give it a look over."

Roger walked to his pickup and pulled from the lot onto Highway 93. They only went a mile or so before he turned onto a dirt road, heading east into the Cerbat Mountains. The landscape became even more barren and empty. He felt at home.

Cyclopic, Arizona does register on some maps—a few—if you search hard enough for the tiny dot that marks its location. As for people, no encyclopedia or atlas indicates any population.

That doesn't mean there weren't people there. There were, a few at least, but you had to know where to look for them. Roger led him to a single-wide trailer on a small rise and waited for him to get out of his truck.

"I use it for hunting or just to get the hell away from people for a while," Roger said, smiling. "Ought to be perfect for a hermit like you."

Roger showed him around. Water was supplied by a well. Electrical power came from a generator. The toilet, shower, and sinks drained into a septic line and tank that

Roger had installed himself. Probably none of it would have passed a building code inspection back in the city, but in Cyclopic there were no codes. If you could do it, you did it.

"How much," he asked after the tour.

"Not much," Roger said. "How about ten dollars a week for as long as you work for me at the garage?"

He thought about it for a minute, turning to scan the horizon. The emptiness was there, comforting and distant, holding back all the secrets. He nodded.

"Okay." He hesitated, then awkwardly put his hand out to shake on the deal.

Roger grinned and shook his hand.

The hermit of Cyclopic had a home. That was how the locals began to refer to him. He was a young man when he became a hermit. Now, an old man, he remained a hermit.

Over the years, he and Roger became close, or at least as close as he could become to anyone. Roger eventually learned that they had both served in Vietnam and that neither wanted to talk much about the experience. War is an ugly thing, and people do ugly things in war, too ugly sometimes to say them out loud.

Some evenings after Roger closed the shop they would drink beers inside the bay. Once in a while, Roger's wife would insist that he come over for supper, but not too often. She and Roger didn't want to pressure him. At first, his stay there was tenuous. Roger half-expected that one day he would not show for work, simply gone again on his wandering.

But that didn't happen. He stayed. The garage and the trailer on the desert hillside became as much a home as he ever expected to have. If he wasn't happy, at least the emptiness of the place made him comfortable.

They had been working together for twenty-five years

when Roger suddenly fell ill. Lung cancer killed him six months later, but not before he deeded the trailer and the property it sat on to the Hermit of Cyclopic.

Twenty more years passed. The hermit remained there in his trailer, working at odd jobs along the highway, changing oil, and sweeping up for the couple that bought the garage after Roger died.

As they often do to those who live solitary lives behind walls of their own making, memories gnawed at him. He began reading the newspapers out of Kingman. Sometimes he drove to the library there and learned how to use the computer and search out names and people. The gnawing grew into an aching need to know, to reconcile with the memories, and face them in the light of day.

And so, the hunt began.

Outside the window, the green hills flowing by grew into green mountains covered with a billion trees. He smiled. Grandma was right. The more things change, the more they stay the same.

TWENTY-FOUR

All In All, Things Went Well

"I have information for you." Chico Saludo was relieved to finally make this call. He had worried that too much time had passed since the visit from Alejandro Garza.

"That's good." Garza's mild tone gave no hint of a threat. Chico relaxed a bit.

"The person you are looking for seems to have gone to …"

"Not over the phone," Garza snapped, his tone changing immediately. "Come see me."

Chico's voice faltered for a moment. The last thing he wanted to do was be in the same room, alone with Alejandro Garza. Such meetings had a history of dead bodies being disposed of in the South River.

"Yes, of course," he said, swallowing down the lump of fear that rose in his throat.

Chico Saludo's team of drug dealers and enforcers had been working overtime to find the information the enforcer from Mexico had requested. The sooner he was out of Atlanta, the sooner Chico could close his eyes at night and not worry that Garza would slip into his home and slit his throat while he slept.

It was an unreasonable fear, he knew, but he worked in a business where the unreasonable was often commonplace. Why would Garza kill him, or any of his team spread around the southeast? They produced well for Los Salvajes, always one of the top revenue providers in Bebé Elizondo's vast network of drug smugglers and dealers. Still, Garza was an unknown entity, a factor in the business equation that could not be predicted.

Would Chico be blamed if he failed to locate the person Garza was seeking? He considered the question and told himself that logically, there would be no reason to blame him. He was loyal to Elizondo, had never betrayed him, and had always carried out cartel orders.

When he said these words to himself, he felt better. Then doubts would creep into his mind and his hand would shake as he sipped his morning coffee, glad to have survived another night. Their business relied as much on controlling others through fear and intimidation as on profits.

It was not inconceivable that an example would be made to encourage others to work harder to find the son of a bitch rat that Garza sought. Chico knew that his position at the top of the local organization made him the ideal example, if Garza chose to make one.

Thirty minutes after the call ended, Chico pulled into the parking lot of a budget motel in Atlanta's west side. With billions of cartel dollars at his disposal, Garza could have stayed in the finest suite in Atlanta, but fine suites and plush accommodations came with advanced and intrusive hotel security. For Garza, invisibility was always critical, especially during this search for the rat.

The motel's parking lot was cracked and heaving up in sections with weeds growing up through the cracks. Except for the few dilapidated vehicles parked outside a few of the rooms, it would have appeared abandoned. Even so, the vehicles were usually only there for a short time as the drivers visited one of the two prostitutes who used the motel as their place of business.

One clerk worked the days shift and another at night. Maid service was minimal and only on request by a guest. Garza made no requests. Happy to have someone rent the room and happier still not to be asked to provide any service, the motel staff ignored him.

He parked his rental car just outside his first-floor room and spent most of his days communicating with Elizondo or seeing to other business over his phone. Twice a day he took a walk, morning and evening, going for food and coffee at a diner a mile away on a busy intersection.

Chico paused before the room, took a deep breath, and then gave a tentative tap on the door. It opened immediately. Without a word, Garza stepped aside for him to enter.

They stood in the center of the small room. Garza did not offer him a seat. Chico observed that the bed had been neatly made. No personal articles were in sight, and except for the presence of the man before him, the room would have appeared unoccupied.

"What information do you have?" Garza asked.

"The man you seek is in Richmond," Chico said, then added for clarity, "A city in Virginia."

"I know where Richmond is. How reliable is the information?"

"We think it is very reliable." Chico's voice almost broke in momentary panic.

Would very reliable be satisfactory? He had no choice but to be honest. Being less than candid would only make matters worse if the information displeased Garza.

"Explain," Garza ordered.

"As you instructed, I have had my people looking for him. A photo of him in a group was distributed. His face is well known and a person like that has only one way to survive on the street. We were sure he must be involved in our business somewhere but using a different name."

Chico paused, thinking that Garza may want to speak or ask a question about the efforts to find the rat. He did not.

"As expected, he has been selling drugs in Richmond, buying them from our local contact. He keeps a low profile and, never buys or sells too much, just enough to survive. It is clear he knows we may be looking for him."

"What name?" Garza said.

"Raul Martinez," Chico said. "Our man in Richmond is waiting for his next contact with him. Usually, it's once a week. Rarely more than that."

"And your contact's name?"

"Roman Madera."

Garza nodded. Madera was Saludo's counterpart in the Mid-Atlantic States.

"Tell him to expect me in the next two days."

"Yes, of course."

His report complete, Chico waited for further instructions. Garza made no notes, entered nothing into his cell phone. They stood looking at each other in the middle of the room.

"Is there anything else?"

"You can leave now." Garza turned away to sit at the small desk across from the bed.

Chico Saludo let himself out of the room, closing the door softly behind him. In his car, driving back to the *taqueria* that served as cartel headquarters in the city, he reviewed the meeting in his mind.

He walked into the room alive and walked out the same way. He nodded to himself and took a deep breath. All in all, things went well.

TWENTY-FIVE

Moving in That Direction

It was a busy day for Benjamin Dupart. Sole stood at the entrance to the alley, watching as he came down the stairs and left through Dupart's front door without a word to his grandfather.

He walked to the end of the block, making no pretense of going to school. Instead, he climbed into an old Chevy Chevelle, waiting for him at the curb. With a little work, it could have been a classic. As it was, the Chevy was just an old car with gray primer paint sprayed over the rust spots.

The car stayed there for several minutes. He could make out two silhouettes, Ben and someone else, sitting in the front seat. Occasionally, an arm would lift, hand extended.

Sole nodded. Good. Sharing an early morning joint to start the day might make them less aware and easier to follow without being detected.

Interference from local police also seemed unlikely. He had noted during his brief stay that police presence in the neighborhood was minimal, responding to calls for assistance mostly. Sole hadn't seen much proactive enforcement during the daylight hours. He made no judgment about that.

If resources were allocated to other parts of the city to suit the agendas of politicians and the city's influential, it worked to Sole's advantage. Whatever the *Demonios de la Muerte* were up to today would probably be unaffected by police cruisers patrolling the area. He should be able to get an idea of Ben's movements with the gang and try to come up with a strategy to intervene.

Ten minutes passed before Ben and the driver of the Chevy finished the joint. The car pulled away from the curb, heading north. Sole stepped back into his pickup, pulled slowly from the alley, and followed to the end of the block.

The Chevy was two blocks ahead now, still northbound. A traffic light ahead provided an opportunity to close the distance. The Chevy stopped for the red signal, and Sole pulled in behind a delivery van, two cars behind. It wasn't a perfect way to follow the car.

He would have preferred to have another vehicle assisting, or even two, rotating the tail every other block or so to avoid detection. Working alone, he was careful not to close on the Chevy too fast. It seemed unlikely that the young driver would be alert enough or experienced enough to pick up a tail, but there was no reason to take chances.

The light changed to green. The delivery van pulled forward and made a left down a side street. Sole waited for it to complete the turn and then closed up again on the Chevy, staying back a hundred yards or so.

Inside the Chevy, Joey 'Keet' Gonzalez and Ben were oblivious to the pickup following at a discreet distance. Feeling the effects of the joint, they bantered the way teenage boys do.

At a corner, Joey slowed and called out the window to a girl standing at a bus stop.

"*¡Oye chica!*" Hey girl!

She turned her head, cast a scornful glance at the car with the two leering young men, gang thugs no doubt, and turned away. A man and an older woman standing at the bus stop ignored the calls from the car. Nothing good could come from engaging with the boys, and a lot of bad things might happen.

"*Chica!*" Joey persisted. "Don't be like that. I got something for you here. Just come sit on my lap."

It wasn't really that funny, but mellowed by the joint, Ben erupted into laughter. The girl turned her back. Laughing, Joey let it go and proceeded down the block.

"I like me some of that," he said, bobbing his head and grinning at Ben. "How 'bout you Benny? That's a sweet piece."

"Yeah." Ben nodded. "Sweet and young."

"We should come by again tomorrow," Joey said. "I bet she's there every day. We get her in the car, take her somewhere and get some of that."

Ben turned to Joey, his brow wrinkled, trying to puzzle out if Joey was suggesting rape. "You mean just take her?"

"Fuck yeah, take her."

"But …"

"But what? Shit, bro," Joey said, pounding the wheel and grinning. "We DMs … *Demonios de la Muerte*." He looked at Ben. "At least I am."

"Yeah, but ... I mean what if she was your sister or cousin or just a friend?"

"She ain't. Never seen the bitch before, but I tell you one thing." Joey nodded, his face serious now. "Gonna see her again. You watch and see if I don't. You want some, you just come along."

Ben was quiet. Somewhere inside he still struggled with a conscience that was becoming desensitized. Part of him tried to push away any guilt about talking of rape like they were going to pick up a six-pack at the store. At the same time, he wanted to embrace the euphoria of being a DM the way Joey did.

The idea of being untouchable, safe in his gang brotherhood, oblivious to societal codes about right and wrong enticed and intoxicated him. If the gang approved, anything became acceptable. In the closed circle of gang relations, no other standard for right or wrong existed.

Joey recognized the concern on his face. "Problem is, bro, you ain't one of us ... yet. Slice been askin' me 'bout that."

"He has?" Ben knew this moment had been coming, an invitation to full membership as a DM. He pushed aside the talk about rape. "What's he been asking?"

"Why you ain't come in yet," Joey said.

Ben shrugged. "I guess I was waiting to be invited."

"Well fuck, bro! You invited. Ain't you seen the way Slice treats you when he around ... like you something special. The man likes you."

"He does?"

"Fuck, yeah." Joey nodded. "We gonna take care of some shit, then we gonna go find Slice and set things up." He looked at Ben for a reaction. "That good with you, bro?"

"It's all good." Ben nodded. "Let's do it."

From behind, Sole watched and pulled to the curb as the Chevy slowed and the driver called out to the girl at the bus stop. He tensed, ready to intervene if they took things farther. They didn't and after a minute, the Chevy continued up the block.

Sole followed, feeling more confident about the tail. It became clear the driver paid little to no attention to anyone behind.

They continued northbound until they were in a suburban area. The Chevy pulled into a mall parking lot and Ben and the driver got out to head inside. Sole recognized the other immediately. He was the passenger in the van who leaned out the window and hollered, "Fuck you!" at Sole the day Salvadore Estevez was attacked.

Sole found a parking spot a hundred yards away to wait and watch. Following them inside the mall would have made him too easy to spot. They wouldn't be going anywhere without the car.

An hour passed before they emerged and walked across the lot toward the Chevy. Ben carried a bag. The boy with him said something. Ben laughed and heaved the bag across the parking lot.

It didn't require any special powers of discernment to know why. Ben wore a new pair of white Converse All-Stars, the DMs shoe of choice that identified them to other gang members. If he wasn't already a blooded member of the gang, it appeared things were moving in that direction.

TWENTY-SIX

The Problem

For three more days he followed Benjamin Dupart. Eventually, Sole relaxed his concerns about being detected. Whatever else they were, the young *Demonios de la Muerte* were oblivious to the possibility that someone other than the police might be tracking their activities.

It was a sign of their arrogance, but then despots tended to be arrogant. The DMs were the rulers of their turf as certainly as the Romans had controlled their empire, at least until the barbarians stormed the city gates.

Sole knew it was only a matter of time before the barbarians, another gang, stormed the DM gates and the turf boundaries changed again. Until then, as long as they stayed within the blocks controlled by the gang with absolute authority, they could terrorize the community at will, and no one would dare interfere.

"Why don't you leave her alone for once," he muttered to himself as he followed the old Chevy past the bus stop. "Keep moving."

It had become a routine. The Chevy's driver slowed

each day to call out the window to the girl waiting for the bus. The same man and woman waited at the stop, no doubt headed to jobs in the city. None of them spoke to each other or acknowledged the shouts from the Chevy.

"That's right. Mind your own business." Sole nodded approvingly. "Ignore them and they'll move on."

His silent admonition was unnecessary. It was clear that the three at the bus stop had no intention of engaging with the gangbanger in the car.

"Good." Sole nodded. "Now move on."

The Chevy did, and Sole relaxed. "Now on to the next stop."

The next stop was a corner where they made their drug buy. Sole could tell it was weed, the dealer undoubtedly one of the DM crew. There was no attempt at concealment. The dealer handed the baggie through the window, they laughed for a second, a fist bump, and the Chevy moved on, its occupants content with their daily supply.

When he told them about the car Ben entered each day, Edgar and Maggie had identified the driver as Joey Gonzales, a friend of Ben's since childhood.

"As I feared," Edgar had said. "Joey has a lot of influence with Benjamin. He's gone bad."

"He was there the day Mr. Estevez was attacked."

"He was?" Edgar's eyes opened wide. "Joey did that? I knew he was going with the gang, but I didn't think he would hurt anyone."

"I don't know if he hurt anyone," Sole said. "I only saw him in the van that was leaving the area when they almost ran into my truck."

"Still, he should not be there." Edgar shook his head. "When he was young, he was a good boy ... used to come to play with Benjamin in the back of the store. How can he be with the gang now? How can a good boy turn into one of those gang people?"

They were valid questions. How did little boys grow up to be gangbangers?

Sole understood. Poverty, abusive parents, absent fathers, an entitlement system that dis-incentivized them to find a more productive way of life, trapped in a dead-end life with no way to escape, a need for societal respect and camaraderie.

It all added up. Then there was the money, more money than they could ever hope to earn in any legitimate way. Probably the only reason Ben still teetered on the edge of gang life was that Maggie and Edgar had provided a solid home for him, even without a father figure.

He said only, "Sometimes young men go bad ... for lots of reasons."

"Don't let my son go bad." Maggie's lip trembled.

And there it was, snared by circumstances once again. He found it impossible to tell her honestly that the prospect of saving her boy was remote.

He swallowed hard and said, "I won't."

"Alright, where now?" he said, spinning the wheel to follow the Chevy around a corner.

Instead of cruising the neighborhood, Joey Gonzales, former good boy, headed straight to the abandoned warehouse where they ended up each day. It was an old industrial area full of similar buildings. With a little restoration, some might even be usable, but no business was going to risk spending money to open a business in gang territory.

The Chevy pulled behind the DM headquarters. Sole proceeded to the end of the block and turned in past a row of buildings, driving to the rear. From his vantage point, he could see across the abandoned lots to the loading dock of the warehouse that the gang used as their entry. He parked and pulled out a pair of binoculars.

It reminded him of a stakeout, waiting for something to happen. TV dramas made it look easy. Sip some coffee, clever banter with your partner, and then close in for the arrest when the bad guys showed up to do bad things.

Sole knew from experience that most often on stakeouts nothing happened—ever. Just mind-numbing, boring, tedium with no clear result.

He sensed that things were about to change on this one.

"You're here early," he whispered. "Something must be up."

TWENTY-SEVEN

No More Pretendin'

The warehouse was full. Ben had never seen so many of the DM gangbangers gathered in one place before.

"What's going on?" he asked Keet as they walked in through the loading dock door.

"Slice called everyone in."

Keet led the way through the crowded room to a stack of pallets against a wall. Ben eyed the surrounding faces. Some he recognized from the streets and neighborhood. Others were new to him, DM members who stayed out on the streets conducting gang business, which meant selling drugs, committing crimes and finding ways to bring in dollars.

A few women, teenage girls mostly, mingled with them, moving from one to the other, offering sexual favors in exchange for drugs. Some DMs took them up on the offers and moved to the shadows in the corners, where after a few minutes of grunting and moaning they would come back into the main area, followed by the girl. Then both would light up a joint or do a line of coke and lean back, mutually satisfied and mellow for the moment.

Keet grabbed two joints from the communal bucket they kept supplied and handed one to Ben. "Here, bro. Light up. Get chill. You gonna need it."

Ben accepted the joint and leaned back against a pile of packing blankets to light up. "Gonna need it? Why's that?" he asked as he pulled a lighter from his pocket. "Already feeling pretty chill."

Keet grinned, shook his head and said only, "You gonna see".

They sat smoking weed, watching the others, listening to the music that vibrated the sheet metal walls. Whenever one of the girls pulled a DM to the corner to service him and receive her reward, the others made catcalls and nudged each other in the ribs as if they were in the stands at a high school football game, gawking at cheerleaders and rooting on the team.

A shadow hovered over them, and they looked up. It was Ape.

"Slice want to see you," he said.

"Who me?" Ben grinned through his buzzed, smoky haze.

"Yeah, you." Ape stood motionless, hulking over them, not threatening but not to be denied either. "Move."

"Yeah, right, man? I'm moving."

Ben pulled himself up straight and clambered down from the stack of pallets. He turned to Keet. "You, comin', bro?"

"Naw, man. Not this time," Keet replied without making eye contact, taking a drag on the joint and staring at the far wall.

Ben walked unsteadily to the lawn chair where Slice

sat enthroned, the undisputed ruler of the gathering. A DM Ben did not recognize, but who wore their colors, hunched over in front of Slice, handing over cash. Slice nodded, said something inaudible, and motioned for him to depart. The gang member turned, gave a curious glance in Ben's direction, followed by a wry smile, and then left the area.

Ape put a hand on Ben's back and pushed him forward. "He's ready for you."

"You havin' a good time?" Slice asked. The light from the single overhead fluorescent lamp illuminating his corner of the room reflected off his dark brown eyes.

It was a simple question, but Ben understood there was more behind it. Slice didn't inquire about anyone's state of happiness without some purpose in mind.

"Yeah, Slice, sure." Ben fumbled for words. "I mean, it's all good ... hanging here and everything."

"I guess it is." Slice nodded, eyes narrowing. The reflected light there became two tiny glinting white points, shining up at him from a distant place.

A tingle of apprehension crawled up Ben's spine. In his time hanging out with the DMs, he had never been singled out or subject to Slice's attention in this way. He had seen how rapidly things could turn for the worse for the unfortunate gangbanger who displeased the gang's leader.

"Did I do ..." Ben began, swallowing hard to get the words out. "Is something wrong, Slice? I mean I didn't mean to ... I mean it's cool hanging here, and I wouldn't do anything to ..."

"Naw, man, it's all good," Slice said with a grin. "We cool. Right, Ape ... we cool with Benny here."

"We cool," Ape's bass voice reverberated behind Ben.

"Gotta be cool," Slice continued, the grin grew wider

on his face, but the eyes narrowed into dangerous points of light. "You got dope, right?"

Ben nodded.

"Girls if you want them, right?"

Ben nodded.

"You one of us, right?"

Ben nodded.

"Hell, no you ain't one of us!" The grin was gone. "You ain't one of us!" Slice repeated loudly enough that others turned to see what was happening.

When they saw that Keet's FNG—fucking new guy—stood cowed before their leader, they nodded and nudged each other. In seconds, the entire crowd was riveted by what was happening. Someone turned the music player off.

"But, I thought …" Ben managed to say.

"You thought what?" Slice sneered. "That you one of us?"

Ben's head swiveled, searching for Joey in the sea of faces that edged closer, penning him in before Slice. He found him standing on the outer edge of the crowd, as riveted as the others, but with no inclination to step forward and intervene on behalf of his friend. Ben realized that Joey had known this was coming.

Slice eyed the Converse sneakers on Ben's feet and smirked. "You got the shoes … the look … but you ain't one of us."

"All I was saying was …"

"What you was sayin' don't mean shit. You know why?" Slice leaned toward him. "You a pretender. You just pretendin' to be one of us." He shook his head. "But you ain't."

Heads nodded. Voices rumbled around the room.

"Yeah, Benny been actin' like he one of us, but he just pretendin'."

"You gotta be one of us," Slice said, his voice milder now, friendlier, now that the reminder about his status had been delivered.

"Right," the voices murmured. "Gotta be one of us."

"Tomorrow you be one of us," Slice said.

"Tomorrow. Yeah, tomorrow." Heads in the crowd nodded as the murmur swirled around the room.

"You know how that happens, right?" Slice asked.

Ben had tried to put the initiation out of his mind. He had known Salvadore Estevez since childhood, and the idea of doing to someone else what Joey did to Mr. Estevez made him queasy. Mellowed by the drugs and safe in the cocoon of gang camaraderie, he had put off thinking about it.

Showing up each day with Joey, it seemed he had been welcomed into the group. He thought—hoped—he had become one of them by default. Things were about to change, and looking into Slice's eyes, an uneasy realization settled over him. More was expected of him.

"Asked you a question, boy. Answer it," Slice snapped at him.

"I have to hit someone. That's how you do it, right?"

"Hit someone!" Slice laughed, and the others followed suit. "You knock them out. One punch in the head and they go down. After that you get blooded and you one of us."

"But I..."

"Tomorrow, you do it," Slice interrupted. "You come with me and Ape and Cheech. We pick the one you gonna knock out. Then you do it and you one of us. Right?"

Wide-eyed and sweating now, Ben couldn't make the words come from his mouth.

"Whatsamatter, boy? You afraid."

"No." Ben shook his head. "I just … I can't." His throat tightened. He had difficulty forcing the words out. "Not that …"

"What you mean you can't?" Slice looked around the room. "Keet, get your ass up here."

The crowd parted and Keet pushed forward, glaring at Ben for putting him in the position of being singled out by Slice.

"Your, bro here don't seem like he want to be one of us, but you been bringin' him in every day. What's that?"

"He do want to be one of us, Slice," Keet said. "I know he do. We talked about it and he told me."

"Then why he sayin' he can't?"

"It's just … he ain't much of a fighter. We was in school together. He never got in no fights," Joey was talking fast, wondering why he hadn't considered the ramifications of recruiting Benny's pussy ass into the DMs. They'd be lucky if they both didn't get an ass beating, or worse.

"He ain't a fighter?" Slice asked, his eyebrows rising. "And you brought him to us?"

"Yeah, he never had the stomach for it … didn't like the sight of blood or some shit like that."

There were laughs around the room. Keet forced a grin, letting the laughter settle for a few seconds, hoping it would relieve the tension, then he continued, "But Benny's smart … real smart. They's all sorts of things he can do for us … smart things … computer shit … planning shit. You know, smart things."

"Smart things," Slice said, shaking his head. "What the fuck that supposed to mean?"

The room was silent as Slice considered the fate of Benny, the FNG, and Keet, who brought him in. Slice's eyes bored into Ben for a full minute. Finally, he nodded and spoke.

"You a lover, not a fighter. Is that it? A smart lover, but you don't like to fight."

Ben managed to nod, and dared a smile. "Yeah ... a lover."

More laughter rippled around him.

"Alright, smart lover boy. We'll figure something out. Maybe we can change things up a little about the knockout, but one thing is for sure. Tomorrow you gonna be here and you gonna be one of us. You seen too much not to. You Understand?"

"Yes," Ben managed to whisper.

"And don't think about not comin' back." Slice's eyes narrowed again and the tiny points of light bored laser-like into Ben. "That old man you live with and your mama ... they protected by us. That don't come free. You don't come back, they gonna pay for it. No more pretendin'. You understand that?"

"I understand." Ben nodded. "I'll be back."

"Now get out." He looked at Keet. "Drop him at home and get back here."

Keet turned and led the way, Ben following close behind. The gang members were silent.

When they were gone, Ape growled at Slice, "The knockout's how it is ... that's how he gets to be one of us ... always been that way. You and me made it that way."

"Yeah, we did, bro." Slice nodded. "But what if I come up with something better?"

"I don't like it, changing the rules," Ape rumbled.

"You gonna like this."

TWENTY-EIGHT

To Pissing on Fences

They were out early tonight. The sun had been down only an hour when the loading dock door opened and Joey Gonzales led Ben out. Sole squinted through the binoculars.

The usual grabass chatter between them was missing. Even at this distance, he could see the looks of worry on their faces. They got into Gonzales' car without speaking.

"Something's up," Sole muttered to himself. "Why would that be?"

They drove off, moving with a purpose, not the usual random wandering back and forth through the city streets. He was surprised when Joey pulled to the curb in front of Dupart's store and Ben got out. Joey said something. Ben nodded and turned to the door as the Chevy pulled away.

"What was that all about?" Sole wondered.

He considered following Joey but then decided against it. He might learn more by being in the apartment. After parking in the alley, he went through the back door and looked into the store before heading up the stairs.

Edgar was behind the register, reading a newspaper. He

looked up and called out, "You're back early tonight. Is everything alright?"

"Not sure," Sole said, stepping into the store and looking around.

"There's no one here," Edgar said. "You can speak freely."

"Where's Maggie?" Sole glanced toward the back room.

"Not here. She went up to start dinner."

"We should probably talk ... all of us."

"Okay." Edgar nodded. "Business is slow anyway. I'll close and be up in a few minutes."

Sole climbed the stairs and pushed the door open without the need to use the key they had provided. He had found that the apartment was always unlocked. At night the exterior doors from the store were secured, but the door to the apartment above was unlocked.

He found Maggie in the kitchen soaking a piece of skirt steak in marinade for carne asada. Ben was in his room, playing music loud enough for the bass to vibrate the walls.

Maggie smiled and made the same comment Edgar had. "You're back early tonight."

"Right." He sat at the kitchen table. "Ben's home early. I followed him back here."

Maggie turned, saw the expression on his face, and her brow furrowed. "You look worried."

Sole nodded. "A little maybe."

"About?" She pulled out a chair and sat across from him. "Tell me."

"I think something big is about to happen," he said, trying to explain the telltale signs he picked up between Ben and Joey. "Not sure what, but I sensed that things were different today between Ben and Joey, and no doubt that probably has something to do with the gang. Whatever it is might give us a chance to intervene in some way."

Hope flooded over her face again, and he felt guilty for giving it to her. Hope could be crushed by reality.

"What is about to happen?" she asked.

"I'm not sure, just signs, the way Ben and Joey are acting, the way they left early." He shook his head. "I shouldn't have said that it might give us a chance. I have no idea, really. It's just that sometimes when a bad thing happens it gives you a chance to step in and remove the bad thing." He shrugged. "There's a chance at least."

That was clear as mud, he thought. *What the hell are you talking about? You're talking in riddles, John-boy.*

The hope faded a little from her face, and Maggie nodded. "I understand."

Edgar came into the kitchen. "You two seem very serious."

Maggie looked up and smiled. "Bill thinks something is about to happen, something that might help get Ben away from the gang."

"I see." Edgar nodded and sat with them at the table. "Tell me."

They talked while Maggie prepared dinner. When Sole finished explaining, Edgar summed things up.

"So, we hope that something bad happens while you are there to stop the bad thing. Is that it?"

"That's about it," Sole agreed. "It's not much, I know."

"It is something, though." Edgar shrugged and smiled.

"I worry I might be giving you hope when there isn't any," Sole said quietly. "The pull from friends to be like them is very strong for a boy his age."

"This is true," Edgar said grinning. "Choosing your friends is like selecting a place to take a piss."

Sole and Maggie looked at him. He paused, allowing their curiosity to build before continuing.

"When I was a boy in Louisiana, my friend, Etienne, convinced me to take a piss on a wire fence that our neighbor had electrified to keep his cows in. I will never do that again."

Sole and Maggie broke into laughter.

"Since then," Edgar continued. "I select my fences and my friends with more care."

Maggie lifted her glass of wine laughing and said "To pissing on fences."

TWENTY-NINE

Thoughts of Home

Sole sat at the kitchen table when Maggie walked in, pulling her robe around her waist. Elbows on the table he looked up and smiled over the coffee cup in hand.

"Morning," she said through a yawn. "You're up early."

"Restless night," Sole said.

"Really? Worried about something?" She poured a cup from the pot and sat across from him.

"Not worried." He shook his head. "Just want to be ready."

"Ready?"

"In case *the something* we discussed last night happens today."

"Sounds like you're in a hurry to get it over with."

"No, not in a hurry." Sole sat the cup down. "Anxious a little I guess, and if it is going to happen, and there's a way to use it to get Ben away from the gang, I'd like to get it done."

"Get it done. Sounds like you're on a mission … something military and official." She smiled. "My husband spoke like that when he was focused on something. Always gave it his full attention." She chuckled. "Annoyed the hell out of me sometimes."

"Just the training." Sole nodded and smiled. "You learn not to be distracted … to see things through, adapt, find a way to get the mission …" He stopped and the smile widened. "Sorry … to get done what you set out to do."

"I know. Jean Paul always found a way to get things done. If he were here now …" She shook her head and glanced down the hallway toward Ben's closed door. "If he were here, Ben's life would be different. Our life would be different."

"Wish I'd known him," Sole said. The mission to help the son of a fallen comrade-in-arms carried more than a little guilt with it.

"You would have liked him." Maggie nodded and added, "He would have liked you."

They sat quietly, sipping coffee at the kitchen table like a married couple, preparing for a routine day. It was a pleasant moment, so pleasant that for a minute or two he lost himself in it.

Then he became conscious of the shared intimacy of the act, sitting alone in the morning, she in her robe, sharing coffee together, lost in their thoughts. Guilt washed over him.

Stop! You should be a thousand miles from here right now!. The voice hollered at him this time.

He watched Maggie staring quietly at the coffee in her cup. No, he realized. You have to be here, at least for a little while, but you should be honest. Tell her now.

"There's something we should talk about," he said.

"What's that?" She raised her eyes.

"I'm not sure how to say it." He grimaced, feeling the

urge to squirm under her expectant gaze. "Whether something comes up, some way to help Ben or not, I …"

"Stop." She raised a palm toward him. "I understood last night. Edgar and I both understand. Whatever you do might not be enough to pull Ben back to us and away from the gang. We understand. What you're doing is more than we could have asked, and you have nothing to feel guilty about."

"Thank you." He nodded. "There's something else."

"Oh? What then?"

"It's just that at some point … soon, really … I need to move on."

A faint trace of disappointment flickered across her face. "I understand that too." She nodded and smiled. "You could stay, you know … if you wanted to."

Now he did squirm in his chair, the look of dismay on his face plain. "I couldn't. I'm not ready … not in a position to …"

"Stop." She laughed. "I'm not talking about staying here for romantic reasons. You're a good man, Bill. I told you that, but Jean Paul was the love of my life. I don't think there will be another, and if there is, it may be years away." She shook her head. "No, I think of you as a friend, a big brother even. Someone I can talk to without any other strings attached and no judgment."

Relief washed over his face and they both laughed now.

"A friend.. I like that. I'd forgotten what it was like to have friends, and a sister too. I never had one before." He nodded and smiled. "But I do have to leave."

"Alright. If that's the way it has to be, just remember that you have a place here with us when you want it. Edgar feels the same, by the way. We talked things over."

"Thank you for that." He nodded and then stood up.

"But I'm not leaving today, so I'm going downstairs to wait in the alley with the tomcats until Ben makes his appearance and do some thinking. I do my best thinking early in the morning. Hell, if morning lasted all day long, I'd be a damned genius."

It was a small joke, a silly one, but they laughed. Then he left her at the table and went down the stairs to the back alley door. Outside, he decided to take a walk. Ben hadn't been stirring yet or they would have heard him banging around.

He walked to the street at the end of the alley and then around the block to the front of the store. It was an hour before Edgar would open and only the night security lights were on inside. Sole passed the store and walked to the corner, stopping at the spot where the *Demonios de la Muerte* made Salvadore Estevez the victim of their initiation. Brown-red bloodstains marked the place where his head hit the pavement.

He walked along the block looking into the shop windows, many boarded or broken out. The ones that were still in business had security bars, alarms, and cameras to dissuade would-be burglars.

Above the locked doors, the rising sun struck the tops of the building. Below, the early morning twilight barely pierced the shadows in the storefronts and alleys.

It was a visually pleasing contrast and reminded him of sunrises in the north Georgia mountains where the sunlight crept slowly down the mountainsides until full day lit the valley. Old-timers always said the day there didn't begin until ten in the morning when the sun finally rose above the surrounding mountains and ended at two in the afternoon when it sank below the opposite crests.

Cassit Pass was a long way from Albuquerque, but for a

moment the feeling was the same. The day crept toward him down the sides of the buildings, like the mountains in Georgia.

Maggie said he had a home with them. He had difficulty relating to that word these days, but standing on the deserted street, watching the sunrise, familiar thoughts—thoughts of home—stirred inside.

THIRTY

Little Man

Despite the suspicion that something big was about to happen, Ben remained in his room until long after the day had begun. It was ten o'clock when Joey Gonzales pulled the Chevy to the curb out front. A few seconds later, Ben thumped down the stairs and out the door without a word to his grandfather.

Sole waited in the alley until the Chevy made the turn at the end of the block. He wasn't too concerned about losing them. The pattern was the same every day. Drive by the bus stop, harass the girl waiting there, cruise the neighborhoods, finish the day at the DM's abandoned warehouse.

He made the turn and caught sight of the Chevy two blocks ahead. "Moving fast today," he whispered.

Joey did not steer the Chevy down the street toward the bus stop where the girl waited every day. As Sole suspected, today was special. Something out of the ordinary was about to happen.

"What are you up to?" Sole leaned forward, peering through the windshield, willing himself into the Chevy so he could listen in on their chatter. He had to settle for following behind.

The conversation inside the Chevy was minimal. Joey focused on his driving for once, not bothering to ogle the girls on the sidewalks or waste time talking to his dealer friends working their corners.

Ben stared out the window, trapped. He felt as helpless to prevent the events coming his way as a man on a railroad bridge with the train bearing down on him and only jagged rocks below. He could jump or face the freight train. Either choice invited destruction.

The intoxicating allure of gang life had faded in the last hours. The sobering prospect of going through with the initiation had caused the euphoria of gang acceptance to evaporate.

He had no stomach for assaulting old men without reason, but defying Slice was unthinkable. He'd seen the sort of justice met out to those who broke the rules, simple and harsh.

And Slice made it clear that the fate of his mother and grandfather depended on his performance in the initiation. During the sleepless night, he resolved to do what Slice ordered, if not for himself, then for the safety of his mother and grandfather.

They were a few blocks from the warehouse when Joey spoke. "Don't fuck this up today."

"I just don't want to hit anyone."

"You are such a fucking pussy!" Joey glared at Ben.

"Me a pussy," Ben sneered. "You go and punch out an

old man, and you call me a pussy." Ben shook his head. "Far as I'm concerned, that's chicken shit."

"Call it what you want, but you heard the man. Do what you got to do today. You don't, and what old man do you think they gonna pick to knock out next time?" Joey warned. "You ain't got no choice. Are you too dumb to see that?"

There it was, the reality of his predicament.

"I see it. Shut up and drive."

"I'm drivin'," Joey softened his tone, trying to reason. "I stood up for you. You owe me. So, just close your eyes and get it done."

"Don't worry about me. I'll get it done, but I don't see how cold-cocking some old man proves anything. How's that show how tough we are?"

"Motherfucker, you are such a pussy!" Joey smirked in disgust. "All I'm sayin' is who you think they gonna blame if you fuck up?"

"Told you. I'm not gonna fuck it up, but if I do It'll be my fault. I'll tell them."

"Yeah, it'll be your fault alright!" Joey pounded the steering wheel with his fist. "Your fault when they beat both our asses and dump us on the street. Be lucky if they don't cut our throats first."

Joey pulled to the rear of the warehouse by the loading dock and got out. They mounted the steps to the back door side by side. Joey made a final attempt, his voice subdued now, fear in his eyes.

"C'mon, man. Don't let me down. We been like brothers all our lives. Don't let it end this way."

Ben pulled the door open without replying. The DMs were gathered in the usual fashion, some smoking pot or listening to music, others with the girls in the corners, most just sitting around bullshitting. Slice sat on his throne.

Like yesterday, everyone was there. The initiation of a new member was a big deal, and Ben's reluctance to go through with it had provided extra drama to the event. All eyes turned as the two entered.

"Get up here," Slice called across the room to Ben.

Ben walked forward and stood before the DM leader, trying not to look terrified. An unusual silence fell over the room. Everyone gathered closer to watch the show.

"So you a lover and not a fighter," Slice said, reminding them how things had ended the day before.

"I still want to be in," Ben managed to croak out, then said more strongly, "But I don't want to hit some old man. That's all."

"Alright. We got something better than a old man to hit." Slice grinned. "First you better take a hit on this."

Slice motioned to a piece of window glass lying flat on a pallet. Three lines of cocaine were laid out.

Ben's eyes moved from the cocaine to Slice and back. He started to shake his head and thought better of it. "I don't do coke, but I smoke weed. Let me smoke some weed. That'd be alright, wouldn't it?"

"Fuck no, that ain't alright," Slice snapped. "You say you ain't gonna hit no old man, Alright then, first thing is hit the coke."

"C'mon, Benny," Joey whispered at his side. "Just get this over with."

All sense of camaraderie and brotherhood evaporated. The faces surrounding him glared. Voices mocked him. Laughter turned to jeering snickers.

"Alright," Ben said, his voice muted and resigned. He

nodded, took a deep breath, and stepped to the makeshift coke table.

A three-inch length of plastic straw lay beside the lines of cocaine. He leaned over, put the straw to his nose, and snorted one of the lines. Then he stood up straight and looked around the room, feeling ... not much of anything.

"What? You think you gonna snort one line and start bouncing off the walls." Slice laughed. "Give it a couple minutes, and you'll see. Ten minutes, you do another line, and another ten minutes after that one. We'll keep you stoked long as it takes."

"Alright." Ben nodded. "That's it? I keep doing cocaine, and it's all good with us."

"No, that ain't it, and it ain't all good, little man." Slice shook his head. "Not yet."

"Hey," someone called out. "That gonna be his name. Little Man."

"Yeah, Little Man," another said and another until they were chanting, "Little Man…Little Man … Little Man."

"Fair enough." Slice nodded and stood before them. He looked down at Ben. "Your name gonna be Little Man. You cool with that?"

"Yeah sure." Ben shrugged and kept talking, the effects of the cocaine beginning to kick in. "Yeah, Little Man, that's an okay name … yeah, I think that'll be good … just call me Little Man, cause that's as good a name as any." He turned to Joey. "That's a good name, ain't it? Little Man? Good a name as any? Fuck yeah, Little Man gonna be my name. Right?"

"It's a good name," Joey said nodding, relieved that things were moving forward, and no one had threatened to beat his ass yet because his recruit turned out to be a fucking pussy.

The loading dock door banged open. Slice looked up from his perch. Everyone else turned toward the door.

"Time for the next part, Little Man. You gonna like this part."

Ben turned to see Ape and Cheech standing in front of the door. His mouth opened and face paled. "But no, I can't …"

"Don't say it, Little Man. Warnin' you now," Slice snarled. "We changed things for you 'cause Keet says you're smart and we can use someone smart like you. So, you gonna do this."

THIRTY-ONE

Something Big Happened

Sole slowed a block behind the Chevy and waited for it to pull behind the warehouse. Once it was out of sight, he made the turn, passed the building, and headed to his stakeout point. He was in position as Ben and Joey stood on the loading dock. Joey said something, and Ben pulled the door open. They disappeared inside.

Binoculars to his eyes, he sat back in the seat, pondering his next move. The big something he'd discussed with Edgar and Maggie could be happening inside right now, and he would never know it. Despite his attempt to put a positive spin on things for Edgar and Maggie, he didn't hold out much hope that anything he did was going to influence the boy.

He was back to square one, and despite all his talk, he still had no real plan. At some point, he was going to have to approach the building and find out what was going on inside. The problem was, as soon as he did, his cover would be blown, and his one chance to do something for Edgar, Maggie, and the boy squandered.

Several more minutes passed as he considered his next move. Sit tight or go in. It was a dilemma, and he couldn't decide. Then the issue was decided for him.

Sole squinted into the binoculars. "Shit."

A van pulled up beside the loading dock. Two gang members climbed, holding the arms of a third person firmly between them—a person he recognized.

He dropped the glasses and threw the truck into gear. The tires squealed as the two men dragged their captive inside and the door banged shut.

"No." Ben's head moved slowly side to side. "I can't …"

"Don't fuckin' tell me what you can't do, Little Man!" Slice warned. "Keet says you a lover. Alright, that's what you do to get in."

"But …" Ben's mouth closed in stunned silence as they dragged the girl forward through the throng of gang members.

It was the bus stop girl. Eyes wide with terror, her head swiveled, trying to understand what had happened, what was going to happen.

Ape and Cheech shoved her forward. She stumbled and fell in front of Ben. Panic-stricken, she attempted to crawl away, but Ape's foot on her back shoved her face-first into the concrete floor.

Ben's eyes pleaded with Slice. "No … I can't … not this."

"Fuck her," Slice said, his voice calm, his face deadly serious. "Fuck her now."

Ben was unable to speak. His mind whirled. What had

he been thinking? Standing wide-eyed over the girl, he could only shake his head.

The knife was in Slice's hand, glinting under the fluorescent lights. "You gonna fuck her, and you gonna do it now, or you not leavin' here."

Another chant began to rise up among the gang members. "Fuck her ... Fuck her."

It grew louder, reverberating through the empty space. The girl cringed, sobbing on the floor. The chanting increased in volume. She put her hands over her ears.

Thunder roared through the building. The chanting ceased.

All heads turned to the loading dock door, focused on the man with the big .45 Colt. The acrid smell of burned powder hung in the air. John Sole lowered the pistol and pointed it at Slice's face.

"Who the fuck are you?" Slice snarled.

Sole sighted along the top of the barrel and smiled. "The man who will put a hole in your dumb fucking head if you move."

"You think you can put a hole in all of us, motherfucker?"

"Seven more rounds in this pistol." He lifted his shirttail with one hand to reveal the Glock in his waistband. "Fourteen more here. I figure I can take out enough of you, pretty fucking quick. And one thing is sure." He stared into Slice's eyes. "You will be the first."

He motioned with the Colt. "Everyone gather around your fearless leader. Do it now!"

The crowd moved toward Slice. The looks on their faces made it clear they hoped Slice wasn't going to tell them to rush the man with the big-ass Colt pistol.

"Ben," Sole said. "Bring the girl here."

While Sole held Slice in his sights and the gang members moved away from the door, Ben reached down and helped the girl to her feet. He put an arm around her and hurried to Sole.

"Good." Sole nodded. "Take her outside. My pickup is by the loading dock. Get in and wait. I'll be right behind you."

The heavy door opened and slammed shut behind him. Sole remained standing in front of it, his pistol pointed at Slice. Unsure what to do, the other gang members shuffled from one foot to the other, avoiding eye contact with the man holding the pistol—all except one.

"Motherfucker, you ain't gonna do shit. You pull that trigger and we'll be on you ... tear your motherfuckin' head off."

Ape came forward. For a moment it appeared others in the group would follow suit. The gun roared again, and Ape fell before he had taken three steps.

"Six rounds left ... and fourteen more," Sole said softly. "Who's next?"

He began backing to the door. "Not gonna give you any warning to stay here for five minutes because I know you won't listen. So, you do what you got to do." He motioned with the pistol at Ape's body. "But I promise you whoever comes through that door first will end up like your big friend there."

He opened the door behind him with one hand and backed through. As it slammed shut, he saw the faces turn from Ape's body to Slice. No one moved, but that wouldn't last long. Without the Colt pointing at them, they would soon recover their courage. The bullshit *machismo* code they lived by required it.

Sole pulled a pallet from a stack on the loading dock

and broke off two slats, then wedged them under the door. Once they decided to come through the door, it would only slow them down for a few seconds, but a few seconds were all he needed.

Jumping from the dock to the pavement, he slid behind the pickup's wheel. Ben stared straight ahead. The girl sobbed between them.

Sole accelerated away from the dock and around to the front of the building. Two gang members were standing in the drive and more were coming from the small office area attached to the warehouse. So much for his plan, he thought.

He floored the pickup, aiming directly for the two gang-bangers blocking his way. They fumbled for the guns tucked in their low hung pants, but he was gone and racing down the street. He heard the report of two rounds being fired, but their aim was as shabby as their attire.

They were several blocks away before the girl was able to gasp and stop sobbing long enough to say, "Thank you."

"No thanks necessary. What's your name?"

"Juanita," she said, wiping her eyes. "And you are?"

"Not important." Sole looked at Ben. "You okay?"

The boy's head turned slowly in his direction, a mixture of confusion and relief on his face. "How did you ... I didn't ..." He shook his head. "I didn't know what to do."

"You were in a bad spot. You're out now," Sole said matter-of-factly. "Thank your mother and grandfather for that."

Ben nodded and looked out the window.

"I'm going to take you someplace safe," Sole said to Juanita. "To the police. You can make a report and they will follow up."

"No." She shook her head, adamantly. "No police."

"But …"

"No," she insisted. "No police. When they ask questions it will only cause more trouble and then they will leave and it will still be the same … except worse."

"Then where?" Sole looked at the girl huddled on the seat.

"To my brother, Carlos. He will take care of me."

"Alright." Sole nodded. "To your brother."

She gave him the directions, and they drove in silence. When they pulled up in front of the abandoned service station, Sole gave her a puzzled look.

"Your brother lives here?"

"Not live … it is where he is. It is his gang place. He will know what to do."

Brother Carlos was a gangbanger, Sole realized. The reason for avoiding the police became clear.

"Are you sure?"

"I'm sure."

"Alright, but I go inside with you." Sole slid out, held the door open for her, and looked at Ben. "Stay here. I won't be long."

But nodded without speaking, content to be told what to do.

"Alright," Juanita said and led the way inside.

As it turned out, Juanita's brother wasn't just with a gang, he was the gang, the leader. Carlos, Big-C to the Cent Killers, listened intently to Juanita's account of her abduction and near rape. When she finished, he turned to Sole.

"You saved my sister. I know what the motherfucker Slice woulda done. I owe you."

"Hoped you would see it that way," Sole said. "There is something you can do."

"I'm listening."

Carlos was silent while Sole explained. When he finished, he nodded and said simply, "Okay."

The drive home only took a few minutes. Edgar and Maggie were both in the store. They looked up expectantly as they came from the alley. Ben climbed the stairs. Sole entered the store, looked around to make sure no customers lingered in the aisles.

Assured that they were alone, he turned to them and said, "Something big happened."

THIRTY-TWO

Pick Your Brothers Carefully

"Is he alright?" Maggie asked as her son plodded up the stairs to the apartment like an old man.

"Physically, he's fine," Sole said. "But he's gone through a pretty severe emotional trauma."

"What happened?" Edgar leaned across the counter, his voice low. "Tell us everything."

He reviewed the events of the last several days. Following the Chevy as it made its rounds through the city, always to end up at the old warehouse used by the *Demonios de la Muerte*. The daily harassment of the girl at the bus stop. The drug deals. The stakeout of the warehouse.

Sole told them everything, almost. He did not mention the death of Ape, the gang member who thought himself Superman, but turned out not to be faster than a speeding bullet.

"And Ben did not do what these others wanted him to do to the girl?" Maggie's eyes narrowed. She wanted the unvarnished truth, with nothing held back.

"No. He did not," Sole said firmly. "When I came in he

was standing beside her, shaking his head, frightened but he made no move to do what they were shouting at him to do. He stood his ground."

"Thank God," Maggie whispered. "What happened after that?"

"After that, we left."

"And the girl?" Maggie asked.

"I took her to her brother."

"Not the police?"

"I suggested it, but she said no." He shrugged. "I didn't think it was my place to argue with her about it. She didn't seem to have much confidence that the police would be able to do anything about what happened, and when they finished their investigation, things would get worse."

"She was right." Edgar nodded. "The gangs rule the streets. The police don't live here. We do. When they leave, the gangs take it out on the neighborhoods. I've seen it. Things can be worse than before the police came."

"And when you left her with her brother, she was alright ... not hurt?" Maggie asked.

"Not physically, but she was terrified while it was happening. That's understandable."

"So, it's over?" Edgar asked.

"I don't know." Sole shook his head. "The gang is not going to be happy. I think they may try to harass Ben, maybe you too ... try something worse in retaliation. We have to be prepared."

"Yes," Edgar nodded. "We would be naïve to believe that it ends so simply. You challenged them ... their control ... their manhood. They won't forget that so easily."

"I made some arrangements that might help."

"What kind of arrangements?" Maggie's eyes narrowed.

"The girl ... her name is Juanita ... her brother is in a

gang. He seems to be the leader of it. That was where I left her."

"You made arrangements with a gang?" Maggie asked, eyebrows raised in disbelief.

"He wanted to repay me for getting his sister out. I told him the only repayment I wanted was for them to put you, Ben, the store, the street under their protection."

"Which gang?" Edgar asked.

"Juanita called them the Cent Killers." He shook his head. "No idea what that means."

"Central Avenue Killers." Edgar nodded. "They are very bad, and that could be good for us. They are strong enough to stand up to the *Demonios de la Muerte*."

"I hope so," Sole said. "Juanita's brother said they would spread the word that you're under their protection … send a signal."

There was a glimmer of a smile on Edgar's face. "That means something very bad is going to happen to someone."

"I need to go up and see Benjamin," Maggie said, stepping from behind the counter.

"Can I have a word with him first?" Sole asked. "It's what I was supposed to be doing all along. Now's my chance."

"Yes, of course. I'll wait here."

Sole climbed the stairs and entered the apartment. The door to Ben's room was closed, as always. He tapped and called through the door.

"Ben, it's Bill Myers. Can I come in for a minute?"

There was no answer. Sole waited a minute, then tapped again and pushed the door partway open.

Ben sat on the floor across the room, knees up, and his back against the wall. Sole pushed the door open wider. "Can I come in?"

Ben looked up and nodded. Sole entered, closed the door quietly, and crossed the room to sit on the floor beside the boy. They leaned against the wall without speaking. Ben rested his chin on his knees and stared at his feet. Sole waited, unsure what to say or how to begin.

Several minutes ticked by before Ben finally spoke. He began as if they had been engaged in conversation the entire time, debating with himself, confused, questioning, trying to understand what had happened.

"Yeah, but ..." Ben began with a shake of his head. "I didn't do a fucking thing." He looked at Sole. "I stood there while they dragged her in. I didn't try to help her, I just stood there ... afraid."

Sole allowed a minute of silence to pass before he said, "You did the right thing, Ben. There wasn't anything else you could do."

"Bullshit. I could have tried to help her ... take her out of there."

"That would have been impossible. You had no chance, and no telling what they would have done if you tried ... killed you ... killed her. They had their blood up. I could see that. The situation was unpredictable and dangerous."

"Yeah, but you did something about it." Ben looked at him and Sole saw the tears in his eyes for the first time.

"I wasn't in your position, surrounded by gangbangers shouting for blood." Sole gave a nod of approval and added, "You didn't run. You stood your ground and said no while they chanted for you to rape the girl. That took courage, Ben. Don't sell yourself short."

"I thought I was going to piss myself," Ben said, disgusted. "Or that I might pass out." He looked at Sole. "But not you. You came in and took control while I just stood there and trying to keep the piss from running down my leg."

"I've probably had more experience with gangs than you. I was prepared."

"You were in a gang?" Ben brow lifted in curiosity. "Where?"

"Yeah, I was in a gang." Sole laughed. "They call it the Marine Corps."

"The Marines aren't a gang."

"Sure they are, in a way." Now, Sole leaned forward, resting his chin on his knees so that he and Ben were on the same level. "The Marine Corps has a code, and once we go through the initiation process, we Marines live by it for the rest of our lives. In the Marines, you are surrounded by your brothers and sisters, people who would die for you if necessary, and you would die for them. Marines never leave anyone behind. You take care of your own."

"Yeah, but you didn't do the things the DMs do."

"You mean break the law?" Sole nodded. "We might not be out on the streets selling drugs and kidnapping girls, but we Marines get into some hairy situations sometimes, but the code we follow has a morality to it. That keeps us from doing those other things. We live by that code."

Sole stopped speaking and waited. Ben sat quietly digesting everything he'd said, then shook his head, the look of disgust back on his face.

"I really fucked up."

"Temporarily." Sole agreed. "But not permanently. There's a lesson to be learned from this, Ben."

"What lesson?

"Pick your brothers … your gang … carefully. Where they go, you will end up too."

THIRTY-THREE

This Ain't Over

"Who the fuck is he?"

"I swear, Slice." Joey 'Keet' Gonzales stood trembling outside the gang's warehouse. "I swear on my mama, I ain't never seen him before."

He had the urge to run like hell, but with Cheech and Poco leaning in from either side, he stood there, trapped. It didn't matter. There was nowhere to run and hide from the DMs, not for a teenage gangbanger who relied on his connections with them for cash and survival.

"You brought him to us."

Slice's eyes bored into Joey until he turned his head away, looking for an understanding face in Cheech or Poco. There was no reassurance there, only icy stares.

"No." Joey shook his head. "I brought in Benny ... Little Man, but I never seen that other dude. He just showed up."

"Bullshit!" Slice snapped. "He shows up just when you and your pussy friend do." Slice jerked a hand toward the loading dock door. "You know what's in there?"

Joey knew, but couldn't make the words come from his dry mouth. He nodded and looked at his feet.

"Fuckin' Ape is lyin' there in his own blood! In our house!" Slice shook his head. "That can't stand. It ain't gonna stand."

"I swear, Slice. I don't know who he was. On my mama's life, I ..."

"Shut the fuck up about your mama," Slice shouted. "She ain't here, but you are. Let's go."

"Go?" Joey's eyes opened wide. "Where we goin', Slice?"

"We gonna find that motherfucker ... that big ass white boy with his big ass gun. Then we gonna find your boy, Little Man, and do to them what he did to Ape."

"Alright, whatever you say, Slice. We find the motherfucker and do him." Joey nodded emphatically. "Do him like he did Ape, except take our time, hurt him bad so he suffers." He turned a hopeful eye to Slice, trying to move the focus to the man who killed Ape. "Fuck, yeah. Make him suffer bad, right?"

"Give me your car keys," Slice said.

"My car? But why my car? Shouldn't we take the van or something?"

"Your car!" Slice growled and Joey shut his mouth. "You brought this shit on us ... brought him into our house. If we get spotted, they not gonna tie it to any of our rides." He smiled. "Gonna be yours."

"Right, man." Joey's head bobbled up and down like a dashboard toy, his words coming fast now, desperate to show he was all in on finding and killing the big white man. "I get it. My fault he came, so I take the hit if anyone has to. Yeah, man, I get it. Let's do it! Let's find the motherfucker!"

He handed the car keys to Slice and moved to the Chevy parked at the foot of the loading dock.

"In the back," Slice said, sliding behind the wheel.

"The back?" Joey said, standing beside the passenger door, a look of apprehension returning to his face.

"Yeah, the back. Don't want you tryin' to get out if you get cold feet."

"Shit, bro. I wouldn't do that." Joey said, trying to put a hurt look on his face. "You can trust me, bro. I been blooded. Remember?"

"I remember. I remember you brought your pussy friend to us. I remember that Ape is dead." Slice started the car. "In the back. Now."

"Right." Joey nodded. "In the back."

He slid into the back seat. Cheech followed and pushed him to the center while Poco got in on the other side. Sandwiched between them, their shoulders pressed tight against him, Joey was trapped. The odor of their bodies mixed with the weed they had smoked earlier was overpowering. He began trembling again.

They drove the blocks of the neighborhood, looking into storefronts and eyeballing people on the street. The big man with the Colt was nowhere to be seen. Neither was Ben or the girl.

Slice pulled to the curb in front of Dupart's Market. Through the glass, they saw the old man, Edgar, behind the counter. A customer walked out, leaving him alone inside.

"Let's go." Slice stepped out of the Chevy.

"Here?" Joey looked around nervously. "In my car ... in broad daylight?"

"Like I said, you the reason we got this problem. Anyone sees what goes down they gonna see your car."

Cheech stood on the curb, waiting for Joey to get out. When he didn't move, he reached in, grabbed him by the shirt, and dragged him from the back seat.

"We go in together." Slice turned for the door.

Cheech and Poco followed, pushing Joey in front.

Edgar looked up from his newspaper as they entered. The usual smile for his customers vanished.

"What do you want," he said without any preliminaries.

"We want your boy." Slice walked up to the counter and leaned across until his face was inches from Edgar's.

"My boy is dead," Edgar said without flinching.

"He means, Benny," Joey said from behind. "They just want to talk to him, Mr. Dupart."

It was a lie, and they both knew it.

"I know who he means, Joey." Edgar looked at the trembling boy standing between the other gangbangers. "You shouldn't be with these people."

"He *is* with us," Slice said. "And we want your boy. Don't fuck with me, old man. You know who I mean. And we want that big white dude too."

"My grandson is not here." Edgar shook his head. "And as for some big white dude, I have no idea who you're talking about."

"We gonna find him. You can't stop it, old man. Best thing for you is to tell us where he is."

"I don't know," Edgar repeated. "Now leave my store."

"You got a girl here, don't you?" Slice grinned. "The boy's mama, right? I seen her. She's one sweet piece of ass for an older bitch. I bet we talk to her, spend some time with her, you be tellin' us whatever we want to hear."

"You lay on a hand on her or my grandson and I will kill you." Edgar's usual mild expression turned to ice. "I said, leave."

"You talk big for an old man." Slice lifted his shirt to reveal the pistol tucked in his waistband. "I think we gonna stay ... look around some ... check that place you live upstairs. That where that piece of ass is hiding ... and the boy?"

"He said leave. Do it now."

John Sole stood in the doorway leading to the apartment stairs. The Colt was in his hand, pointed at Slice's head. The men standing beside Joey reflexively moved their hands to the pistols concealed under their shirts. Sole shook his head, the warning in his eyes plain. Their arms dropped to their sides.

"You." Slice whirled to face the Colt and the man holding it.

"Me." Sole nodded. "Now leave."

"You spilled blood ... DM blood." Slice shook his head. "This ain't over. It's a war now, between you and us."

"I've been to war before." Sole smiled. "Now walk out or you'll leave here in a body bag." He motioned with the Colt. "All of you."

"We'll be back," Slice said with a defiant sneer. "You got the gun in our face now, but there ain't no place you can go that we can't find you."

Slice backed away from the counter and turned for the door. Cheech and Poco, with Joey between them, followed.

As the Chevy pulled away from the curb outside, Sole turned for the back alley door.

"Where are you going?" Edgar asked. "You need to stay away from those boys. They'll hurt you."

"Maybe," Sole said. "You heard him. This isn't over."

"So what are you going to do?"

"End it."

Edgar nodded. "Alright, but I have a question."

Sole stopped and looked at him. "Ask it."

"Did you spill blood, like he said? Did you kill?"

Words were unnecessary. Edgar saw the truth in his eyes. Sole turned and left through the alley door.

THIRTY-FOUR

War

"Where we headed?" Joey squirmed in the seat, his head swiveling nervously back and forth between Cheech and Poco. "Hey, really, where we goin'? This isn't the way to …"

Slice's cold eyes moved from the road to stare at him in the rearview mirror and then back to the road. Joey trembled now, scared shitless.

The newest blooded member of the *Demonios de la Muerte* knew the penalty for failing his gang brothers. It had all sounded so good, felt so good, to be one of them, to have respect, to be feared by others because he was a DM.

Cheech elbowed him in the chest. "Stop jerkin' around."

"Sorry," Joey whispered. "I just …"

"Shut the fuck up," Cheech snarled and elbowed him again, but Joey could not stop trembling.

Slice wheeled the Chevy off the main road. They crossed the railroad tracks headed south out of the city. A minute later, they were coming out of the surrounding brush and into the clearing beside the Rio Grande.

Joey recognized the place. It was the spot they had dumped the stolen van the day he played the knockout game for them. A second vehicle waited there, engine running, a gang member behind the wheel.

"Please, don't." Tears flowed over his young cheeks. He blubbered, "I'm one of you. I'm a DM ... blooded ... *un hermano* ... a brother."

But gang brotherhood was a tenuous bond, and for Joey 'Keet' Gonzales, it was coming to an end. Slice stopped the Chevy near the river. Cheech dragged him out. He stood, head bowed and hands folded over his groin in a reflexive, self-protective posture.

His head shook back and forth, the tears falling in cascading arcs to the ground. Joey sputtered, spit and snot flying, catching the sunlight as the droplets flew through the air to plop into the dust.

"Slice, don't. I'll make things right. I'll find him for you. You won't have to do a thing. I'll find him and take care of it. I'll slit that pussy's throat ... the girl too ... I'll..."

Joey was talking fast, making the most of the seconds that remained.

Slice walked around from the driver's side of the Chevy. He shook his head. "You know the rules."

"But it wasn't me. It was Ben ... Little Man ... he did it ... his grandfather too. He must have sent the big white dude. You need me to find them."

Slice laughed. "Naw, Keet. We don't need you for shit."

"Please." Joey shook his head, his eyes closed now. "You can't."

"I can."

Slice lifted a hand. The pistol in it barked once. The bullet plowed through flesh, skull, and brain matter. Joey Gonzales crumpled into the dirt.

"Let's go." Slice turned to the waiting car. "We gonna finish this war."

They climbed into the waiting car. Before they had traveled half a mile, gunfire erupted from ahead and the brush on one side of the dirt road. Police investigators theorized that it had been planned by someone with military experience. The theory was correct.

After leaving Dupart's, Sole walked to the end of the street where a nondescript van waited. Seven Cent Killers gangbangers crammed into the back. Carlos, Big-C, sat behind the wheel. Sole climbed into the passenger seat.

"They came here just like you said. I got a man followin' them in another car. Figured this van might be too easy for them to spot. He'll let us know where they go."

"Good thinking." Sole nodded.

Carlos had his phone on speaker as he drove, listening to the directions relayed by the Cent Killer tailing Slice and the DMs.

"Shit. I been there before. Good spot," Carlos said when they pulled off the road and across the tracks, in the direction of the river. "I know just where they headed."

The van carrying the Cent Killers stopped on the dirt road a half-mile short of the clearing. Sole and the gang members piled out. Carlos' tail man was standing beside a tricked out low-rider Chevy S-10 pickup, smoking a joint.

"Let's do the motherfuckers." Carlos strode down the center of the road, his pistol in his hand.

The others clustered around him, moving toward the clearing. Two carried AK-47s. The rest had their pistols out.

"Wait," Sole said.

Carlos stopped. "What?"

"Let's do this right. I have some experience in this sort of thing."

"What you mean, experience?" Carlos' eyes narrowed. "You some kinda killer?"

"Some kinda," Sole replied without flinching under his stare.

"A killer, huh." Carlos scowled and then shrugged. "Alright, he saved Juanita. Let's see what this white boy got planned.

"Good," Sole said and began moving at a trot to a bend in the road before it opened out into the clearing. "Do what I say."

The other Cent Killers looked at each other, shrugged, and followed Sole's lead. They covered the distance in a minute. Sole stopped a hundred yards short of the bend in the road and motioned them into position. The two men with the AKs along with two others armed with pistols were set as the blocking force in the road.

"Stay in the brush along the road. When their car comes around the bend, you let them come. When you fire, you shoot up the road at the vehicle coming toward you and at anyone who gets out on the right side. That's your firing lane. Don't shoot anywhere else. Stay quiet and wait. Hold your fire until I fire the first round. Understood?"

The four men looked at each other, then at Sole, finally at their leader, Big-C.

"We gonna do it from hidin' like a bunch of pussies?" One of the Cent Killers smirked.

"You're gonna do it and live," Sole said. "Wait for my shot, then open fire until all of them are down."

"Do like he say, and be quiet." Carlos turned to Sole.

"Except one thing. I fire the first shot. That motherfucker Slice was gonna rape my little sister. I do him. No one else."

"Alright." Sole nodded. "Wait until Big-C fires the first round." He turned to their leader, adding, "And you don't fire until I say so. We do this right and everyone goes home ... except the DMs."

Big-C nodded. "Do like he say."

Sole took the rest of the Cent Killers and positioned them along the left side of the road. Big-C crouched in the brush beside him. Once the firing began, they would keep shooting until everyone in the car was down, dead or dying.

It was a classic military-style, L-shaped ambush. If executed according to Sole's instructions, none of the shooters would be caught in their own crossfire and all of them would be able to pour fire into the DMs.

They were in position as they heard the sharp crack that sent Slice's bullet tearing through Joey's brain. A minute later, they heard the car coming down the dirt road. As it rounded the bend, the Cent Killers tensed. The car carrying the DMs was just passing when Carlos rose from his place of concealment.

"Shit," Sole said and rose to stand beside him.

"You motherfucker!" Carlos shouted and opened fire on Slice in the front passenger seat.

Trapped, the DM leader reached for the door handle to push it open and confront his attacker, but it was far too late. Carlos kept pouring rounds into Slice's body from a distance of four feet. He emptied the magazine in his Glock19, inserted another, and emptied it. Slice's face was unrecognizable when he finished.

Every Cent Killer weapon opened fire when Carlos shot Slice. It lasted for thirty seconds, more an execution than murder, but a lifetime for the DMs taken by surprise in the car. When the slaughter ended, they were all down.

Cheech in the rear passenger seat had been the focus of the Cent Killers on the long leg of the L-shaped ambush. Like Slice, his body was riddled with bullets.

Poco, sitting in the rear beside Cheech, managed to push the door open and fall out onto the dirt. The blocking force of AKs and pistols fired until he stopped moving. The driver, taken out by an AK-47 7.62 millimeter round to the head when Carlos opened fire, never had any idea what was happening.

Sole walked around the vehicle, making a quick inspection of the bodies. Slice was lying on his back in the dirt where he had fallen from the car. His eyes stared into the sun from his mutilated head.

The Cent Killers stood, gawking at their handiwork. This was no undisciplined drive-by shooting, no gang free for all with bullets flying in all directions. The one-sided devastation of the attack impressed Carlos and the others.

"Man we could use you," he said, giving Sole a nod of approval.

"No, I'm leaving, but I'll tell you what to do, how to do it, after that it's up to you. I just want one thing.

"Yeah?"

"Nothing happens to the Dupart's, their customers, friends, family, the neighborhood. They stay safe, always. You target the DMs and that's it."

"Promised you we gonna look out for them for what you did for my sister."

"Good." Sole nodded, then barked an order to the group. "Move out now. Leave the scene."

He turned and trotted back down the road toward the Cent Killer van. The others followed silently.

Over the next few weeks, the Cent Killers took their revenge on the *Demonios de la Muerte*, decimating their ranks. Police were impressed with the military-style precision of the killings. Ambushes, sniper hits, back alley commando-style knifings. There were never witnesses or evidence left behind. It was as if a new killer had come to Albuquerque and set up shop, but strangely, he only seemed to target one gang.

The surviving DMs understood what was happening. With their leadership dead and no one willing to step forward to take control, they laid low. Those who could left town.

A few, without the finances or ability to flee, sent word to the Cent Killers that they wanted peace, swearing they had nothing to do with what happened to Juanita. Big-C heard them out and was going to order their execution anyway when a miracle happened.

Juanita intervened. She was tired of the killing and verified that, while the remaining DMs may have been present in the room, they stood in the background and had nothing to do with her abduction or the threat of rape.

Like most wars, it ended slowly. Now and then, hostilities would flare up, but gradually, the Cent Killers and their military tactics evolved to the point that no other gang dared challenge them.

The murders were never solved, the police were relieved when the killings finally abated, ending up in the cold case file until new evidence or suspects were uncovered. Gangs continued to roam the streets, and the neighborhoods saw little change, except for one. The area previously terrorized by the *Demonios de la Muerte* came under the protection of the Cent Killers and transformed into a haven of calm and relative peace amid the gang occupation of the neighborhoods.

Dupart's Market continued to be a gathering place for locals. Edgar maintained his role as the transmitter of the latest neighborhood news.

THIRTY-FIVE

Peace
___

The van pulled to the curb at the corner where they had picked him up. Sole climbed out and gave a parting nod to Carlos.

"When you leavin' town?" The Cent Killer leader asked.

"Soon."

"Alright. Be chill, man. We got this."

"Right. You too."

Sole turned toward Dupart's Market. The van pulled away from the curb. The operation to end the threat the DMs posed to the Dupart family was complete. He had done what he could.

The street was quiet. A lone car, a sixties-era sedan, painted purple with chrome wheels and enormous dragon's head hood ornament rolled past him. It slowed and the driver and passenger nodded at him as he walked by. Big-C already had his people out patrolling the area, maintaining order, the gang equivalent of a neighborhood watch.

It was modern-day vigilantism, locals taking upon themselves the right to enforce their own justice. Sole wasn't naïve. Like all vigilantes, the Cent Killers had an agenda and were driven by self-interest. When those came into conflict with the locals, they would enforce their will in the harshest way.

He also understood there were no other good alternatives. Understaffed and overwhelmed by the growth of gangs, law enforcement agencies struggled to protect citizens who lived in a war zone. They couldn't be everywhere at once, while the gangs could be anywhere they wanted, whenever they wanted.

In the end, the real battle wasn't between the police and the gangs. It was a fight for the souls of the youth drawn to the gangs from a society that had seemingly lost its moral compass.

He had no illusions about the peace that Carlos promised. Eventually, the Cent Killers would be pushed out by another gang, and a new occupying force would take over. The rules would change again. There was no way to prevent that, but for now, it was the best he could do.

He found the store closed when he arrived at the door and had to use the key Edgar had given him. He turned to give the street a final look, and went inside.

Edgar and Maggie waited for him in the kitchen upstairs. A pot simmered on the stove, the aroma of chilies, onion, and garlic filling the air. They had waited dinner for him.

It was a homey setting, just a family having dinner together. Sole sat across from Maggie, and she put a beer in front of him.

"Here. You look like you could use this."

"I could." He lifted the bottle and took a long sip. "Where's Ben?"

"In his room," Maggie said. "I asked him to wait there for a while. He didn't seem to mind." She paused before adding, "He said you told him some things ... about gangs ... about the Marine Corps."

"I did." Sole nodded and put the bottle on the table. "Sorry, if I was out of line. I didn't know what to say."

"No, it's fine. It was the sort of conversation I hoped he would have with you at some point. I just didn't realize it would be on a day like this." Her eyes were intent, her brow furrowed. "I have a question, though."

"Okay. Ask it."

"Edgar tells me you killed someone today. Is that true?"

"It is," Sole said, without adding that he had participated in ending the lives of several someones.

"Did Benjamin see it?"

"No." He shook his head. "He was outside with the girl, Juanita. I did what I had to do to get them out and to get myself out. That's all. If that's a problem for you, I understand. I'll leave, and you can report it to the police. I understand that too."

His morality was not theirs or that of normal society. There was no way to explain it, but if having a killer under their roof offended them, he would respect their feelings and leave immediately. He had no intention of being arrested or of drawing them into his flight from the police.

"No." Maggie shook her head. "Not a problem. You did what you thought you had to. I just wanted to make sure that Benjamin was not part of it."

"He wasn't."

"Things have been quiet on the street," Edgar interjected, changing the topic. "Since those gang people left the store ... and you ... it's been quieter than usual." His eyes met Sole's. "A couple of different cars cruising back and forth, not bothering anyone, just keeping an eye on things."

"That so?" Sole looked through the kitchen to the living room window facing the street below. "I think it will be quieter around here for now."

"I see." Edgar nodded without making further comment.

He remained with them for another two days. A few times, he and Ben took walks around the neighborhood. They talked little. Sole figured he'd said enough. Ben just seemed to like to have him there while he walked and thought things through.

On one of their walks, Ben said, "They found Joey."

"Did they?"

"Yeah. I saw it in the news … out by the river it said." Ben stopped and looked at Sole. "There were some others nearby, Slice and some DMs. They'd all been shot. Police called it an execution."

"How's that make you feel?"

"Sad. Joey was my friend, growing up."

"That's understandable," Sole said, nodding.

"Yeah, except one side of me is sad, but the other side is relieved. I mean, he turned on me in front of the DMs said I should do it … rape the girl, Juanita." He looked up at the sky and shook his head, trying to understand. "He changed … wasn't the same Joey."

A boyhood friend had become a willing accomplice to rape. It was a serious, illusion-shattering lesson about the human condition and the fine line that some people, even people we think we know, walk between the darkness and the light. There was nothing to say. When Ben was ready, they continued walking in silence.

On the third day after the ambush by the river, he rose

early. Maggie and Edgar found him drinking coffee at the kitchen table. They poured a cup and sat with him without speaking for several minutes.

As he finished his first cup, Edgar said, "You're leaving today."

It was a statement, not a question.

"I am," Sole agreed. "It's time, and I have …"

"Other business," Maggie interjected. She stood and walked around the table, leaned over and kissed his cheek. "Thank you for being here … for everything you did. Remember you always have a home here, if you want it."

She choked off the words, turned, and left the kitchen, brushing a hand across her eyes. Edgar sat and stared at his coffee cup.

"Sorry, to see you go, son." Edgar looked up, his eyes damp. "It's been …" He shrugged. "Having you around has been good for all of us."

Sole nodded. "It's been good for me too."

More words would only make things harder. Sole rose, gathered up his duffel from the living room, gave Edgar a final smile, and left.

Pulling his pickup from the alley, he caught the sun making its way down the sides of the buildings. It was a sight he had come to appreciate, one that he would remember.

An older couple strolled past, walking a dog. Two teenagers ran down the sidewalk, without threatening or harassing them or anyone else. A woman waited alone at the corner bus stop, reading a book. For now, peace reigned in the neighborhood.

THIRTY-SIX

The Hunter - No Ghosts

Nothing had changed.

In Cassit Pass, the tidal waves of change rushing around and over the world, merely swirled in eddies like the surf around boulders along the seashore. Like the boulders, the rock-solid society of Cassit Pass remained impervious, eroding around the edges a little perhaps, but mostly the same from one generation to the next.

Even so, he stood before the tiny house and marveled. It looked as if the woman and young boy who had lived there once might step out onto the porch and wave to the stranger staring at their house.

"Come on up," the woman would say. "What are you waiting for? Hurry and I'll set a place for you at supper."

Her son would stare and wonder what to think of the man, the hunter. When he put his hand out to touch the boy's head and ruffle his hair, he would pull away. Embarrassed at being so forward, the man would put his hand back in his pocket and offer a nervous smile.

Brow lowered, sending creases across his young forehead, the boy would stare for seconds until he asked, "Who are you and what do you want?"

"You boy. I want you ... I've been hunting you for these past few years."

"Why?" The boy's face would be deadly serious now, all business, ready to meet whatever threat the man posed to him and his mother.

The hunter stared at the spot on the porch where the boy would be standing while his mother clattered the pots and pans inside, readying their supper. How could he tell the boy why he was hunting him? He couldn't.

"You'll grow up to be a man one day, and I will come to find you."

"Why?"

There was the damned question again. "You're too young now to understand."

"Bullshit," the boy would snap out and his mother would call from inside for him to mind his language.

Then the boy would continue, "I'm not so young. You just come on ahead and find me if you think you can."

He would stare defiantly at the man standing at the edge of the yard, waiting, ready to take him on, to take the world on if necessary. The man would remain silent, respecting the boy's innocent fearlessness.

Finally, the boy would speak. "You're just talk ... hot air ... wind blowing in the trees. You ain't nothing to be worried about, and I sure ain't scared of you." Then the boy would bark a final warning, "Get the hell out of here."

Another rebuke for his language would be called out by his mother, and he would turn with a final sneer and go into the house, closing the door firmly behind him.

Standing at the edge of the yard, the man who would come to find the boy one day imagined the meeting in every detail, as he had a thousand times before. The difference was this time he stood before the little house that had not changed in all these years.

He walked across the yard and stepped up on the porch, almost expecting the boy from the past to come outside and challenge him. But the house was empty. A gust from the north washed away the images of the boy and woman. With clearer eyes, he saw that the house was not just as it had been. It was run down and bore the signs of having been abandoned years earlier.

The porch creaked. The planks had warped, and the nails popped loose.

A window on one side was broken. He found a tree limb under the window inside, blown through, probably in the wind from a spring thunderstorm.

The back door hung at an angle by one hinge. Someone had forced their way in to scavenge what was left after the house had been abandoned.

He entered and stood in the center of the kitchen, then moved into the living room and found a spot where he could see out through the broken window. He sat down and leaned against the wall, taking everything in, sniffing the air, trying to pick up a scent, a thread of the boy who had lived there once with his mother. He listened for ghosts rustling in the other rooms. There were no ghosts and no trace of the one he hunted.

Outside, the night came on. Shadows stretched across the floor until they met the night outside, filling the empty house with darkness. There, in the abandoned home where the boy and woman once lived, he slept soundly for the first time in years.

THIRTY-SEVEN

Bogey Man

Driving north on Interstate 85, Alejandro Garza passed through country that vaguely reminded him of semitropical regions in Mexico. The trees were different and the landscape flatter, but the same brilliant green covered the countryside.

There was history here, too, and he had always been a student of history, using the lessons of the past to reinforce the ones he taught to the cartel's enemies. Virginia was home to the first permanent English colony in America where John Smith and his party established set up a camp in what would become Jamestown in 1607. Many battles of the American Revolution and the War Between the States had been fought on this Virginia ground.

The North Americans thought that their history had given them some sacred claim to the region. They had begun by driving out the native inhabitants and claiming the land for their own. Then they flagellated themselves for their harsh treatment of the people they had conquered.

"Foolish weakness," he thought as he drove, contemplating the land, farms, fields, quaint villages, busy cities, and burgeoning industry he passed.

None of it meant anything to him. The Norteamericanos were weak, and the English were inept peasants when it came to colonization. For him, the real history of the Americas began a century earlier, in 1519, when the Spanish established a colony on the Mexican Yucatan Peninsula. The Spanish knew how to conquer and colonize, adding brutality upon brutality, extracting vast wealth from the land, and taking it to their homeland on galleons to enrich the sovereigns and adorn the churches.

The descendants of those English colonists were soft, insecure, fools. He felt no pity for them as the cartel took their wealth back to Mexico in exchange for the drugs they craved. The North Americans were now the peasants, and he and Bebé Elizondo the sovereign lords, enriched by those same peasants who hunted them with their law enforcement agencies.

He was close now. A few miles south of Petersburg, he took his foot off the accelerator and allowed the car to slow, entering the ramp to the rest area. He drove past the line of parked cars, picnic tables, and restrooms to a space at the far end of the parking area.

A man waited for him there, leaning on the fender of a gold Mercedes. Tall and thin, he wore a white, short-sleeved cotton shirt over designer slacks and tan moccasins. He grinned widely as Garza rolled to a stop beside the Mercedes E-class sedan and stepped out of his rental car.

Roman Madera's parents were Marielitos, Cubans who had fled the island in 1980 during the days of the Mariel

Boatlift. The event became a policy and credibility crisis for the Carter administration. For the Madera family, it was salvation.

Unlike the cinema portrayal of Tony Montana in Scarface, the Maderas were descended from slaves once owned by landed Spanish gentry. In Miami, they managed to open a small cigar shop with a loan from other Cuban ex-pats. Law-abiding and grateful to be in America, they avoided the drug culture that had immigrated along with the legitimate asylum-seekers, terrorizing the city in the eighties.

Their son, Roman, followed a different path. Born in the States, he had no memory of the deprivations and persecutions his parents had suffered in Cuba. They were just stories the old people told at gatherings. In his teens, he was a known runner for local cocaine smugglers. After being accused of theft by one of the Florida narcotics lords, he fled to the north to avoid a midnight bullet in the brain.

Virginia seemed as good a place as any to stop and see if anyone was following. When it appeared he had been forgotten by his pursuers, he immersed himself in Richmond's drug culture. Eventually, he became a trusted member of the local drug hierarchy and when *Los Salvajes* moved into the region, he was among the first to recognize the writing on the wall. He went over to the cartel as a dealer and enforcer and worked his way up through the organization, taking the places of others who had proved untrustworthy or disloyal.

Now, he led the cartel's distribution network in the Mid-Atlantic States, and his region was always one of the top producers. Once he had even been honored with a phone call from Bebé Elizondo, commending him for his efforts. He was warned by the man standing before him now never to discuss the call or even mention it to others in the organization, but still, he had spoken to Bebé himself.

"Señor Garza," Roman said, the smile widening.

He made no effort to extend a hand to Garza. Such familiarity with one as elevated and universally feared was unthinkable.

"You have what I want?" Garza said without preliminaries.

"Yes." Roman nodded. "He has been spotted."

"Where?"

"In Richmond. Another forty miles from here."

"Is he aware we are looking for him?"

"No." Roman shook his head. "I have handled this personally, making inquiries but making no mention of you or your visit. I told his street supplier, one of our people, I was interested in expanding the streets where he works as a reward for his sales." He smiled, proud of his deception. "I am told he was pleased by this."

"Good." Garza nodded. "Let's hope that he doesn't see through your ruse and disappear." Garza's dark eyes bored into Roman's. "That would be unfortunate."

"Yes, yes. I think it has worked and we should be able to find him quickly."

Roman said a silent prayer—*Dear Mary, mother of God, please make sure we find the sneaking little rat bastard quickly.*

He wished he could make the sign of the cross the way the nuns taught him, but Garza's intense stare made that unthinkable. He put forward his most confident expression and cleared his throat.

"Of course, I could have my men pick him up and hold him for you, if that would be satisfactory."

"It is not." Garza's eyes narrowed. "I handle this alone. I will extract the information I require and ensure that it is accurate. You will be with me to assist if I should require it. Otherwise, you will remain silent."

"Certainly, I understand," Roman said quickly. "As, I said, we have not mentioned your visit. I was only suggesting …"

"Don't," Garza snapped.

Roman's mouth clamped shut.

"Lead me to him," Garza said.

"Yes, of course."

Roman climbed behind the Mercedes' wheel, conscious of Garza's stare of disapproval. He should have driven a more modest car. What was he thinking? Clearly, a man like Garza did not approve of such ostentation.

Roman led the way down the ramp to the interstate in the very visible gold Mercedes. Garza followed in the rental.

The drive north to Richmond took half an hour. Roman prayed that his people had everything in order.

As they approached the James River crossing into downtown Richmond, Roman took an exit ramp. A few minutes later, they were winding through streets lined with small frame houses. It was an older section of the city, once a suburban enclave of working-class homes. Now the long-time residents were struggling to hold on to their quality of life as drugs and gangs seeped into the area.

Roman pulled into a shopping center parking lot and got out of the Mercedes. Garza waited in the rental.

"He is in a small house that he shares with two other dealers not far from here," Roman said standing beside Garza's open driver's window. "They will not be there. I sent them on an errand to check sales in another part of the city, gave them some cash so they would not lose revenue from lost sales today."

If he expected a compliment for his ingenuity, none was forthcoming. Garza was focused on one thing.

"How can you be certain he is there?"

"We know he is low on inventory." Roman smiled. "He's been working hard, making money."

"And you are certain he will be there?"

"He needs inventory. One of our runners, a twelve-year-old boy, is supposed to deliver a package with the inventory. He won't leave until the runner comes with the package."

"Good." Garza nodded. "Get in."

"Get in? Here?" Roman cast a glance at the gold Mercedes. "This is not a good area to leave a car like this. Perhaps I can take it to a garage in the city first, then we …"

"Get in. If you are worried about your car, you should have driven another." Garza waited, hands on the wheel, staring at him.

"Yes, of course. You are correct." Roman said, going to the passenger door. "It was thoughtless of me not to have considered that you would want to arrive in the same vehicle."

"Direct me to the house," Garza said when Roman was seated.

They wound through another series of streets. The farther they drove the more rundown the houses appeared. Block by block, the neat working-class homes morphed into ramshackle hovels, bearing the signs of urban decay—broken fences and gates, trash in yards, windows broken or missing, paint that had faded away or chipped off decades earlier. As they came to a corner, Roman pointed.

"There. The third house down this block."

It was a house like all the others. A four-foot-high chain-link fence surrounded the yard. In one section the fence was bent over, apparently from the impact of a vehicle that left the street and plowed into the yard. A lone shutter hung at an angle from one of the windows. There were no shutters on any of the others. Garza drove past and pulled the rental to the curb a block from the house.

"When is the runner due to arrive?" Garza asked, his eyes not leaving the house.

Roman checked his watch. "In another half hour."

"Good. We will wait, and I will tell you how to proceed."

Luis Acero sat on a frayed sofa, smoking a joint, waiting for the runner. He eyed his personal stash of cocaine and thought better of taking a hit now. Later, when it was time to work the streets. Then he could do a line to clear his head. For now, he needed to conserve his resources.

If shabbiness marked the neighborhood, filth was the identifying trait of this house. It was a shit hole.

The air reeked of old food, burned food, rotting food, the pungent smell of urine and unflushed toilets. Dirt and debris littered the floors. The only furniture, the sofa and two chairs of the same type, were stained and soiled with body fluids from sexual encounters and bladders that had released while one of the occupants slept through a drug-induced coma. Scratching noises in the walls marked the passage of mice and rats, scurrying back and forth.

Luis Acero ignored it all. This shit hole was home for

now. When he had put together enough cash, he planned to move on, find another city and another dealer to work for.

He had left Atlanta two years earlier with a pocket of cash supplied by John Sole. The detective had killed the drug lord who was going to kill Luis. Since then, they had spoken three times on the phone Sole provided. He had no idea what the former cop was doing, but he knew he wasn't a cop anymore. That had been in the papers.

Part of him hated Sole. If he had not been a snitch for him, Luis would still be in Atlanta, selling drugs on his corner, making money, and living large.

Another part of him knew that John Sole was the only person he could trust. Sole could have abandoned him, let the cartel slit his throat and dump him in the river, but he didn't. Instead, he made sure Luis had some cash to start over somewhere and took the cartel on a chase away from Luis. That counted for something.

A knock came at the door. About fucking time. Luis rose from the sofa, joint clenched between the fingers of his left hand. He pulled the door open.

"Here."

The young black boy held out two plastic shopping bags bearing the markings of a local grocery store. If anyone stopped him, he was just getting some groceries for his mother. That was the cover story he had been given, but no one ever stopped him.

Luis took the bags without speaking. No names were mentioned. Nothing else was said. Luis nodded and closed the door.

He returned to the sofa and placed the bags on the floor between his feet to examine the packages inside. Several heavy brown envelopes in each held cocaine packaged in plastic bags. One of the shopping bags held gram packages, the other eightballs—an eighth of an ounce of cocaine each.

He took a long final drag on the joint, dropped it to the floor, and stepped on it with the heel of his shoe. Then he pulled the rickety coffee table close and started to cut three lines of coke from his supply. The jolt would get him jump-started for the day.

He rolled up a twenty-dollar bill and leaned over to snort the first line from the filthy tabletop. A knock at the door, three sharp raps stopped him. His head lifted, nostrils expanding as if to sniff the air for danger. Every nerve in his body tensed. No one should be visiting. No one ever visited. There was no reason to visit. He found his customers, not the other way around.

He pulled the slats of the blinds apart and peered out. No car sat at the curb, but that didn't mean anything. He rose and went to a side window where he could see the front stoop. He relaxed and moved to the door, a smile on his face.

"Roman," Luis said as he pulled the door open. He nodded and grinned like a high school athlete happy to have pleased his coach on being told he was moving him to the starting team. "Man, it is good to see. I got your message … expanding my area … gonna make you proud, bro. I promise."

"I'm sure you will."

"Come on, in, man. Get off the street. This ain't your usual hood."

Roman remained stationary, expressionless. Luis' forehead wrinkled, confused. They stood face to face without speaking for several seconds.

"What's the matter, Roman? I thought …"

The sound behind him was faint, just a slight movement

of air as someone passed into the room. He turned and would have screamed out his terror if Alejandro Garza had not clamped a gloved hand over his mouth.

Garza forced him down on the sofa, the muscles in his arms sinewy steel as Luis beat helplessly against them. Roman entered, and Garza nodded.

In a matter of seconds, he wrapped the duct tape Garza provided around Luis' feet and hands and over his mouth, making a complete pass around his head. They sat him up straight on the sofa.

"Do you know who I am?" Garza asked.

Eyes wide, his breath coming in gasps, Luis nodded.

"Then you understand what is going to happen."

Luis' eyes grew even wider. It was the stuff of nightmares.

In the world he inhabited, Alejandro Garza was the phantom bogey man who sent terror through every heart. And here he stood, towering over him, all-powerful, the decider of fates, the man who could give him the simple speedy death he prayed for at this moment, but who could also send him into an endless, agonizing hell of torture that would only end when the bogey man was satisfied.

"You will give me what I want. You know that."

Trembling, Luis nodded.

"All of it. I promise that you will have no choice." Garza's voice was like the drone of a machine, heartless, passionless, and irresistible. "It is inevitable, only a matter of time. The question for you, and it is an important one … one that will determine how you end your wretched life … is how much time will I waste here with you. Do you understand?"

Luis nodded again, and this time he wept.

PART III
Life

THIRTY-EIGHT

The Hunter - A Place for Ghosts

The grave was much as he had imagined it. Nestled in a corner of the town's lone cemetery, the tree-covered slopes of the mountains rose above it. Towering oaks, hickory, and maple surrounded the site, casting cool shadows. It was as if nature cradled the place in her palm, ensuring that peace would preside here.

He knelt by the grave, peered at the stone, and nodded. This was the one. There was no mistaking it. Though it had been dug and then covered twenty years earlier, the chiseled words engraved on the marker were still clear.

Clara Barker Sole
1951 - 1998
Beloved by all;
May the tender mercies of the Lord be upon her as she showed tenderness to all.

He reached out and touched the stone marker, then leaned forward and rested his forehead on its polished surface. It was cool and soothing. Minutes passed. He remained like that, soaking in the coolness, letting it ease away the fever that had possessed him most of his life.

An hour passed, and he was still alone by the grave. He hadn't expected anyone to come, but still, there had been the chance that the man he sought would be drawn to the place.

A cardinal in a nearby tree called to the strange man invading his domain. He looked up. It was unmistakable, brilliant scarlet against the green background, and one more sight he had forgotten. There were no cardinals in the Mojave Desert.

The bird turned its head side to side, watching the man. It gave another less musical call, a metallic chip sound that seemed to say, "Watch out. You're on my turf, human. I know where the bodies are buried."

The man smiled and muttered, "I'll bet you do."

The smile felt strange, pulling at the corners of his mouth like an article of clothing that had shrunk and been forgotten. It spread across his cheeks in an unaccustomed way until he accepted it. Gradually, it grew wider. He looked at the grave, whispering to her ghost.

"I'm smiling. Can you see it? Can you believe it?"

He could almost see her throw her head back, her laughter deep and throaty, womanly. "No, I don't believe a bit of it."

A breeze rustled the leaves in the trees, and he looked around as if she had sent the wind as an answer from beyond. He shook his head. "I guess this is a place for ghosts, if ever there was one."

Many of the graves were old, some dating back more than a hundred and fifty years to the founding of Cassit Pass as a crossroads stop for travelers. Traveling by horse, mule, wagon, cart, or foot, they made their way from the eastern coastal regions to the Cumberland Plateau and beyond, searching for fertile farm country not already claimed by wealthy planters in the slave states.

A few stayed in the mountains. This was far enough, and as good a place as any to make a life. They lived here and died here, and now, Clara rested with them.

He spent the afternoon sitting by the grave, waiting. After a while, even the cardinal ceased calling, accepting his presence the way it accepted the dead when they arrived periodically to take their place in one of the graves.

An occasional breeze moaned through the trees, rustling the leaves and branches the way a sob shakes the shoulders of a mourner. He looked around the empty cemetery and wondered. Were the dead beyond weeping? Or did they shed their tears for the puny mortals left behind?

He sat through the afternoon listening to the trees whisper and moan, their limbs creaking as they swayed until the sun lowered and the shadows lengthened. It was clear that the man he hunted was not going to show today. He hadn't really expected him to. It was just a reason to visit the grave.

He took a small medallion from his pocket and laid it on the stone, then stood and walked away. The hunt continued.

THIRTY-NINE

Moments

The layers of tape wrapped around his head and eyes were ripped away, taking part of his eyebrows and lashes with them. Luis Acero blinked and squinted. The transformation from pitch black to bright day was instantaneous, and the dim light from a lamp on a nearby table was like looking into the noonday sun. The light stabbed into his eyes, and he squinted in pain.

He sat upright on a wooden chair in the middle of a bare room. He had no idea where the room was located. He had no idea where Alejandro Garza was, but Roman Madera towered over him, holding the duct tape in his hand.

"Do you know where you are?" Roman asked.

Luis shook his head and looked around the room at the bare plank walls. Somewhere behind him, light shone through a window.

He sobbed and whimpered, his throat too choked with fear to plead. They had covered his eyes with the tape, then dragged him from his home and placed him on the rear floor of a car where he lay for hours.

Sounds of the city faded. A while later, noise from passing cars also disappeared. When the car came to a stop, he was dragged out and into a structure where they sat him in the chair and left him. He had no idea how long he sat there. It could have been hours or days. Sensory deprivation distorted his sense of time. At one point, he thought he must have slept, but that could have been merely a wish to sleep so he could wake up from this terrifying dream.

"You are in a room in a cabin in the mountains of western Virginia," Roman said, his voice firm but the expression on his face regretful and full of empathy. "This is a place far from the city and that shit hole of a house you rent, a place where no one will hear you if you cry out and where no one will come to save you."

Roman paused. His eyes softened with what appeared to be true sympathy, and Luis shuddered.

"This is the last place on earth you will see, Luis," Roman continued sadly. "I am sorry it has come to that, but you see that it can end no other way. The only thing you have power over now is how it ends for you."

Luis' shoulders shook with his sobs. Tears poured down over the duct tape that sealed his mouth shut. He struggled to speak.

Roman patted him on the back and ripped the tape away from his mouth. "Don't drown in your tears, Luis."

"Please," Luis begged. "There must be a way ... something I can say." His head moved side to side in denial, flinging tears to the floor. "I will give you what you want. I will do whatever it takes, but let me live. I beg you, Roman!" He gasped, barely able to speak through his tears. "Please let me live."

"*Hombre*, be a man!" Roman said in harsh tones, annoyed that Luis was making this hard for him. "You know who waits in the next room. He allowed me to come in and try to prepare you so that you would reconcile yourself to the inevitable and offer him what he wants quickly. Do that and he will make things easy for you, painless and quick." Roman shook his head. "If you do not, it will be very hard on you ... harder than you can imagine."

"I want to live!" Luis cried out.

A door opened behind him. A tall man stepped around the chair and looked down at his quivering frame. Roman stepped to the back, reconciled to what would happen next even if Luis was not.

The tall man spoke. "You will not live. That has been explained to you. You will tell me what I want to know one way or another. Tell me quickly and I will send you to your ancestors quickly and without pain."

Luis's head sunk to his chest, weeping in desperation. Without warning, a hand struck him in the side of the face, the force of the blow twisting his head to the side. The sobbing stopped as he caught his breath, stunned by the blow.

The point of a knife pressed into the bottom of his chin, lifting his head until he looked into the eyes of Alejandro Garza.

"We will begin." Garza spoke quietly, without threat, as if he were asking about the weather. "Where is the man, John Sole?"

It was a simple question, and Luis was terrified to give an honest answer. Trembling, he whispered, "I don't know."

Eyes clenched shut, Luis waited for the blade of the knife to slice into his quivering flesh.

"Very good," Garza said, nodding approval.

Luis' eyes popped open. "Good?" He was confused.

"I do not believe this man would be so careless to make his whereabouts known to the likes of you. If you had answered differently, it would be proof that you are going to try to lie to me, and there would have been consequences before I asked the next question … painful consequences. Do you understand this?"

Luis nodded.

What passed for a smile flittered briefly across Garza's stone-like countenance. "Are you ready to continue?"

Luis nodded.

"Good. Have you been in contact with him since leaving Atlanta?"

"Yes."

"How many times?"

"Not many. Three maybe." Luis looked up, thinking, and nodded. "Yes, three times."

There were tears in his eyes. With each question, he drew closer to the moment when Garza would run the blade across his throat. Yet, each moment was one more of life. He tried desperately to devise a plan to extend the moments and avoid the knife.

"Have you seen him in person, when you have been in contact with him?"

"No, never."

"How do you contact him?"

"I call him."

"You call him?" Garza's eyes narrowed. "You have been warned to speak only the truth." He lifted the tip of the knife blade in front of Luis's eyes. "This man would not have a number you could call and reach him so easily."

"It's not like that!" Luis spoke rapidly. "I didn't mean I just call his phone."

"Explain."

"There is a voice mail account. I dial the number for the account and leave a voice message. It is not the number to his phone, but we can both listen to voice messages on it." Luis' voice and eyes pleaded in desperation for Garza to believe him. "I leave a message. He checks in from another phone, one I don't have the number to ... a burner. Then he calls the same voice mail number and leaves a message for me. He tells me how to reach him ... what number to call. It's always a different number. He never uses the same phone."

"Simple and clever." Garza considered the explanation for a moment, then extended a hand to Roman. "Let me have his phone.

Roman handed over the phone they had taken from Luis' pocket. Garza scrolled through the contact list.

"This number, is it in your list?"

"No." Luis shook his head, and a spark of hope flickered in his heart. He might be able to prolong his moments of life for a few more minutes. "He told me to remember it, not write it down, or add it to my phone."

"You will give me this number."

"Yes."

Luis spilled it out immediately. Garza thumbed it into his phone and saved it.

"If you left a message for him that you were with me, that he must come to me to prevent me from ending your life, would he come?"

The spark of hope burned a little brighter, fanned by the possibility that this might not be his last day on earth.

"Yes," Luis said quickly, praying that he was right.

Garza was silent, considering the possibilities, and Luis lived for several more moments, each one a lifetime in his feverish brain. If he could survive until Sole showed up, there might be a way to go on living. Garza looked at the phone in his hand.

"If I leave this message for him, he will come right away?"

"No," Luis said, and recoiled as Garza lifted his dark eyes, menacingly. "Not at first, I mean. He checks the voice mail, but sometimes it takes a few days. He doesn't check every day, but he will, and then he will get your message and ..."

"And he might come to help you, or he might not," Garza interrupted. "I warned you to speak truthfully."

"I am. I swear it," Luis pleaded. "I mean he saved my life I Atlanta when he ..."

"When he killed our man."

"Yes." Luis' words came out rapid-fire filling the air in the hope that as long as there were words floating between them, Garza would keep the knife away from his neck. An idea came to him. "But there is someone else. Someone he will come to protect. I am certain of it."

"Who?" Garza's eyes narrowed.

"A woman."

Sole had fled Texas with a woman and her son to protect them from the men Garza sent to kill them. This was a bonus he had not expected.

"And how did you hear of this woman?"

"I helped get fake IDs for them so they could stay hidden."

"And Sole contacted you himself for this task?"

"No. He sent someone ... a friend he said." Luis gave the sales pitch of his life. "He will come for me, but he will come faster for the woman I think. I'm just a snitch to him, but they are friends ... I am sure there is something between him and the woman."

"Something?"

"Yeah, like they were together ... like she was his woman and he was protecting her ... like she ..."

"I understand," Garza broke into Luis' sales pitch, staring at him as he weighed this new information. "Then why do I need you?"

"Because I'm the one who contacts him on the voice mail number. He would expect a message from me if there's a problem. If I don't leave the message, he will think it's a trap and not show up."

Luis's mouth clamped shut. He had given it his all, and the spark of hope still glowed. The next few seconds would determine whether it sprang up into full flame or sputtered and died as the blood drained from his slit throat.

After several seconds, Garza asked, "The number of the person who contacted you about the fake IDs, is it in your phone?"

"Yes, in the list of calls. I don't keep an address book or anything." The hope in his eyes flickered a little brighter.

"Show me." Garza held the phone in front of Luis' face and scrolled through the call history.

"There, that one," Luis said as the numbers went by.

Garza pointed. "This one?"

"Yes."

Garza turned to Roman. "Keep him secure here, but release his hands and feet. Let him have food and clean up. We will need him for a while yet."

Roman nodded without speaking.

Garza turned to Luis. "This changes nothing. You betrayed us by working with the police. For that, there is only one punishment, but for now, you will live a bit longer."

Garza turned and left the room. Roman pulled out a knife and cut the tape binding Luis' hands and feet.

The room swirled around Luis like a kaleidoscope. He almost toppled from the chair when the tape fell to the floor. Less than five minutes ago his life was about to end in this room.

Now he had a reprieve. The extra moments of life dangled in front of him on a thread of hope. The moments might be uncertain, and they could end at any time, but he clung to the thread the way a drowning man clings to a life preserver.

FORTY

Still Here

In Winslow, he pulled off the interstate to check a map and consider his next move. Albuquerque was four hours and two hundred fifty miles behind him. The goodbye with Maggie and Edgar haunted him. His time there and sudden departure gnawed at him. Things felt incomplete, unfinished.

You did what you could, he reminded himself. The mission, focus on the mission. You can't fix everyone's problems. Move on.

He sighed. Alright then, focus. Ahead lay the metropolises of the western deserts and Pacific coast. Flagstaff, Phoenix, Tucson, Las Vegas, Reno, Los Angeles, San Francisco, Portland, Seattle. Sole studied the road atlas and outlined a zigzag course in his mind.

A quick stop for gas and a convenience store sandwich in a plastic box, and he was on the road again. It was time to resume the game of cat and mouse with *Los Salvajes*, time to remind them that he was still there, waiting for the inevitable.

He muttered to himself as he drove, a habit that he engaged more frequently when solitude closed in around him.

"I'm still out here, boys. Catch me if you can."

There was new purpose in her life. In a month, she would be married. The word sounded almost strange to her, a foreign custom she embraced to comply with the expectations of her new life. Despite raising a son, she had never been married, never thought she would be.

Her reflection in the mirror stared back, the same person she had always been, but changed too. John had done that, changed her, and changed her life. Despite the turmoil and fear accompanying their departure from Texas, she knew in her heart that she would still be there if not for John. Worse, she might have lost her son and Jacinta.

It was the great contradiction in her life. Without John, she would not have escaped the prison of her life in Texas, but because of him she met Sam. She had a new life, and the new person in the mirror could move on.

"Thank you, John," she whispered and continued brushing her hair. "We're still here, thanks to you."

He sat on the cabin porch, smoking a cigar with his coffee. The sun was still far below the surrounding hills. Gray early morning light filtered through the trees.

Alejandro Garza considered the situation. Bebé Elizondo expected him to return soon. In one regard, Elizondo was correct. The hunt for Sole could not continue indefinitely. There must be an end. They had other pressing business.

So where was John Sole? The question preoccupied Garza night and day. Had he dropped off the face of the earth?

There had been no reports of his movements for several weeks. The cartel's vast distribution networks had not had any contact with him. No bodies of local dealers had turned up in alleys with bullets in their heads. No one had called frantically to report he had been spotted.

He had vanished. No, that wasn't true, Garza decided. If he remained unseen, it was because he preferred it that way. The question was why. What had changed?

Garza had come to realize that Sole was leading them on a chase. The rat, Luis Acero, had made it clear that there were others about whom Sole cared, and so he forced the cartel to pursue him and ignore those others.

He tossed the coffee from the cup across the yard and stood up. It was time to remind Sole that the cartel was still here.

FORTY-ONE

Death Row

"Make the call."

Alejandro Garza handed the phone to Luis.

"Right," Luis nodded and took the phone from Garza's hand.

"I'll be listening. You leave the message … you want to speak to him. Nothing more. No signals of any kind. Do this as I have instructed and your life will continue for a while. If you say anything other than what I have said, you will die in the next minute."

Luis nodded.

"Say it."

"I understand. Leave the message. That's all … nothing else." He looked up at Garza, pleading. "I want to live. Don't you know that? I'm not gonna say anything else. I do this right, and you'll see you can use me, I can help you. … just give me another chance to make things up."

"Make the call," Garza replied without emotion or promise.

"Okay." Luis looked down at the phone and punched

the number for the voice mail service they used to communicate.

Thirty seconds passed while the call connected and the recorded female voice advised him he had reached the voice mailbox of Bill Myers. It took another fifteen seconds to go through the menu options—press the one numeral to leave a voice mail, two to enter a PIN and hear messages, three to change the greeting and manage other services. Sole had warned him never to enter three.

Luis pressed the one numeral on his phone, waited a second, and spoke.

"We gotta talk. It's important. I'll check messages every day until you get this."

Luis disconnected the call and handed the phone to Garza.

"Good," Garza said.

"That's all?" Luis asked.

"For now." Garza pocketed the phone. "When will he call?"

"Like I said. I call back and check messages every day. When he gets this one, he'll leave a message and set up a time for us to talk, a number to call, that kind of thing. He's pretty careful about how he does it."

"I'm sure he is. How long?"

"How long before he gets the message?" Luis shrugged and answered truthfully. "No telling. Sometimes it's quick, just a day, or two. Other times it takes a while because he's … busy."

Luis saw Garza's eyes narrow at that and repressed a smirk. No doubt when Sole was busy he was fucking with the cartel.

Garza turned and walked from the room without comment.

Luis Acero looked out from the single window in the room. It was barred, but beyond the bars, the Blue Ridge Mountains undulated to the horizon. A billion trees covered their slopes. How easy it would be to hide out there without them finding him, if he could only get out there.

He couldn't. The cabin was his prison and the room where they had kept him for the last several days was his cell. Bathroom visits and a few minutes a day to stretch his legs in the yard outside under the pine trees were his only breaks from the monotony of the room. Always, Roman Madera remained at his side as fearful of displeasing Alejandro Garza as Luis was, even more so since he would eventually leave the cabin alive to return to trafficking drugs for the cartel.

Luis had no illusions. He was under a death sentence, serving his last few days on death row. With no hope that his sentence might be commuted or pardoned, delaying the execution became his only purpose in life.

Take your time, John Sole, he thought. Find something else to do. Every day he delayed answering the message would be another day of life for Luis Acero.

FORTY-TWO

The Hunter - Rotten Son of A Bitch

The bartender leaned over the bar, his fists planted on each side of a newspaper spread open before him, a cup of coffee at the side. He looked up as the customer walked in.

"What can I get you?"

"Beer, I guess." The hunter slid onto a stool and looked at the waiting bartender. "Got a Sam Adams?"

"Yep."

"Make it a Sam."

"Right." The bartender turned away and added, making conversation with the customer. "Most people order coffee this time of day. Beer crowd doesn't usually get here before four or five."

"No law against it is there?"

"Nope, not a one."

The hunter noted his size and figured he must tip the scales at about three-fifty. It was the first thing everyone noticed about the man who ran the place. The second thing was the wide, round face filled with a perpetual grin.

The bartender put the beer on the bar, folded his arms,

and the grin grew wider. It was a perfect pour, an inch of white foam atop dark amber. He watched, waiting for the customer to lift the glass and appreciate the perfect pour.

The hunter obliged, nodded, lifted the glass, and took a swallow, then put it back on the bar. "Good. Thanks."

He swiveled on the stool, examining the interior of the small bar. It was early still for public drinking in this out of the way place, and he was the only customer.

Located on the square in the center of Cassit Pass, the bar was tucked between a craft's shop and an old five and dime store that still managed to attract locals who didn't want to drive to the big box stores closer to Atlanta.

Space was at a premium. A few tables and chairs were scattered around the room, and ten stools lined the bar that faced the front door and street outside. From the street to the bar's back door wasn't more than forty feet with a width of twenty. Friday nights must be elbow to elbow at the only bar in Cassit Pass, or maybe it never got busy.

He turned back to the bar and his beer to find the bartender watching him, arms folded over his belly, his eyes curious above the grin.

"Who's Derek?" he asked, nodding at the sign high on the wall over the bartender's head—*Derek's Bar*.

"That'd be me. I own the place.

"Don't remember any bar around here," he said, not really interested in conversation, but the bartender's inquisitive stare showed no signs of moving on to something else.

"You been here before?" The grin remained in place, but the furrows in his forehead marked the bartender's curiosity.

"Yeah." The hunter nodded. "Long time ago. Back then couldn't get a beer in town ... not legal anyways."

"Yep, we used to be a dry town, but the council finally

gave in and decided to permit us." The bartender chuckled. "Figured they were losing too much revenue to the big city. Money talks, even out here amongst the hillbillies. Been here about ten years now."

"So, I expect you know most everyone in town."

"A good many," Derek said with a nod. "If they drink at all, they eventually make their way in, except for the hardcore Baptists and Pentecostals."

"How about a man name of John Sole?"

Derek's eyes narrowed, and the grin faded somewhat. "He was from here. He's not around anymore."

"Oh." The hunter nodded and lifted the beer. "Just that I read some things in the paper a couple of years back."

"True enough. There were some things in the paper, terrible things ... family murdered. Then he disappeared. No telling where he is now." Derek shook his head sadly. "Thing like that would ruin a lot of men ... maybe kill them."

"I expect so," the hunter agreed. "Thing is, I'd like to find him if I can. I was hoping someone around Cassit Pass might be able to point me in the right direction."

"Don't know that they can, but I have a question for you." Derek's demeanor changed. He leaned forward, peering into the eyes of the stranger who had come into his bar, digging into what most people in Cassit Pass considered the worst event to have ever occurred to one of their own. "Who the hell are you to be asking questions about John Sole, and why do you want to find him?"

The hunter looked into the bartender's eyes and said the words he hadn't said since young John Sole was born to Clara in the house on the mountain. "I'm his father."

"The hell you say." Derek's usually open, friendly face clouded with disbelief. "John Sole didn't have a father. I grew up with him. He was a couple of years ahead of me in school, but we knew each other and everyone knew how his father deserted him and his mama when he was a baby. He never made mention of anyone he called a father."

"I'm sure that's true."

"I can see a resemblance, but that doesn't mean a damned thing." Derek leaned a little closer, like a man examining a faded photograph in an album. "All I can say is, if you're who you say you are, you are one rotten son of a bitch."

The hunter, the man who claimed to be John Sole's father, did not argue the point. He simply nodded and returned the bartender's gaze.

"Still, I don't suppose you'd be in here claiming to be that rotten son of a bitch if you weren't him," Derek said. "What's your name?"

"Lamont Sole … people back then … Clara … used to call me Monty." He took a deep breath and shook his head. "What I'm saying is true. You can check it out, and whatever you say to me can't be worse than what I've said to myself over the years."

"That supposed to be some sort of excuse or an apology to your dead wife?" Derek shook his head emphatically. "It doesn't excuse anything. That boy grew up without a father, and his mother, Clara, she spent her life alone in that little house. If that isn't an evil way to treat people, I don't know what is."

Monty Sole sat, hands folded around the glass, and lowered his head. He had expected this sort of reception, had prepared himself for it, but that didn't make it any easier. He had no desire to meet the bartender's outrage. A silent minute passed between them before he spoke.

"I'm looking for my son. Can you help me contact him?"

"Why should I? If I did know where he was, and I do not, but if I did, why should I believe he even wants to hear from the deadbeat who abandoned him and his mother."

"Maybe he doesn't," Monty said, nodding. "But that's his decision, isn't it?"

"I suppose that's true." Derek scowled and crossed his beefy arms over his chest. "If anyone should tell you what you are to your face, it ought to be him."

He turned and pulled a stack of business cards from beside the cash register, flipping through several before he pulled one out.

"Here, take this." He held the card out to Monty. "Billy Siever and John were best friends in school. I don't suppose you know anything about that, but if anyone knows about John Sole or his whereabouts, it'll be Billy. They reconnected after Clara died. I heard Billy say they kept in touch … at least until the day John disappeared off the face of the earth."

"Thank you." Monty reached for the card.

Big Derek the bartender held it tight for a moment, his eyes boring into Monty's. "Don't make me regret giving this to you."

"I won't." Monty looked into Derek's eyes. "I promise."

Derek released the card. Monty pushed it down in his shirt pocket and stood, reaching for his wallet.

"Beer's on the house," Derek said. He shook his head. "Rotten son of a bitch or not, after all that's happened to your boy, if he's still alive, I reckon I don't feel like charging his father for a beer. Go find your son."

Monty Sole nodded and walked out into the noonday sun. He stood alone on the curb in front of Derek's Bar, his heart pounding in his chest. Derek had known John growing up. Meeting the bartender was the closest thing to contact with his son he'd had since the day he walked off into the mountains, running from his demons. He'd been running ever since. It was time to stop.

He pulled the card from his pocket. It read:

William Siever, Attorney at Law

They were best friends, Derek said. He hoped that was still true.

He punched the number on the card into his phone and waited. The call went to voice mail and he ended it. Maybe it would be better to do this in person.

Or maybe he shouldn't do it all. Derek's words rang in his ear.

"You are one rotten son of a bitch."

FORTY-THREE

Wedding Gowns and Robo-Calls

It was a family excursion. With the dates for two weddings and a baby shower approaching, there was a lot to plan, and planning involved a good deal of shopping.

They began at the Mall of Georgia in Buford, mostly because it was the first in proximity to Gainesville on the drive to Atlanta. Accompanied by Billy and Vera Siever, Isabella, Sam Goodwin, Sandy, and Jacinta were on an excursion, determined to make all the arrangements and necessary purchases in one day.

Their route would take them on to Perimeter Mall, then to the upscale boutiques of Buckhead. While the ladies shopped, led by Vera Siever who had jumped in to help in the planning with the enthusiasm of a favorite aunt, the men found a bar and grill with seating in the mall concourse and drank coffee.

"Guess I'm out of practice for this sort of thing," Sam said as the ladies disappeared into the Saturday crowd. "Forgot how much goes into a wedding."

"It's a defense mechanism." Billy grinned and winked at

Sandy. "We forget to protect the next generation. Otherwise, young fellas like Chris here would get cold feet, marriage would end, and society would crumble."

They chuckled and sipped their coffee, staring vacantly at the passing throng of weekend shoppers. Like men castaway on an island watching ships pass in the distance, they hoped for the return of the one that would take them to safety and home.

Meanwhile, in the bridal department of a well-known department store, an important debate regarding wedding attire ensued.

"I'm just not sure," Isabella said, looking at herself in the mirror outside the dressing room. "Maybe something simpler and less ... white."

"Don't be silly, Abby. You look beautiful in that gown, and of course, you can wear white," Vera said to Isabella and looked at Jacinta, adding, "You too Margarita. Forget that baby bump. It just makes you look more beautiful. For heaven's sake, it's the twenty-first century. Those old traditions are for ... well, the old folks and neither of you qualify as old, believe me."

"So you think I should buy it?" Isabella said, looking in the mirror and smoothing the silk fabric over her hips.

"I love it," Jacinta beamed.

"Heavens no!" Vera interjected. "We just started. Lots more shopping and more gowns to try on before you make a selection. This is just a warm-up stop to get ourselves ready for the game," She beamed at them. "We're in this for the long haul!"

An hour passed, and then another. At noon, Billy suggested they order a burger for lunch as the cafe management eyed the coffee-sipping customers occupying prime table real estate on the concourse.

"I could eat a burger," Sam said. "Is it too early for a beer?"

"Not for me." Billy looked at Sandy, teasing.

They ordered the grill's famous half-pound burgers for lunch. Sandy drank a Coke while Sam and Billy sipped beers. When the server came to clear away the plates, Sam stretched and started to stand.

"What's the hurry?" Billy asked.

"Thought I might go find the ladies … see what's keeping them."

"What's keeping them? You really have been a bachelor for a while haven't you?" Billy laughed. "Sit down and relax. They'll be a while."

Billy's phone chimed. He carried two, his personal cell, and one for clients and his law practice staff to reach him.

"We've got this young man as our designated driver if we need one, and judging by how long the ladies have been gone, we just might."

The call came in on the business phone. He looked at it, wrinkled his brow, and put it back in his pocket without answering.

"Somebody you don't want to speak with?" Sam asked.

"928 area code. Probably a robo-caller."

"Arizona," Sandy said between sips of Coke.

"I'll let it go to voice mail. For now, the ladies are not in sight and I'm having another beer."

FORTY-FOUR

Safe Words

The trip through Flagstaff was a quick one. At first, he thought the city at the foot of San Francisco Peaks might be a washout, a waste of time, more an attraction for tourists, hikers, and skiers than a hotbed of gang activity and drug use. He was wrong.

Exiting I-40 onto Old Route 66, he only wandered the street for half an hour before cruising through the Sunnyside district. The indicators were all present. Low rent housing, much of it dilapidated intermixed with blue-collar businesses—plumbers, contractors, body shops. Three blocks from an elementary school, he noticed three young men standing along the curb in front of a run-down house.

As he watched, a car with three teenagers pulled up. The pass was quick, two of the men kept an eye on the street in both directions, while the third made the pass through the window and received the money. The transaction took no more than fifteen seconds, and the car left with the teens laughing and chattering loudly enough for him to hear as they rounded the corner and left the area.

Good enough, he decided and fell immediately into character as he climbed out of the pickup. Head slumped forward with his chin almost on his chest and a ball cap pulled low over his eyes, he began his shuffling, ambling walk toward the three dealers.

"Shit, man. What the fuck we got here?" The dealer who handled the drugs and money bent down to get a better look at his face.

Sole stood up straight, pulling the Colt from his waistband as he rose to his full height. He smiled.

"Afternoon, boys."

"Who the fuck you callin' boys?" the dealer snapped back. "And what you think you gonna do with that? Best put that thing away before we shove it up your ass."

It was a good effort at bravado, but the dealer's eyes never left the pistol. His two companions maintained a much less confrontational demeanor, clearly more intimidated by the yawning muzzle of the .45. Sole had their complete attention.

One of the watchers said, "Shut the fuck up, Fonso. Man's got a gun."

"He's right," Sole said. "Shut the fuck up Fonso."

"So what you want, *cabrón*?" Fonso said. "Money?"

"Sure, I'll take the money and whatever drugs you're holding."

"The fuck you will!" Fonso glared at him over the end of the pistol.

"I will." Sole moved the pistol back and forth to encourage him. "Hand it over now or you won't like what happens next."

Without speaking, Fonso pulled a wad of cash from his pocket. One of his watchers turned and pulled a plastic garbage bag containing the drugs from behind the front wheel of a rusted out car parked half on the sidewalk and half on the street.

"Put the money in the bag."

Fonso grabbed the bag and shoved the cash inside.

"Now put it on the ground."

"What the fuck is wrong with you man?" Fonso shook his head in disgust. "You know who we are, what gonna happen to you?"

"I know what's gonna happen to you if you don't do what I said." He motioned with the Colt. "On the ground."

Fonso dropped the bag on the ground between them. "Now what?"

"Run."

"The fuck you say. That's bullshit. I ain't runnin' nowhere …"

Sole raised the pistol so that the bore was inches away from a spot in the center of Fonso's forehead.

"Run."

The three men began trotting down the street.

"Faster," Sole called after them.

They picked up speed. He waited until they had gone a good two hundred yards, turned and trotted back to the corner where he had parked his truck.

It was a different approach, and he wondered why he hadn't thought of it before. A white man taking their money and drugs was sure to draw the attention of dealers in the area. It wouldn't take long for word to filter back to *Los Salvajes*. The tactic might even be more effective than leaving a dealer with a bullet through the brain.

Fifteen minutes later, he was southbound out of Flagstaff on I-17 toward Phoenix, his next stop. As the sun was setting, he pulled off the highway and stood at a guard rail looking down into a deep ravine. After removing the cash and shoving it in his pocket, he gave the plastic bag a toss and watched the drugs plummet to the rocks below. When it hit bottom, he turned with a satisfied smile on his face and climbed back into the truck.

Relaxed now, cruising along with one hand on the wheel, he took out his phone. He hadn't checked the voice mailbox since leaving Albuquerque.

There was only one message, and it came from Luis Acero.

"We got to talk. It's important. I'll check messages every day until you get this."

Sole was no longer relaxed. He sat up, tense and alert. It wasn't that Luis sounded nervous. Luis always sounded nervous. In his mind, Sole was still a cop, and he was still a snitch, and snitches were always nervous around cops.

What concerned Sole was what the message lacked. It was a critical component, the one thing that should have been there, and Luis never mentioned it.

When Luis had been an informant working with Detective John Sole in Atlanta, they always began each call with the words—*It's all good*.

They were the safe words, the signal that they could speak freely. They had continued the practice after Sole left Atlanta and began wandering around the States to leave a trail for the cartel. Luis would never forget to say the words.

If he didn't use the safe words it meant one thing. He needed help.

FORTY-FIVE

One Little Smile

"Excuse me for interrupting, Señor Garza."

Roman Madera stood in the center of the cabin's great central room. Garza sat at a desk before a window that looked out over the broad, green valley below. It was picturesque, a scene out of a magazine. The well-appointed cabin was, in reality, a mountain estate. Roman had purchased it from a retiring investment banker who cashed in to go live in the islands of the Caribbean.

When Garza made it known that he required a private space to conduct his business, Roman offered it up. Garza moved in, took the master suite for himself, and relegated Roman to the role of butler and Luis Acero's jailer. Roman did not object. He didn't dare. After all, the money to purchase the cabin had come from his dealings with *Los Salvajes*, a fact that Garza would certainly remind him of if he dared voice an objection.

"What is it?" Garza raised his eyes from the laptop on the desk.

"I wondered ... I don't mean to inquire into your business, of course ... but, I wondered how long we will be keeping the rat in this room."

"Why do you ask?" Garza leaned back, his cold eyes regarding Roman with the sort of empty interest that a cat looks at a mouse once it has become boring.

"Only because, if you will want me to get rid of ..." Roman swallowed. "If you want me to dispose of him at some point, I should make arrangements."

"No. We will need him for a while longer. I'll let you know when and what arrangements you should make."

"Yes, of course." Roman nodded and turned to leave.

"Sit down." Garza pointed to a chair beside the desk.

"Certainly."

Roman slid into the chair, cursing himself for coming into the room. The last thing he wanted to do was spend more time than absolutely necessary with Elizondo's enforcer.

"I have been doing some research," Garza began.

He said nothing more, and after several seconds, Roman realized he was waiting for him to inquire into the research. He repressed an inward smile. Even the great Alejandro Garza, it seems, was given at times to a bit of drama. It was the first time he had seen signs of a chink in the armor that Garza used to cover his humanity.

"May I ask about your research?" Roman said.

"The number on his phone ... the person who called to arrange the false identification for the woman."

Another pause and Roman said, "Yes?"

"The number is for an attorney's office in a place called Dahlonega."

"I've never heard of this place."

"You wouldn't have. It is a small city in the north of the state of Georgia."

"So we ... I mean, you ... have found the person who made the arrangements for the false identification papers, which means ..."

"Yes." Garza nodded.

This time Roman could have sworn that a smile crept across Garza's face. It wasn't much of one, barely perceptible, but its brief flickering across his face revealed much about the importance of finding this man, John Sole.

The number of people, men and women, sent from this world by Alejandro Garza in the service of Bebé Elizondo was a thing of awed conjecture. While the exact count was unknown, all of them had been sent coldly, efficiently, and without passion out of this world.

All reports from those present at the murders made it clear that Garza killed with the same emotion that one might have in swatting a fly. It meant nothing to him, even less than nothing.

But this, this one little smile, told Roman much. Finding Sole meant a great deal to Garza on a personal level.

"Then this means ...," Roman began.

"This means we need the rat, and I will require your services a while longer."

Shit! Roman fought to control the disappointment from showing on his face. He nodded politely.

"Of course. I am always in your service, *jefe*."

FORTY-SIX

The Hunter - An Unfaltering Eye

Billy Siever's desk phone intercom beeped. He had asked his assistant to hold calls while he reviewed the documents setting up a trust for one of his more prominent clients, one of the wealthiest citizens in the county and a member of on the county's board of commissioners.

When his lawyer hat was on, Billy had a tendency to be brusque with others. Today, he was under a strict deadline. He punched the button to answer the call with more than a little annoyance.

"I asked you to hold my calls, Doris," he said, his tone abrupt.

"Sorry, Billy," Doris replied unruffled, not one to take offense or be intimidated by abrupt tones, one of the key reasons she had lasted as his assistant for ten years. "It's not a call. You have a visitor, Billy."

"A walk-in?" He sighed. "Have them make an appointment for later this week."

Muffled conversation filtered over the line, and he was about to disconnect when Doris came back on.

"I'm sorry, Billy. He's being insistent ... said his name is Lamont Sole and to tell you that you know his son."

The papers dropped from Billy's hand. He rose from his chair, strode across his office and jerked open the door.

The man standing over Doris' desk was not impressive. Billy figured he had to be in his seventies. Frayed blue jeans and work shirt, white hair brushing his collar, and a week's growth of beard made him look more like a homeless person than the father of his best friend.

He looked hard into the old man's face. There was a resemblance. He could be John's father, but so could a lot of other old men.

"You say your name is ..."

"Lamont ... Monty ... Sole." The old man nodded and held up the business card. "Derek at the bar gave me this. Said you might be able to help me."

"Come in and sit down." Billy opened the office door wider and stepped aside. "Doris, hold my calls, please."

"Of course." Doris adjusted her glasses in a business-like way that meant, mind your tone with me next time, mister.

Billy closed the office door behind Monty Sole, indicated a chair in front of his desk, and walked around to sit across from him. He was quiet for several seconds, studying the man's face. Then he asked the most important question. "How do I know that you're who you say you are?"

Monty sat erect in the chair, alert and attentive but not nervous. He had the posture of man who was there on business.

"I have a driver's license," he said, pulling out his wallet. He placed the license on Billy's desk. "Don't know if that's as much proof as you'll want, but it's all I have."

Billy picked up the license. "Arizona?"

"Arizona." Monty nodded. "Been living there for more than twenty years."

Billy pushed the license back across the desk. "You're right. That doesn't prove much."

Dealing with Luis Acero, setting up the new identities for Isabella and her family, he knew that obtaining a false identity was merely a matter of knowing where to look and having the money to pay. While this man's financial resources were questionable, he did have the appearance of a street person who just might know where to look.

"Fair enough." Monty nodded calmly and asked. "You a good friend of my son ... of John Sole?"

"I like to think so."

"Then you probably know something about his past."

"I do."

"Ask me some questions."

"What?"

"Questions. You're a lawyer. You ought to be good at asking questions. Ask me questions to prove who I am ... or who I'm not."

"Alright." Billy nodded. "What's your birthday?"

"April 5, 1949." Monty shook his head. "You can do better than that. That doesn't prove anything. It's right on that driver's license I showed you. If I was an impostor, I'd be a fool not memorize that."

He nodded encouragingly. "Go on. Ask me some more questions. Just remember, I left when John was a baby, so I won't have any answers about things that might have happened to him after that." He smiled. "Except for one thing ... something that made the papers. Seems he took a preacher's car for a joy ride when he was a teenager, and he wasn't alone. I believe you were there, weren't you, Mr. Siever?"

"I was." Billy nodded. "But as you say, you found that in the papers where anyone could have read about it."

"True enough, so ask me some more questions."

Billy did. John's date of birth, again too easy to discover.

Clara's birth date. The date of their marriage. All discoverable by someone who took the time to search. He needed more proof.

"Where did you live with Clara and John?"

"To be exact, I lived there with Clara mostly." Sadness filled his eyes. "John was just a newborn when I left."

Monty described the small house on the mountainside in detail. The number of rooms, how they were laid out in the house, which way it faced. How you could watch the sun rise from the front porch and see it set from the back porch. He talked in detail about the surrounding landscape, the mountains and trails he wandered, where he would disappear to when he need to be alone after his return from Vietnam.

Billy became convinced. The man before him was probably John Sole's father. He asked the most important question last.

"Why did you abandon your wife and child?"

"Honestly, I've been trying to understand that all these years." He looked up, tears in his eyes. "It was a terrible thing to do. I was afraid, I suppose."

"Of what?"

"Of what I'd become ... of what I remembered." He shook his head and looked down. "Of things I did. Felt like I couldn't find a way to make it all the way home from Vietnam. Seemed like I was poisoning everything around me ... Clara and then the baby, John. I couldn't do that to them, so I left." He gave a helpless shrug. "I know it doesn't make sense. Nothing made sense then ... or now.

It's just how it was … what I did … I have to live with that."

"You ran out on them."

"I did."

Monty Sole made no excuses. He sat across the desk, accepting Billy's scorn for his actions. It was that more than anything that convinced Billy that Monty was who he claimed to be. He had the same unfaltering eye as his son when examining his own imperfections. He would not make excuses for his failures.

"Alright. Let's say I believe you." Billy sat back in his chair, his eyes fixed on the old man's. "Why are you here? What do you want?"

"My boy's in trouble," Monty said plainly. "I want to help him."

FORTY-SEVEN

To Snare a Wolf

The call from Alejandro Garza came in after midnight. A little drunk and a lot stoned, Chico Saludo retained enough of his faculties to recognize the number on his phone display. He answered immediately.

"Señor Garza. It's good to hear from you," he lied. "How may I be of service?"

"I want you to find someone and watch him."

"Yes, of course. Give me the name and I will have my people find him for you."

"Not your people. You will find him and watch him … personally. No one else."

"Me?" Chico sat up in his bed and nudged the bare-assed, auburn haired woman stretched out beside him. When she didn't move, he put his foot on her hip and shoved until she rolled off and fell to the floor. She landed with a thud on her bare backside.

"What the fuck?" She sat up, dazed, rubbing her ass with one hand, blinking her eyes.

"Get out," Chico hissed trying not to be heard over the phone.

"What … why?" The woman looked around the room. "Ain't nobody here. Wassamatter?"

"Get your clothes and get out … now."

"You said something to me?" Garza's voice growled over the phone.

"No, no , Señor Garza. Just a small interruption."

"Send your interruption away."

"I am doing so right now, Señor Garza." Chico motioned to a wad of cash on the bedside table. "There. Take it and get your ass out."

"Small interruption." The stripper scooped up the cash and smirked at the flaccid member shriveled between his legs. "You got that right."

Bottom undulating in a tantalizing way as she stumbled around the room, she gathered her clothes. At the door, she turned, giving him a full view of what he would be missing for the rest of the night and before breakfast in the morning.

"Fuck you," she snarled, flipped him off, and slammed the door.

"Is your interruption gone?" Garza heard the door slam.

"Yes, Señor Garza." Chico stood propped a pillow against the headboard and leaned back, scratching between his legs. "Who is it that you want me to find?

Garza's explanation was brief. There was a lawyer by the name of William Siever in a place called Dahlonega. Chico's mission was to go to his office, watch him without being seen, and track the lawyer's movements and people he met. Garza concluded, giving him Siever's office address.

Chico scribbled the address down on a pad by his bed and then ventured a comment. "I will make sure that this is done, but ..."

"What?"

The acid in Garza's tone caused him to hesitate. He took a breath and continued.

"I only wonder, that's all, Señor Garza ... just wondering if it might not be better to have others involved. More people to track this lawyer. I have people who are very expert at ..."

"You," Garza broke in. "No one else. We are out to trap a wolf, a very clever wolf with sharp fangs. The more people who know what we do the greater the chance of one of your experts giving away our intent. I intend to snare this wolf. You will do as I say."

"Yes, of course," Chico replied.

Any further comments or suggestions were out of the question. They might even be dangerous.

"One more thing," Garza said.

Shit! Now what, you murderous demon, Chico thought.

"Yes?" he said mildly.

"From this point on, until the assignment is completed and we have snared the wolf, no drinking, no drugs and no whores. I do not tolerate interruptions of any kind. Is this understood?"

"Completely."

Son of a bitch! Not even a sip of tequila!

"Good. Now, prepare yourself and go to Dahlonega. Be in position to watch the office and Siever's arrival this morning. I will expect hourly reports from you."

"It will be done."

Garza ended the call without further comment or

instructions. Chico sat on the bed staring at the wall for several seconds, sighed, and began to pull himself together. The day ahead would be long and God only knew many others would follow until Garza snared his wolf.

FORTY-EIGHT

Stranger from the Past

He was a particle speeding along in a stream of particles, vehicles hurtling along the interstate. Like neutrons careening around the core of a reactor, some streamed along in the same direction. Others sped toward him in the opposite. Still more veered off at exit ramps to be replaced by others entering on another ramp.

John Sole pointed the pickup east on I-40, another anonymous particle. Other vehicles were a blur to him. Isolated in the tiny world of his pickup, he considered his next move.

Trouble was brewing. Luis Acero had lived and survived too long on the streets to make the mistake of not giving the all clear signal in his message. The question now was what kind of trouble and who was behind it.

Ignoring the call was out of the question. Luis might be a drug dealer, snitch, and a generally unsavory character, but circumstances had bound their lives together. The last time Sole heard from him, Luis was in Richmond. That meant at least another full day's drive, time to figure things out, get closer, and come up with the best way to contact Luis and help him if he could.

He thumbed his phone and dialed the voice mailbox again. If Luis left a follow-up message, it might shed light on things. As it turned out, there was another message, but not from Luis.

"Semper Fi. You know who this is."

Billy Siever sounded excited.

"I need to speak with you, or rather there is someone you need to speak with. Trust me on this. You should speak with this person. I know it's not protocol or procedure or whatever you call it, but for once if you could just call me direct as soon as you get this message, I'd appreciate it."

The message ended.

Semper Fi was the all clear signal he and Billy had arranged for their communications. A call from Luis followed by another so soon from Billy could be coincidence or they could be connected. He decided to ignore the protocol he'd put in place for once. He punched up Billy's cell number.

Billy answered on the first ring. "Yes?"

"Semper Fi."

"I'm glad you called." Billy still sounded excited though he'd left the voice mail hours earlier.

"What's up? This about our friend in Virginia?"

"What? No." The sudden concern in Billy's tone was plain. "Why is there a problem there?"

"You tell me," Sole said, cautious about saying too much in the event Billy was under duress or facing a threat of some sort.

"Look, enough of the cloak and dagger shit. I don't have any idea what you think is happening with our friend in Virginia. If there's something I should know about for the sake of our other friends," he said referring to Isabella and her family. "Tell me now."

"No, if you don't know, it doesn't concern you or them. Sorry to have worried you. So, you said there is someone I have to speak to. Who?"

"Lamont," Billy said bluntly.

It was a name Sole hadn't said a dozen times in his life. He would have been happy to never say it or hear it again. He drove in silence for a minute before Billy spoke again.

"It's a shock, I know. He showed up here at my office. I didn't believe him at first, but I'm satisfied." Billy paused, waiting for a response. When there was none, he repeated the admonition he'd left in the voice mail. "You should talk to him."

"What makes you think I want to talk to him?" Sole stared straight ahead down the highway as if he could see all the way to Billy's office in Dahlonega. "He would be the last person in the world I want to talk to."

"He's your father, John," Billy said softly, violating protocol once more by saying his name.

"He abandoned us. He's just a man, less than that as far as I'm concerned." He shook his head as he spoke. "No way he's my father, not really."

"What he did was wrong. There's no excusing that, and I'm not saying you should forgive him, but you are carrying a lot of baggage, my friend. I worry about you."

"You don't have to worry about me."

"No, but I do, and maybe it's not my place to say it, but you need to shed some of the baggage. Tell him what you think, how you feel, why you feel the way you do, get rid of it and let it go. Then send him on his way if you want to, but don't let the chance for some sort of closure pass, if not for you, then for Clara's sake."

"That's not fair. Leave my mother out of it."

"She's part of it, and you know what she would tell you to do if she were here," Billy said. "Talk to him. Air things out and get rid of some of the baggage."

Another minute passed. Billy was prepared to end the call and concede defeat when Sole relented.

"Alright. Is he with you now?"

"No, he came in this morning, proved to me who he was, and left. I told him I'd try to get hold of you. He checked into a motel and said he'd be around until I made contact with you. He wants to meet you, John, said he believes you're in trouble and he wants to help you."

"Trouble? Why did he say that? What kind of trouble?"

"He didn't say. Just that he wants to help." Billy paused. "Are you in trouble, John?"

"I'll be there tomorrow," Sole said, ignoring the question. "Where is he staying?"

Billy named a fifty-year-old motel on the outskirts of town. "Call me when you get in town."

"Alright."

"Tomorrow then?" Billy said to reinforce that his friend was actually committing to the meeting with the stranger from his past, who happened to also be his father.

"Tomorrow," Sole said and ended the call.

FORTY-NINE

Son of a Bitch

Chico Saludo was cold, wet, and, miserable. Rain had been falling since his arrival in Dahlonega just after sunrise.

For thirty minutes, he had driven around attempting to locate the law office of William Siever. His phone's map app kept pointing him to a residential neighborhood where he could see no offices, or anything that resembled an office building.

He was beginning to think that Garza had given him the wrong address. Stopping to ask directions was out of the question. Despite his efforts to convince Garza that he was not expert at this sort of work, he was experienced enough to realize that a newcomer in town with a Mexican accent, asking questions about a local attorney was something people would remember.

Desperate to make Garza happy, and terrified of failing, he parked on a side street and got out to walk the street in search of the office. He'd been up and down the block twice, passing the stone house with the address numbers that matched the ones Garza had given him when he noticed the sign.

"*Mierda*," he muttered. Shit.

A sign carved from stone sat low to the ground, nestled under, and partially concealed by a bank of shrubbery. It reminded him of a tombstone. The lettering was highlighted in black and just barely visible in the misty, early morning light—William Siever, Attorney at Law.

A new problem arose. He'd found the office, but how in the hell did Garza expect him to watch it? He couldn't park along the curb in this neighborhood. An office in a business district would have been different. There he could blend in and pretend to have other business. Here, there was no blending in.

Walking along the sidewalk, he passed a small park. It was at the end of the block across from the corner where he'd left his car out of sight on a side street.

It wasn't much of a park really, just a fifty by fifty patch of grass with a swing set and slide for children, but there was a bench under a small gazebo, where he could sit and watch the house down the street. Everything was wet from the blowing overnight rain and drizzle that continued to fall. He wiped the bench off as best he could and sat.

The water soaked through his pants. Chilled to the bone, he trembled and waited. There was nothing else to do. The thought of calling Garza to complain of his situation was out of the question.

At eight o'clock a large sedan driven by a matronly, gray-haired woman who reminded Chico of his mother's sister in Mexico passed by the park and pulled into the house-office driveway. It disappeared around the rear, and a few minutes later lights came on inside the building. Chico noted the time on a memo in his phone.

A half hour later, a BMW driven by a male passed on the wet street. He was in his late forties or early fifties. The car pulled into the driveway as the woman had, to disappear around the rear.

Chico made another note. It was time to call Garza.

He answered on the first ring. "Yes?"

"I am watching the office, as you directed. Two people have come and parked behind the building. The lights came on. One is a woman the other a man. I believe that is the person, you are looking for, this William Siever."

"Is there a way to verify who he is?"

"Not that I can see. I would have to go inside and make inquiries, and that would make them suspicious, I believe."

"Of course it would," Garza snapped back at the obvious and unnecessary comment. "Remain in place. It is probably the lawyer. When he leaves, follow and see if you can verify."

"Yes, as you say," Chico said, then thought he might at least hint at the uncomfortable conditions he was forced to endure. "It is raining at the moment, has been raining since I arrived and I am very …"

The call disconnected without any further comment from Garza.

"*Hijo de puta.*" Son of a bitch, Chico muttered, pulling his light windbreaker tight around his shoulders.

A few more vehicles came and went during the day. Once, an old, white-haired man cruised by slowly in a pickup truck. He seemed to be searching for an address as Chico had been earlier. He braked as he passed the lawyer's office, put the truck in reverse, and then turned up the driveway. He was inside for more than an hour before the pickup came down the drive, drove past Chico once more, and left the area in the direction it had come.

Chico noted it all in the memo app on his phone, muttering all the while about the man who had sent him out to sit on a bench in the rain until he was as waterlogged as the bench.

"Motherfucking, son of a bitch."

FIFTY

Prisoners

"How much longer?" Bebé Elizondo's usually tranquil tone held just the hint of an edge.

"Soon," Alejandro Garza replied, unruffled. "I have a plan to bring things to a conclusion in the next few days."

Elizondo did not ask about the plan. Garza would never go into details over the phone

"So I can expect you back in a week." It was a statement, not a question.

In his subtle way, Bebé hinted that the mission to find John Sole and eliminate him was becoming an obsession for his chief lieutenant and cartel partner. It was time to get back to work. The trail of dead drug dealers left by the American was of no consequence and had no real effect on their business.

Los Salvajes had been taken by surprise, but now that they knew his methods they were alerted and more watchful. Sooner or later, he would make a mistake, and one of their people would end his rampage and collect the million dollar reward Elizondo had offered for his head. Until then, John Sole was nothing more than a distraction.

"Yes, in a week or so, but I cannot promise the time exactly," Garza replied with his usual scrupulous adherence to the truth, despite Elizondo's obvious impatience for his return.

"I see."

Bebé sat back in the chair on his veranda, puffing hard on his cigar, looking out over the Pacific, taking the time to renew his patience with his deputy. A minute passed as he considered how to handle the situation.

Despite the unalterable fact that both men were ruthless killers, the bond of brotherly affection between them was real. They had grown up on the streets together, protected each other, even fought for each other. As time passed, their roles evolved. Elizondo became the senior business partner and planner. Garza took on the role of chief enforcer and protector of all business decisions and activities.

The arrangement worked well, but on this one issue of the American, they disagreed. Garza considered him to be the cartel's premier long-term threat both to their persons and their business. Elizondo thought of him as a sideshow, a lesson from which to learn and then to move on.

Patience restored, Bebé took a breath and asked, "What is your plan to end this and come home, Alejandro."

Garza reviewed the steps he would take over the next few days. Elizondo listened, a blue-gray cloud of cigar smoke circling his head to be whisked away by the ocean breeze. When Garza finished his review of the plan, Elizondo nodded.

"As always, my friend. Your planning is meticulous, and I look forward to your report of its success." Bebé stared into the distant blue horizon as if he could see into Garza's eyes. "Now I have something to ask of you."

"Ask it."

"I am worried about you, Alejandro. I can't rest peacefully until you are well away from the North Americans and safely back in our country. Besides, the children miss *Tio* Alejandro." He paused, knowing that Garza maintained a stern but sincere affection for Bebé's children. "When your plan has been executed, and I have confidence that it will be successful, it is imperative that you come home."

It was Bebé's way of compromise, give his deputy space to pursue his goals, but set a limit. Garza paused considering the question. If he did not eliminate John Sole, his plan would be a failure, but Elizondo skillfully removed failure from the equation, instead making Garza's safe return the primary concern.

"I will," Garza promised.

"Good. I look forward to seeing you soon, Alejandro."

The call ended.

"All is well with Señor Elizondo?" Roman Madera asked nervously.

Garza turned toward Roman Madera, seated across the room from him. "You heard the plan, as I reviewed it?"

"Yes."

"See to the rat. We leave in the morning. Take everything. We will not be returning."

Roman rose and left, closing the door gently behind him. He had listened to Garza's side of the conversation with care, heard the review of the plan, and also his final words to Bebé, "I will."

Without any context, those two simple words sent an arrow of dread into his gut. They could signify anything.

Will you please bring me a souvenir from America?

I will.

Roman thought that seemed unlikely.

When you are done, will you kill that idiot Madera?

I will.

There was no reason for the cartel chief to want him dead, at least none that he could think of. He had gone out of his way to be helpful and to provide Garza with everything he requested. Still, life and death blew through the cartel ranks randomly at times like springtime tornados and often for no apparent reason.

Roman hurried about, making preparations for their departure, knowing that he was as much a prisoner as Luis Acero. He had no more liberty to leave or deny Garza's requests than Acero. The difference was the rat already knew his fate. Roman was left to ponder words like—*I will.*

FIFTY-ONE

Very Good

Chico Saludo had finally dried out. He sat in his car with the heater on letting it take the chill from his bones. A front had settled over the area and the drizzly weather was held in place all day.

At the end of the day, the BMW pulled from around the back of the stone house that served as the office and proceeded slowly to the outskirts of town. Chico followed until the BMW turned up a sloping drive toward a large house partially hidden on a wooded hillside.

Now what? He drove slowly past the driveway. It was certainly the lawyer's home. He picked up his phone and punched in Garza's number.

"Yes?"

"He has gone home for the day."

"You know the location of his home?"

"Yes."

"Good. Watch it and follow him again when he leaves."

It was too much. Chico swallowed hard and ventured a thought. "It has been a very long day. I have been sitting in the rain and am very cold and tired. I worry that I may fail you, Señor Garza. I might lose him, or miss something important if I don't get some rest. I was only wondering if you would allow me to have some of my people assist?"

For once, Alejandro Garza paused to consider a request from a lesser mortal. It was not an act of compassion but one of necessity for the sake of the mission.

Accustomed to working with the trained assassins on his payroll, he was discovering that these drug peddlers were soft in comparison. His usual team of killers were mostly former military, many from the Cuban *Commando Tropas Especiales*—Special Forces. All were familiar with long periods of privation in the pursuit of their duties, and the compensation provided by the cartel far exceeded anything they could earn in a lifetime of service to Fidel and Raúl Castro. Complaining about their work conditions was unthinkable.

But bringing them into the United States would have run the risk of attracting attention, and anonymity was crucial. This drug dealer was soft, but he was all Garza had to work with at the moment.

"You will watch him, no one else. Garza said and Chico's heart sank.

"As you wish, *jefe*."

"We are coming to you, and you will have help by tomorrow," Garza continued. "Give me the address of the lawyer's home, then go find a place to rest for the night. Be back early in the morning and follow him again. Stay with him until you hear from me."

"Thank you, Señor Garza," Chico said his spirits lifting at the unexpected reprieve.

A short while later, he found a small country motel, checked in, and took a hot shower to warm up. After a dinner of greasy American fried chicken at the adjoining cafe, Chico went to back his room and slept with the heater on all night.

By six in the morning, he was back on the street where the lawyer's hillside home was located. He parked in the dark along a side street curb and waited. At eight o'clock, the BMW came down the sloping driveway and turned toward the office in Dahlonega. Once more Chico followed.

An interlude in the continuing drizzle made him think that the rain was passing. Chico offered a quick thank you to the heavens—*Gracias Dios*.

A short time later, as he settled in under the little park gazebo, the rain started again. He looked up at the sky again. *¿Qué carajo?* What the fuck?

The BMW pulled out early in the afternoon. Chico followed it to the house on the hillside and pulled into the side street to watch. He didn't have long to wait.

Fifteen minutes later, the car came back down the driveway. He could see a woman in the car with the lawyer as it passed.

After a thirty minute drive, they arrived in Gainesville. Chico followed them to the small house in the middle of the block. A woman and man came out onto the porch to greet the lawyer and his wife. Another young man walked out from the garage followed by another younger woman. Happy smiles, handshakes, and greetings were exchanged. Chico drove past the house, pretending to ignore the little gathering by the front door.

An empty church parking lot at the end of the street made a good place to wait and watch. He parked and dialed up Garza's cell phone.

When he reported on the location of the small house

and the gathering of people there, Garza said two words instead of his customary one word reply. "Very Good."

Chico spent the rest of the afternoon and evening in the parking lot watching the house, and fighting off the temptation to take a nap. With Garza arriving at any time, napping was out of the question.

Luis Acero sat in the rear of the SUV, his hands, wrists, and ankles zip-tied together. Roman Madera was at his side. Garza drove, periodically lifting his cell phone to hear a report from someone. He said little on the calls, usually one word replies, or brief instructions for Chico Saludo to stay in place.

Once, Luis heard him say, "Very good."

Senses keenly attuned to the minutest changes in his situation, the words made his heart leap into his throat. The words "very good" coming from Garza could not mean anything good for Luis.

A short time later, they passed the Gainesville city limit sign. Luis shivered in his seat and fought back the desire to cry out and beg for his life once more. The time was close now. The moments of existence he had tried so hard to prolong were slipping away like sand clenched in his trembling fist.

They pulled into a church parking lot at the end of a residential street and parked beside another car. Garza opened the window. Luis recognized the man waiting for them—Chico Saludo, one of the cartel's drug lords.

"They are all in that house down the street," Saludo said. "The one with the cars in front."

"How many?" Garza said, peering in the direction Saludo pointed.

"Six. Three men and three women ... a party of some kind."

"Very good," Garza said, nodding.

Luis shivered again. The words rang cold and clear in the misty evening, settling into his terrified heart.

On the street where the gathering was in progress at Isabella's home, a pickup slowed as it drove past the house. After a few seconds it crept forward to the end of the street to turn back toward the city center. Chico Saludo watched with interest, but the driver was invisible in the evening gloom.

FIFTY-TWO

Let Them Be Happy

After more than twenty-four hours on the road, he was exhausted. John Sole took the exit ramp from I-985 into Gainesville, Georgia and stopped for the red signal at the top. It was all he could do to keep his eyes open and his chin from dropping down onto his chest. The need for sleep finally overpowered him.

The light turned green. A car behind him tapped the horn. Sole's eyes popped open.

Enough. He'd drifted off to sleep in the minute before the signal changed.

It was time to find a place to get some rest. He made the turn and passed a truck stop at the intersection. The all-night diner inside was open.

Coffee, he thought. Black, strong coffee. That's what you need, John-boy. Then you can keep going.

No. He shook his head. You need rest. A few hours' sleep and you'll be able to think clearly. Right now you're no use to anyone, and as likely to get yourself and everyone else killed as get Luis Acero out of whatever trouble he stumbled into.

Then there was the issue of the man who claimed to be his father, waiting for him in a motel in Dahlonega. He thought about ignoring him and continuing on to find Luis, but Billy was right. Clara would have wanted him to at least meet the man.

He could hear her voice.

Tell him he's a son of a bitch for what he did, if that's what makes you feel better, but look your father in the eyes for the first time in your life.

"Alright. Find a motel and get some sleep," he muttered.

First, there was one place to visit. He cruised through the streets of Gainesville. He'd only been there once, but the location was burned into his memory.

It only took a few minutes to find the street. He slowed as he passed the house midway down the block. The lights were on inside. Several vehicles filled the driveway and lined the curb outside. Through the picture window's partially open blinds he saw people moving about.

A family gathering was in progress. He smiled as Jacinta walked from the kitchen into the front room carrying a tray with glasses on it. Sandy rose from a chair to help her with it. He turned and held it out for two people seated side by side on the sofa. Their faces were not visible, but he knew that the arm that reached up for a glass belonged to Isabella. That meant that the man seated beside her was Sam Goodwin, according to Billy Siever, a good man. They made a happy family.

What the hell are you doing? The voice was asking questions again.

I don't know.

He took his foot off the brake and let the pickup roll down the street, turning at the corner past a church, back toward the interstate. Winding through the city, he found a budget motel that claimed to always keep the lights on for weary travelers.

Ten minutes later, he was stretched out on a bed, his clothes in a pile on a chair. The image of a happy family behind a picture window floated before him as he sank into sleep,

"Stay away. Let them be happy," he muttered

FIFTY-THREE

Stakeouts

"Where are they?" Alejandro Garza stepped from the SUV to stand beside Chico Saludo in the church parking lot.

"The house in the middle of the block with the car on the street in front." Chico pointed.

"Don't point. Someone might notice."

"Right." Chico dropped his arm instantly. "Sorry. I wasn't thinking."

"From now on, think," Garza snapped.

"Yes, *jefe*." Chico might be the drug lord of Atlanta, but he understood who the boss was tonight.

Garza stood quietly for a few seconds, assessing the quiet residential street. Then he motioned to Roman Madera to join him for a conference. "Here's what we will do."

Three hours later, Chico Saludo found himself once again parked on the side street near the lawyer's residence. The rat, Luis Acero, lay prone in the back seat, unconscious. The zip ties on his hands and feet and the duct tape on his mouth had been cut away.

Garza had ordered Chico to drag Acero from the SUV and place him into his car as they sat in the church parking lot. Then Chico watched in horror as Garza leaned over Acero with a hypodermic and shoved the needle in the squirming man's arm. What if he killed him with poison and ordered Chico to drive around with a dead body and dispose of it somehow? How the hell was he supposed to do that?

Garza turned to Chico and explained, "Rohypnol, a strong sedative. The North Americans call the pill form rufies, a drug their weak men use to rape women while they are unconscious. He will appear intoxicated if anyone should see him with you, a friend who had too much to drink." His eyes narrowed. "But do not let anyone see him with you."

"Of course not," Chico said, ignoring the nervous bead of sweat on his brow that threatened to trickle into his eyes.

He looked over the seat into the back. There seemed to be no danger that the unconscious man would cry out for help. Chico doubted whether the rat would ever be able to do more than sob, which he was doing now in his sleep. The potent drug Garza had used acted within seconds and had transformed the terrified man into little more than a teary-eyed vegetable.

Chico snarled, "Yes, cry all you want now, rat. I don't think you have much time left for tears."

Acero's head moved back and forth, his eye wide, staring vacantly at the ceiling of the car. Snot dripped from his nose to accompany the tears. Chico gave a wolfish grin and turned to stare back down the street toward the hillside house.

For now, his assigned role in Garza's plan was to follow the lawyer and his wife when they left the party and then wait outside the house through the night. When the lawyer left for work in the morning, he was to advise Garza.

What does he think I am, a fucking *poli*—a cop? This must be what it is like on one of their stakeouts. Wait and watch, watch and wait.

He had to stay put until the great mastermind, Alejandro Garza, decided how to deal with the real cop, John Sole. His mouth twisted into a wry smile. The cop had become a boil on Garza's ass, he thought, and the smile grew wider. It felt good to think these things, to vent to himself alone in the night, sitting in a car with a rat in the back seat.

It felt good, but he would never speak such words to Garza's face, and saying them did not change the fact that he was cold, tired, and hungry. This work could be accomplished by one of his underlings, someone dull and without imagination, capable of sitting idly for hours and following orders.

Is that what cops were? Dull and unimaginative?

John Sole did not seem dull and unimaginative. Up to now, he had stymied Garza at every turn.

Chico shrugged. It didn't matter. He only knew that sitting in this car in the middle of the night did not suit someone with the abilities of a Chico Saludo, drug lord of Atlanta. Unfortunately, Garza did not share in his sentiments.

He settled back into the seat and fought off sleep, mostly in case Garza called or drove by unexpectedly. Through half-closed eyes, he could make out the lawyer's house on the dark empty street. How did the fucking cops do it, anyway?

Twenty miles away, Garza and Roman Madera sat in the church parking lot watching the house down the street. Roman's head nodded and his chin sank to his chest repeatedly. He opened his eyes wide and shook his head to clear it, casting a sidelong glance at Garza, hoping he had not noticed.

The cartel enforcer sat ramrod straight in the passenger seat. If he blinked, Roman could not detect it.

A robot, Roman thought. The son of a bitch is a robot, or an alien.

"You slept," Garza said without turning his head from the house.

"Sorry." There was no sense denying it. Roman stretched, wrapped his hands around the wheel, and sat up straight. "My apologies," he said, and added nervously. "It won't happen again."

"Sleep if you must. I will watch," Garza replied, unconcerned. "You will need it. Tomorrow we have work to do."

Roman folded his arms over his chest and leaned back on the headrest. He wondered how Chico Saludo faired in Dahlonega on stakeout outside the lawyer's house.

He only wondered for a second, before he drifted off to sleep. Trapped in this car with a cold-eyed, murderous robot from another world, he did not doubt that Chico had the best of things.

FIFTY-FOUR

I Ran Away

The seedy, rundown roadside inn on the outskirts of Dahlonega had been there since Sole's youth. He remembered driving past it into town on Friday nights with Billy Siever when they were looking for more distraction than Cassit Pass had to offer two high-spirited teenaged boys.

It had probably been there more than half a century. Located on the highway into the city, he figured there had been some sort of stopping place there since the days of horse-drawn coaches that once used the route to cross the mountains into Tennessee.

The pavement was cracked. Weeds grew in every corner. The building hadn't seen a coat of paint in decades, and what there was of it was cracked and peeling. Dirt and trash blown in by the wind collected in every corner, crack, and doorway. It was a forgotten place. As far as John Sole was concerned, it was perfect for the man who claimed to be his father.

He parked in front of the room number Billy Siever had given him and stared at the door. You have to do it, he told himself. Have a reckoning with the old bastard, if not for you, then for Clara. After that, you can leave with a clear conscience and go find Luis Acero.

Sole got out of the pickup, walked to the door, and gave three hard raps. It opened immediately.

The man staring back at him didn't smile or try to throw his arms around him. He simply stood there, silent, emotion flickering in his eyes. He seemed afraid to speak or move as if the slightest gesture, a breath of wind, an uttered word, a whisper might cause the vision to evaporate before him.

Monty Sole had not laid eyes on his son since the day after his birth. Now he couldn't take his eyes off of him, examining his face, seeing Clara there, and yes, a little of his father too.

Seconds passed before he stepped aside, opening the door wider. "Do you want to come in?"

Sole stepped over the threshold without speaking. He looked around the shabby room and nodded, then turned to the man still holding the door open.

"Why are you here?" Sole said, his stare icy, disgust the only emotion visible on his face.

"Hard to say." Monty Sole closed the door, nodded and looked at the floor. "You'll only hate me more for the reason."

"I don't think that's possible."

"Alright. I'll say it." Monty paused to suck in a deep breath to force the words from his mouth. "I love you …. I loved your mother. What I did …" He shook his head, and now tears glistened in his eyes. "I know it was wrong … inexcusable … it was just that …"

"Don't!" Sole barked. "Don't do that. You're no

prodigal son. You're nothing but a stranger who showed up." Sole turned for the door. "You're nothing to me."

"Don't go." Monty's voice broke, the tears falling down his cheeks now. "Please, only a few minutes, then leave if you want, and you'll never hear from me again if that's what you want."

"It's what I want," Sole sneered. "I'm only here because my mother would have wanted me to see you. That's it. Nothing more."

"Can I show you something?" Monty's trembling hand reached for the duffel on the bed.

"What?"

Opening the bag, Monty pulled out a stack of envelopes bound with several rubber bands. He placed them on the bed in front of his son. Sole recognized his mother's handwriting immediately.

"What are these?" He picked up an envelope, staring at the address written in her careful hand, perfectly spaced, each letter and numeral exactly as he remembered from the letters she had written him before her death when he was still in the Marine Corps.

"I think you know what they are," Monty said. "I see it in your eyes."

Each envelope had been carefully opened, slit along the top with a knife, not ripped. Once read, Monty returned each to its envelope, securing it in the duffel that had stayed under his bed over the years.

Sole bent over to examine them. "She wrote all of these … to you?"

"Yes." Monty nodded solemnly. "They're yours now. I suppose you have more right to them than I do."

The letters spanned several decades, sent to Monty infrequently but regularly. The last letter arrived a few years after their son had gone off to the Marine Corps. Sole realized they stopped when Clara passed away. He looked up.

"I never knew she wrote to you."

"I asked her not to say anything about our letters."

"Why?" Sole's mind spun, trying to come to grips with the unmistakable fact that his mother remained in touch with the man who abandoned her.

"There're things about me ... things I've done ..." Monty shook his head. "It was better you didn't know ... better you didn't have to live with the knowledge your father did those things."

"What things?"

Monty shook his head and said nothing.

"You wrote her back?"

"I did." Monty nodded. "Not as often as she wrote, but I let her know where I was. That's how she knew where to send the letters." He hesitated. "I loved your mother, son."

"Don't say that!" Sole shouted. "Do not tell me about your love for my mother and do not call me son! You lost that right."

"Alright. I'm sorry."

"It's forty-five years too late for that."

"You're right." Monty shrugged. "I don't know what to say."

"You said you wrote back to her. I never saw any letters." Sole shook his head. "All those years living in the house with her, I never once saw a letter from you."

"I wrote them just the same and sent them. There wasn't any return address on them or name. You wouldn't have known who they were from."

"Where are they?"

"She hid them in the house, behind a loose wallboard in the closet."

"They should still be there then," Sole said. "I think I'll stop by the old house and see if they are, or if this is just a lie from an old man."

"They're not in the house anymore," Monty said, his eyes fixed on his son's.

"That figures," Sole sneered.

"They're here." Monty reached into the duffel again and pulled out a smaller bundle of envelopes. "I stopped by the old house … spent a night there and took these."

Stunned, Sole sat on the bed, slid a letter from the envelope, and began reading. One by one he read through the account of their lives in Cassit Pass. John's birthdays, Christmases, their anniversary date, Clara always sent an update on their son, what he was doing, his progress in school. Some held pictures of John as a boy, then a teenager, then as a newly enlisted Marine in his uniform.

They were full of news about him and what was happening in their lives. Some were chatty. Others serious, somber even, out of keeping with his mother's buoyant character.

Sole imagined his mother late at night huddled over the kitchen table writing. Clara and Monty had stayed in touch through the years, but the letters showed more than that. Clara loved Monty. In every one, she told Monty she loved him. At first, she pleaded with him to return to her and his baby son. After a few years the pleas ended, but her affirmation of love for her husband never faltered.

An hour passed, and Sole read on. The years of his life passed by, recorded in his mother's neat handwriting. He came to one his mother had written when he was three years old, and his brow furrowed.

Come back to us, Monty. We can protect you from the memories. We can give you new ones. Just come back to us.

"What did she mean ... protect you from the memories?"

"Doesn't matter ... not anymore." Monty shook his head and his eyes moved from Sole's to stare at the floor.

"Bullshit! You show up here after forty-five years, hand me a bunch of letters and call it good?" Sole's voice rose for the first time. He shook his head, glaring at the man he was forced to accept as his father. "That's not good enough. Whatever you think I couldn't handle knowing about you as a boy, I can handle now."

Monty raised his head and nodded. "Maybe you're right, but it's an ugly thing."

"Say it." Sole snapped at him.

"I was in Marine Corps ..." Monty began softly, speaking without emotion. "Vietnam, 1972. Things had begun to wind down, but they kept the pressure on the North Vietnamese to get them to the negotiating table. Peace talks, they called them, but there wasn't much peace where they sent us, especially if we had special skills."

"What special skill?" Sole asked.

"Yeah, that." Monty nodded. "Not much of a skill really, not for someone from around here. I spent most of my life wandering these mountains and hills, hunting, fishing, doing the things country boys did back then." He shrugged and added modestly, "Turns out I was pretty good with a rifle, at least better than most of the new recruits. They took me aside and made me an offer I couldn't refuse. No slogging through rice paddies for Monty Sole, no sir, none of that. No, they said I'd have a special place, a safe spot, not out on point waiting for an enemy ambush or booby trap. I'd be in the rear of things. My job would be to deliver long-range precision fire on the enemy."

"They made you a sniper," Sole said.

"That they did." Monty nodded. "And all that talk about staying in the rear, well, that was bullshit. I slogged along right beside the other grunts, taking my turn on point, in the middle of it all. Anyway, there I was, defending our democracy, trying to keep those Communist dominoes from falling the way LBJ had warned. Mostly, I just wanted to get home to Clara. Then one day …"

Monty's eyes focused on the wall above his son's head. He had the look of a man staring at a distant horizon. Sole had seen the look before.

"Our company worked with an ARVN unit, Army of the Republic of Vietnam." He gave a wry laugh. "Wasn't much of a republic though, run by dictators and generals pretending to be elected presidents. Anyway, we went out on this operation to take out a Viet Cong unit that had taken over a village. They said the village was supposed to be ours. Don't know how anyone would know the difference. The villagers were caught in the middle of it all and went along with whoever had the guns. That day the VC had the guns, at least until we got there."

Sole had been a Marine, been to war. It wasn't Vietnam, but people died and soldiers were killed. He pushed back the feelings of empathy for his father. Lots of people go to war, but they don't come home and desert their families.

"Anyway, things were going along pretty smoothly. We surprised them. Wasn't much of a firefight, just some random shooting. Then the VC disappeared into the bush … all except one … the village chief. Turns out he was Viet Cong too; at least that's what the commander of the ARVN unit with us told my platoon leader.

"They hollered at him to surrender, but he wasn't inclined. So the ARVN sent some troops forward to take him into custody. The village chief let off a burst with his

AK, and they came scampering back for cover. It was kind of comical, to tell the truth.

"That's when my lieutenant called me forward. It's simple, he told me. Find a good position and wait for him to poke his head out of his hut, then take him out. So I said, yes sir, and found a good spot to set up on the edge of the village.

Monty paused. When he continued, his voice droned in a soft monotone, as if he playing the account back on a recorder.

"We took cover, directly across from the hut where he'd taken cover ... not more than seventy-five yards. Under normal circumstances, you couldn't miss. Hell, they didn't even need a sniper to do it. Any one of us could have taken the shot, but it was my job, so they called me forward to do it.

"I probably sat there waiting for five minutes or so, but it might have been longer. Things get kind of compressed in those situations."

Another pause. Sole remained silent, waiting for the story to come to its conclusion.

"Finally, I saw some movement. I was ready, safety off, just the slightest pressure on the trigger, breathing controlled. It was routine, like all the other shots I'd taken. Then, he came charging out of the door, his AK slung over his shoulder. He probably figured we weren't going away and was trying to get to his buddies who had skipped out on him. Thing is …"

Monty took his eyes off the wall and looked at Sole. This part he had to say face to face.

"He had a woman with him, a mother holding a baby. He had his arm around her neck, holding her by the hair. The other hand held a knife at her throat. She was screaming and crying, struggling, so he pressed that knife into the baby's throat and she settled down, sobbing and speaking fast. I didn't understand the words, but I knew she was begging him not to hurt her baby.

"Take the shot, Sole, my lieutenant said from behind. He was watching the whole thing. I didn't. I hesitated. I mean, I was a good shot, but with the woman and baby there, I kind of froze. My hands shook so bad I could hardly hold the rifle. It had to be a perfect headshot, no margin for error. Then the captain came up close behind me and yelled, take the goddamn shot, Sole!"

A single tear rolled down Monty's cheek. Sole listened silently to his father and for the first time understood the pain he had not wanted to share with him.

"I took the shot," he said. "The village chief just sort of crumpled to the ground. The woman and her baby fell on top of him."

He shook his head. "It wasn't full dark yet, just sort of a gloomy fading twilight. I'd made tougher shots before, but I didn't make that one. I was only off by a few inches, but it was enough."

Monty sighed, bringing the story to its conclusion. "Two ARVN rushed forward, pulled the woman off the VC, and put a couple of rounds in his head for good measure. I walked out of the bush and checked the bodies, hoping there was a chance they were still alive. They weren't."

They stood facing each other in the seedy motel room without speaking.

"The worst of it was, the baby died first. My bullet tore through his little body, his mother, and finally the VC chief. I had one target, but I squeezed that trigger and killed them all."

John Sole regarded the man who told the story and felt

chastised by his pain. For the first time was able to think of him as his father.

"You could have stayed with us, me and Mom. She begged you to," he said.

"I tried." Monty shook his head. "Clara and I married. She got pregnant. We tried to do the things you're supposed to do in life, but one day I came back from wandering the hills and she'd had the baby, and there you were. I held you. Looked into your eyes, saw you smile and put you down. How could I hold you, be a father to you after what I did?" He shook his head. "But I couldn't. I ran and kept running. It was better than looking at you and being reminded of what I am … a baby killer."

"PTSD," Sole said quietly and put a hand on his father's shoulder. "Post-traumatic stress disorder."

"I suppose," Monty said, tears filling his eyes at his son's touch. "They didn't have a name for it much back then, so I ran away.

FIFTY-FIVE

Arrangements

"There is movement."

Alejandro Garza's whisper jarred Roman Madera from his doze.

"Movement?" Roman jerked himself upright in the seat.

"There." Garza nodded down the street into the glare of the rising sun.

Roman rubbed his eyes and tried to focus on the old pickup pulling from the driveway of the house they had watched through the night. It passed by the church, the young man behind the wheel oblivious to the SUV and the two men inside watching.

"Follow?" Roman asked.

"No." Garza shook his head. "Wait."

Almost an hour passed before another vehicle, a small car driven by a woman, pulled from the driveway. It too passed by the church, the driver unaware that she was being watched.

"That's her," Garza said softly.

"Who?" Roman turned and asked.

"The one we seek," Garza said, his eyes narrowed, a viper, intent, sensing its prey. "Follow."

Roman had no idea who the one they sought was, but he obeyed and shifted the SUV into gear. He pulled from the church lot, yawning and trying to focus on the car that was a block ahead now and turning at the corner. He accelerated quickly, fearful of Garza's reaction if he lost sight of the car.

"Do not draw attention to us," Garza ordered.

Roman eased his foot off the accelerator. The woman's car was still a block ahead. He prayed it would not disappear from view around a corner.

As it turned out, the drive was short, less than ten minutes. The woman's car turned into the parking lot of a small shopping center and parked in front of a simple shop entrance. Goodwin Insurance Agency was stenciled on the large glass window that took up most of the front of the store.

Roman slowed and turned into the parking lot. He tried not to stare as he drove past the building where the woman stopped to take a key from her bag and unlock the door. She was attractive, forty-something, and despite the low budget clothes she wore, her figure held his eyes for a few seconds. He wondered what she had done to attract the attention of *Los Salvajes* and Alejandro Garza.

"Continue driving," Garza said. "Pull back out onto the street."

"Continue?" Roman looked to the side, puzzled. "If she is the one we seek, should we not …"

"Continue," Garza said, cutting him off in mid-sentence. "We have what we need for now."

Roman nodded without response and pulled through the parking lot. Garza took out his phone and punched in a number. Roman could hear a muffled voice on the other end. It was Chico Saludo.

"Where are you?" Garza asked.

"Near the lawyer's office," Chico responded. "In a small park nearby where I can watch."

Over the last few days, he had become a fixture there under the gazebo. A couple of elderly locals out for their morning walk had even smiled and nodded as they passed by. At least it wasn't raining today, Chico thought, pulling his jacket tighter around him.

"And the rat? Where is he?" Garza asked.

"In the car, unconscious. He mumbles in his sleep, but does not try to move or escape."

"He will be like that for several more hours." Garza put the phone on speaker and opened the notepad app. "Give me the location of your hotel."

"It's not actually a hotel," Chico began. "It's only a …"

"The address," Garza snapped.

"Yes, of course."

Chico gave him the location of the seedy motel in Dahlonega. Garza punched it into the notepad.

"Meet us there. Stay in your car until we arrive."

"As you say," Chico said as Garza ended the call.

Like Roman, Chico had no idea what Garza was planning, but at least he could leave the gazebo and get back into his warm car. That was good enough for now.

He was waiting in the parking lot of the motel with the engine running when they arrived in the SUV thirty minutes later. The motel clerk had peeked from the office window several times, watching him. Chico was afraid he might come out to investigate why the out-of-towner guest was sitting in his car. Once, he came from the office and stared in Chico's direction, but Chico ignored him, and after a minute, the clerk returned to his station behind the desk.

Chico breathed a sigh of relief when the SUV pulled in and Garza stepped out. He climbed from his car to greet him.

"I trust everything went well through the night," Chico said.

Garza ignored him and opened the rear door of the car. Luis Acero stirred, lifting his head, his eyes half open for a second before they glazed over and he dropped back onto the seat.

Garza reached in and pulled him upright by the arm. "Help me get him into your room." He turned to Roman. "You too."

"Give me your key," Garza said and Chico fumbled in one pocket for the key while he held onto Acero.

Garza checked the key for the room number, and then turned to the door a few feet away. The two drug lords supported Luis under the arms and dragged him through the parking lot toward the motel room door, the toes of his shoes leaving a trail in the gravel.

"Hey!"

The three men turned toward the shout. The motel clerk stood on the cracked sidewalk outside the office staring at them.

"What's wrong with him?" the man called out.

Garza turned, a friendly smile on his face. "Just had a little too much to drink last night. We want to put him to bed," he said in perfect English.

"Well ..." The clerk wrinkled his pudgy brow as if considering a puzzle and added, "But you can't all be in that room." He nodded at Chico. "He paid for a single."

"I will be happy to pay for the additional guests,"

Garza said amiably. "In fact, we'd like another room with two double beds. I'm afraid we may all have had a bit too much to drink last night. If you've got the room, of course."

The deserted parking lot was evidence that there were rooms available, as many as they wanted.

"Okay," the clerk said, nodding. "I suppose that'll be alright."

"Fine," Garza said with a smile. "I'll be right there to register and pay for the rooms and guests.

"Okay. I'll be waiting right here." The clerk gave a firm nod as if he had won some sort of victory and turned back to the office door.

Garza turned back to Chico and Roman. "Get him inside on the bed."

While Roman and Chico carried Luis Acero inside, Garza paid for the rooms. At the sight of the wad of cash in the stranger's hands, the clerk instinctively inflated the price of the rooms, adding on a special handling fee.

Garza thumbed through the bills. The clerk's lips moved, counting as each bill was placed on the counter. He could have kicked himself for not overcharging even more. When the office door closed behind the stranger, he pulled two twenties from the pile of cash and stuffed them in his pocket.

Garza returned with a second key and handed it to Chico. "You two will take the second room. Get some sleep. Later, we have work to do."

The two underlings nodded and entered the room next door. Five minutes later, they lay sprawled on the two double beds, snoring.

Garza went into the first room where Luis Acero had flopped face-first on the lone queen-sized bed. There was no room for Garza, but that was of no consequence. He had no intention of sleeping.

Taking a seat in the plastic chair by the small desk, he took out his cell phone and punched up a familiar number. Bebé Elizondo answered immediately.

"I will be home soon," Garza said.

"Excellent," Elizondo beamed back.

"First, there are a few arrangements to make."

"Tell me what you need."

Garza explained for several minutes.

"It will all be done," Elizondo said as his deputy summed up what was required. "We look forward to your return, Alejandro."

FIFTY-SIX

Troublesome Old Man

"I want to help."

"You have no idea what you are saying."

They spent the night speaking about the letters Clara and Monty exchanged over the years. The conversation was tender at times, tense occasionally, and painful a lot. By the end of the night, Sole's anger had dissipated. Acceptance set in.

He found himself able to see the old man through softened eyes. His war had been fought almost five decades earlier, but was Monty much different from any other veteran suffering from PTSD? A pang of guilt knifed through his heart, and he regretted the hatred he had harbored for the man over the years.

"I may be old," Monty said as dawn was breaking. "But I figured out you have a problem, that you are on the run from something or toward something,"

"Nothing for you to worry about." Sole shook his head.

"Maybe, but like it or not, you are my son. I've followed your trail … the bodies left behind, the timing after the murder of Shaye and the children. You disappeared, and it all started. It took time, but I had plenty of that, and I pieced it together."

Monty's eyes locked on his son's. "She was my daughter-in-law. They were my grandchildren. I want to help."

"No." Sole shook his head again. "This is my fight. I have to fix things, and this time I can't put someone else at risk … not even you."

"So why did you come back here?" Monty persisted. "Coming here means you had a change of plans, something that took you away from your mission. I didn't expect to find you here, not really. I came here to get those." Monty nodded at the letters stacked in rows on the bed.

"You have things pretty well figured out." Sole shook his head a final time. "No. I won't bring anyone else into this."

"Don't you think I want justice for my family?" Monty asked softly. "We aren't so different in that. Someone should make things right for what happened to your family … our family."

"And what does that mean to you … make things right? How would you have any idea what I intend to do to make things right? You never even knew them… our family. Never saw your grandchildren, never met my wife, the woman who brought them into the world."

He regretted the words as soon as he spit them out. Monty's head lowered, avoiding his son's stare.

"I was a terrible father and worse grandfather," he whispered, then looked up. "Maybe it's my way of asking for atonement. Not even sure myself. I only know that I've stopped running from the past now. You are my son, and I want to be with you and part of what you are doing."

"This isn't about giving you a way to atone. It's about …"

"Justice ... balancing the books for what they did," Monty said, his voice firmer now. "I'm not going anywhere, son. I found you once. I'll find you again."

"You are a troublesome old man," Sole sighed.

"That sounds like something your mother might say." Monty smiled. "And true, so tell me why you came back."

"Alright," Sole sighed. "I'll tell you. Then we part company, at least until this is over."

"No promises," Monty said with a smile, "But I'm listening."

Sole explained. Monty listened. The morning sun sent a shaft of light through the slightly parted curtains. The time had come to depart.

John Sole stood and faced his father. The bag holding the Monty's and Clara's letters lay on the bed, each letter carefully refolded and placed in its envelope.

"Take the bag. I brought it for you, for the day when I would find you," Monty said. "I found you."

"No." Sole shook his head. "They're yours. She wrote them for you. You wrote them to her. It's enough to know that you have them ... that you kept them."

"Alright." Monty nodded. "But they're yours any time you want them."

"Someday, maybe." Sole reached for the door, paused and turned to his father. "I'm glad that you found me, Monty. I won't say that being abandoned by you is forgiven." He shook his head. "It's not, but I understand now what happened."

"Will I see you again?" Monty asked.

"One day." Sole nodded. "I have your cell number. Keep it, and I'll call when I can."

He turned, opened the door, and walked out into the

day. Monty Sole sat on the bed, the bag of letters beside him, and wept.

"Goodbye, son."

Crisp morning air blew down from the Georgia mountains. Sole sucked it in to clear his head. Part of him wanted to stay with the old man for a while longer, but that was impossible. Three days had passed since he received the cryptic message from Luis Acero that they had to talk.

Sole went to his pickup, sat behind the wheel, and pulled out his phone. Dialing into the voice mailbox, he left a message for Luis.

"Arriving Richmond tomorrow."

He ended the call and dialed another number. When it was answered he said simply, "I'm in town."

"Here? In Gainesville?" Billy Siever was surprised.

"Close enough. Can we get together?"

"Yes, sure, of course. I'm just surprised you called?"

"Wanted to thank you." Sole didn't add that the odds were high he might never be able to see his friend again.

"You did?"

"Spent the night with my father talking."

"Get things worked out between you?"

"Worked out?" Sole thought for a second. "Not sure that's how to describe it. More like an understanding."

"That's good," Billy said sincerely. "Guess I'm a bit surprised you called me on this phone, violating your protocols."

"Figured this once would be alright. I'll get another burner and trash this one when I hang up. So, when can we meet?"

"I'm in court this morning," Billy said. "How about this afternoon, say five, the place we used to go?"

"I'll be there."

The place was the bar where they had met and reconnected after his mother's funeral. Growing up in Cassit Pass in the seventies and eighties, it was the only place in the county to get a beer legally, although he and Billy had used fake IDs to get beers illegally more than once. But the old place remained in business, thriving in the midst of a community of bible thumpers and holy rollers, or maybe because of them.

After a quick trip to the electronics department of a local big-box store to pick up another prepaid phone, he drove from Dahlonega into the surrounding mountains. He had hours to kill before meeting Billy, and there was someone he wanted to visit.

FIFTY-SEVEN

Understood

Had Alejandro Garza known that his adversary was only twenty miles away his plans would have been different. As it was, he had no idea the man he sought was in a nearby motel room rehashing life with his father. By necessity, the strategy he devised grew in complexity and involved more people than he would have preferred.

He spent the morning arranging one of the most critical elements of the plan, an important rendezvous for the evening. The need to travel undetected within the United States coupled with the usual requirements for weapons, operational security, and escape and evasion contingencies complicated things, but if all went as planned, John Sole would come to him.

At one-thirty in the afternoon, he decided that his assistants had slept enough. He picked up his phone and punched in a number. A groggy Roman Madera answered.

"We leave in ten minutes. Get Saludo and come to the other room."

He ended the call and turned to examine the rat still

lying on the bed. Luis Aceros' eyes were open now, the effects of the drug wearing off. Garza went to his briefcase and took out the syringe, filling it from a bottle procured legally in Mexico.

Luis' eyes widened. His head moved feebly side to side, but he was powerless to prevent Garza from plunging the needle into his bare arm. He was unconscious again in seconds.

There was a brief tap at the door. Garza opened it, and Chico and Roman hurried inside. Neither had any idea what Garza planned or their role, and neither was thrilled at the prospect of being involved. Overseeing the cartel drug sales in Atlanta and Richmond was undoubtedly safer.

"Here is what we will do," Garza began.

It took only a few minutes to outline everything. When he completed the briefing, neither man dared offer up their concerns, although there were many of those. North America was not Mexico. Law enforcement would not look the other way if they happened upon them as they executed Garza's plans. Prison in America might not be as harsh as prison in Mexico, but it was still prison, and the State of Georgia still had the power to impose the death penalty.

In any event, their concerns were irrelevant. Elizondo and, by extension, Garza and *Los Salvajes*, owned them. They had no choice but to accept their assignments.

They nodded and replied in unison, "*Entendido, jefe.*" Understood, boss.

FIFTY-EIGHT

Savages

"What do we do now?" Roman Madera leaned forward, peering through the SUV's windshield.

"We wait," Garza replied.

In the back seat, Chico Saludo said nothing, silently whispering a prayer that they could quickly do what Garza wanted and get back to the much safer and predictable business of taking money from people in exchange for drugs.

Roman decided not to ask what they were waiting for. One question was sufficient.

They didn't have long to wait. As he watched, a portly man with a round smiling face came from the office, got into a car parked in front and backed out carefully. Sam Goodwin drove past the SUV, unaware of the three men watching his office.

"Drive to the front door," Garza ordered. "When we get out, go to the rear of the shopping center. There will be a driveway there, and the back doors are numbered." He nodded at the number over the glass front door. It read

Suite 204. "That number, 204, will be stenciled on the back door. Wait there for us."

"Right." Roman nodded and pulled to the front of the Goodwin Insurance Agency.

Garza exited the SUV, followed by a reluctant Chico Saludo. They were through the front door as Roman made the turn to circle to the back of the shopping center. Isabella looked up from her desk and smiled.

"May I help you?" The smile faded. The tall man's intense stare and his companion's nervous glances through the front window immediately telegraphed that these were not ordinary insurance customers there to see Sam. "Mr. Goodwin is out just now, but if you will come back later ..." She slid the center drawer of the desk open as she spoke, her hand poised to reach for the small pistol Sam had placed there for her protection when he was out.

The tall man stepped forward before she was able to lift it. His movements were incredibly quick, practiced and confident. He had done this before.

Grasping her by the throat, a powerful hand closing off her trachea so that she could make no sound, Alejandro Garza physically lifted Isabella from her chair. He motioned to Chico.

"Come."

Chico scurried forward and followed them into Sam Goodwin's adjacent office.

"Sit in the chair," Garza ordered.

Chico sat in a chair facing the desk. Garza spun the struggling woman and pushed her down onto Chico's lap.

"Now place your arm around her neck. Hold her tightly and wrap your legs around hers so that she cannot struggle."

Chico complied. As he adjusted his arm around her

neck, she gasped for air and tried to scream. Panicked, Chico clamped his arm tighter, and she choked, struggling for air, but with his legs wrapped around hers, she was nearly immobile.

It wasn't a very dignified manner of restraint. It felt awkward and ridiculous, but Chico found that the woman's struggles subsided as she used up the oxygen in her lungs.

With her rump pressed into his lap, their position was almost sexual. She was a very attractive woman, with curving hips and long legs. In other circumstances, her body pressed against him in that manner, she would no doubt have become aware of his erection building.

But there was no erection. Chico was almost as terrified as she. What if someone came through the door and discovered them? He knew what would happen. Garza would dispatch them in his efficient manner, and that terrified Chico even more.

As he held the woman, who was barely moving now, Garza took a hypodermic syringe from his pocket. It was already loaded with the drug he had used to quiet the rat, Luis Acero. Garza uncapped the needle, ripped up the woman's sleeve, and plunged it into a vein.

Within seconds, her struggles ceased completely. Chico worried that she might be dead, that Garza had used too much of the drug. Then he felt the gentle rise of her chest as she breathed.

"You can release her now," Garza said and pulled Isabella's limp form from Chico's lap. "Help me take her to the back door."

They dragged her through the small office to the rear, her feet bumping limply over the floor. Garza pushed open the door, looked outside, nodded and then pulled her out into the sunlight.

Chico was relieved to find Roman waiting there with the SUV as ordered. He had feared that his counterpart might be tempted to say, to hell with this, and drive away as fast as possible. But Roman would never dare defy Garza any more than Chico would.

Chico opened the SUV's rear cargo door. Garza lifted and tossed the woman in beside Luis Acero's unconscious form. Chico thought they looked like a couple, lying peacefully together after making love.

Garza climbed in the front passenger seat. Chico sat behind him. They had been inside no more than two minutes. As the office's back door closed, they heard the phone ringing. Eventually, someone would report that the woman was missing. By that time, they would be far away.

"Drive," Garza said calmly, and as Roman stepped hard on the accelerator, he added, "Not fast. Do nothing to draw attention to our vehicle."

They may have been skilled drug dealers, but his assistants were clumsy in this sort of work. Even so, the plan had begun successfully, and the critical part was that they had the woman. Garza held no illusions about executing the next part of the plan. It would be unavoidably messy.

Blood pounded in Roman's ears. He licked his lips. The plan was for him to follow Garza inside this time while Chico waited in the SUV with the engine running.

Pulling up the driveway of the old stone house that served as Billy Siever's office, Chico backed the SUV around so the nose pointed toward the street, ready for a quick exit. Garza got out, followed by Roman, and walked to the door at the side of the house. A few seconds later, Chico flinched in the seat, ducking his head behind the wheel for cover.

Three roars in quick succession echoed through the

afternoon air. Even muffled inside the heavy stone building, the gunshots were unmistakable. Chico lifted his head, his eyes darting nervously around, certain that someone must have heard them, but the afternoon outside remained undisturbed. Birds chirped in the trees, a car drove by on the street out front, a dog barked a few houses away. Maybe the dog heard the shots, but no one else did. After a few seconds, even the dog settled down.

Inside, things moved quickly. Roman followed his *jefe* through the door. Before he could even lift the pistol in his trembling hand, Garza fired three times, instantly killing the three women seated at desks in the main office area.

He was a machine, efficient and deadly, no motions wasted. The receptionist lifted her head to greet them as the door opened. A pleasant, inoffensive smile on his face, Garza returned the greeting with a bullet through her brain. Another woman, standing beside a row of file cabinets, was dispatched in similar fashion. The third had just begun to rise from her chair behind a desk when the pistol barked again. She slumped forward, the hole in her forehead pooling blood on the faux leather desk blotter.

It was over in seconds. Garza moved quickly to a closed door behind the woman's desk. A sign on it that read, William Siever. The door jerked open as Garza reached for the handle. Billy Siever stood there, wide-eyed, mouth agape, a small .38 revolver in his hand, hanging at his side. At Vera's insistence, he kept the pistol in his desk as protection, although she could never say exactly what it was to protect him from, and Billy had never actually expected to have to use it.

As it turned out, he had no time to use it now. The tall man with hard eyes held a much larger pistol, inches from his face. The man reached out and took the pistol from Billy's hand, then nodded at his companion.

Roman pulled out the duct tape Garza had made him carry in his pocket and passed the roll twice around Billy's head, sealing off his mouth, but allowing him to breathe. The tall man jammed his pistol up under Billy's chin and whispered.

"Do not attempt to escape. If you do, we will kill your wife. We know where you live."

Then he jerked Billy forward, dragging him through the office area. As they passed Doris' slumped body and blood-soaked desk, Billy gave out an anguished howl. Muffled by the duct tape, it came out as a mewling whimper. Roman thought he sounded like a kitten whining and terrified before being flung into a river to drown.

They pulled the lawyer through the side door, down the three stone steps, and pushed him into the rear seat of a waiting SUV. As he stumbled in, Billy saw Isabella and Luis Acero, crammed into the rear cargo area. Both were unconscious.

The man who pushed him in climbed into the seat beside Billy. A third man sat in the driver's seat, waiting, fists clenching the wheel and nervously eying the tall man who took the front passenger seat. The tall man gave a nod and the driver started the SUV down the driveway. A few minutes later, they were leaving the City of Dahlonega, heading into the mountains on a state highway.

Billy had never seen any of these men before, but he knew who they were. John had warned him that the cartel would never give up, never stop looking for him and anyone close to him.

Los Salvajes—the savages, John had called them. The dead bodies in Billy's office testified of their savagery.

FIFTY-NINE

Rules of Engagement

He sat by the grave for hours. It was his first visit to see his mother in years.

A few times, he had brought his family to see the place where he had grown up and to visit the grave. He wanted the children to know the grandmother they would never meet.

That was when he still had a family. Today, he was there to report to Clara.

"I saw my father," he whispered, eyes closed as he sat on the ground beside the gravestone.

He could almost see Clara smile and nod in her familiar, patient way.

"I know, son. Did you make peace with him?"

John thought about that for a few seconds and nodded. "I think so." Then he shrugged and whispered, "But I'm still angry."

"He knows that. He understands that. He's a good man, son. Just confused. Are you confused?"

"No." He shook his head. "I have a mission, a purpose."

"That's good. As long as you are certain."

He opened his eyes and his mother's face faded away, her voice receding into the distance.

"As long as you are certain."

He shook his head. He wasn't certain about anything except that he had to protect those he had dragged into this mess and put at risk.

He said goodbye to his mother and left the cemetery to stop by the old house, much as his father had done a few days earlier. The familiar green hills and mountain valleys surrounding Cassit Pass pulled at him. The aching desire to return home pulled at him too, to forget the pain, or at least let it heal. He could move into the old house, fix it up, and spend his life there.

Maybe in time, he thought, when he'd done what he had to do, but he knew it was a lie. He shook his head. There was no escape or hiding from it. The old life was gone. The problem was this new one felt old and used up too.

He wandered through the rooms of the house remembering. He moved out to the porch and sat on the top step listening to the birds. No doubt they were the descendants of the birds he had listened to as a boy, returning to the same nests each year, passing the family home on from one generation to the next.

The sun was lowering when he rose and left the house. It was time to meet Billy Siever before he went to pull Luis Acero out of whatever trouble he'd stumbled into.

For years, Gurney's Bar in Sexton had been the only place to get a drink legally in Winscombe County. Sole and Billy had managed to drink there illegally as underage teens a few times. That was before old man Gurney got caught looking the other way and the sheriff gave him a stern warning.

From that point on, they had done what every other underage drinker of the day did. They drove a couple of hours to a liquor store on the outskirts of Atlanta and paid one of the winos standing outside to go in and make their purchases.

This satisfied everyone. The wino was happy to be able to buy more booze. The boys were happy to get their booze. The liquor store manager, who understood exactly what was happening, was happy to sell more booze. The business arrangement, as far as everyone involved in the transaction was concerned, seemed a perfect example of free-market capitalism at work.

On this day, Sole sat at the bar in Gurney's and legally sipped a beer. Five o'clock came and went. He ordered another. At six o'clock he figured some problem had delayed Billy. He took out his phone to leave him a message and reschedule for the next time he passed through the area.

He punched in the number. It rang twice before a voice answered. It was not Billy.

"I've been waiting for your call," the voice said. It was deep and calm, businesslike, with a peculiar old-world formality.

"Who is this?"

"Come now. You are much too astute to ask such a question. You know who I am. We have been playing a game of chase, hide and seek, a child's game." There was a pause, and Sole imagined the smile on the face he had never seen. "It is time to bring the game to an end. Don't you think so?"

"Where is he?" Sole demanded.

"Mr. Siever, you mean?" the man replied calmly. "He is with me, as are two more of your friends."

"Who?" Sole's voice rose in volume and the bartender looked his way.

"We call him the rat. You would remember him as Luis Acero from your days as a detective in Atlanta. I think then you would have called him a snitch." The man gave a small laugh. "That name does not sound any more flattering than rat."

"Who else?" Sole snapped back, already tired of his pretentious bullshit.

"I think you already know, but to make things plain for you. Your friend from Texas, the woman you fled with after killing my men. Her name is Isabella, I believe, although her identification shows a different name, a forgery no doubt."

"They have nothing to do with what happened … with what I am doing."

"Yes, but they do share a common trait that makes them valuable to me. You care about them." The voice paused and then added, "You understand what I want, of course. You are much too intelligent for me to have to say it."

Sole knew exactly what he wanted. The offer would be to release the others if he turned himself over to the man who killed his family. Sole also knew it was a lie.

"Why would I do that? You will kill them whether I come to you or not." Now Sole paused for effect. "And when you do, I will hunt you down and kill you."

"That is already your plan, is it not? And you are correct. In normal circumstances, I would kill them … and you." The man on the phone sighed. "But these are not normal circumstances. We have wasted too much time with your juvenile games. There must be a resolution to the matters between us. I make a simple proposition."

"Say it," Sole said, his jaw clenched.

"You are too intelligent to sacrifice yourself, knowing that I will kill the others in any event. I know you, perhaps better than you know yourself."

"You think so?"

"I know so. In any event, I have no doubt you would willingly give your life to save theirs, but not if the result were merely to die along with them."

Sole remained silent. Exchanging words with this man was pointless and only played into his hand, strengthened his position and weakened Sole's.

"I, on the other hand," the voice continued, "would allow you to kill my associates without a second thought, if it meant hunting you down and ending this."

"I'm sure you would. Get to the point."

"I detect the disdain in your voice, as if you are somehow morally superior to me. You are not." The voice on the phone paused, as if about to explain some great truth. "It is true that by your standards, I am without moral constraint or conscience, but I do live by a code, just as you do. My code requires me to win, to conquer, to obliterate those who oppose us, and I will."

"You can't win by harming my friends. It won't stop me. It will only make me more determined."

"Yes, I know this too well, but I am also a pragmatist. Your game has cost us too much time and money and blood. So, to bring things to a speedy conclusion, I propose a new arrangement, outside of my usual practices."

"What arrangement?"

"I will allow your friends to live, in exchange for you ... and your life, of course."

"Just like that? I'm supposed to believe the man without moral constraints has turned over a new leaf?"

"Not at all. You know better than that." The somber voice almost chuckled. "If I could kill you and them, I would. But as I said, I am a pragmatist."

"Say what you have to say," Sole interrupted, annoyed with the pretentious bastard's lectures. "Or we can end this call, and you can wait for me to find you ... and kill you."

"Very well. You force me to make exceptions in order to conclude our business," the voice continued, unruffled. "Your friends may live. In that way, you have won a sort of victory. I will also have a victory. You will die. Our little game, our war, will end with your death."

"What if I just say, do what you want with them? Kill them if you want. It changes nothing. I will find you and kill you."

"Please, Detective Sole. Do not speak to me as if I were a child. We both know you would never let that happen if you were able to prevent it. The rat, Acero, yes, perhaps you would let him die for you." There was a brief pause before the voice continued, thoughtful as he considered the possibilities. "But no, I believe you would not even let the rat die for you. Your honor would not permit it. That is where you and I differ, Detective. That is why you cannot win this little war we have between us."

The man on the phone was confident. He had reason to be. It was a checkmate move, forcing Sole to step into the trap his opponent had laid.

"Alright," he said. "And if I accept your proposal, how do we go about making the exchange, me for them?"

"Simple. We both know you will not accept my offer if I

set the rules of the exchange. You would not trust me and would have no reason to sacrifice yourself for no reason. Therefore, I propose that you make arrangements to receive your friends. We will exchange them for you at a place of your choosing ... as long as that place is in Mexico."

"Mexico? That seems to put the odds in your favor."

"Absolutely!" The man laughed out loud now. "Now you understand! Make the arrangements to free your friends. You may bring whoever you wish to receive them, as many as you wish. Make sure they have the means to transport your friends safely out of Mexico. They can even be armed, to provide security and safe escort, but you will remain behind."

"And you? How many will you bring?"

"Ah, yes. That will depend on the location you choose, the people you bring with you, and the terms of the exchange. I will be prepared for any eventuality. You will not escape."

It was arrogant. The man on the phone, the man who had murdered his family, was supremely confident in his abilities to win in a face-to-face confrontation.

"The odds don't seem very favorable," Sole said quietly.

"In your position, I would agree. I would say not more than a fifty percent chance for your friends to survive and for you ...zero ... but there is one certainty."

"What?"

"If you do not agree, the odds are one hundred percent that I will kill Isabella, your friend Siever, and the rat. You know I will do it." He paused and let the words linger in the air for a few seconds. "Surely, you see that a fifty percent chance of survival is much better than none. Is it not?"

It was. Sole had no choice.

"Alright. I agree to your terms. Me for them at a place of my choosing in Mexico. I make the arrangements."

"Excellent!" the voice beamed at him over the phone. "I am aware of your exploits against us and that you may be traveling. It may take a little time to make your arrangements, and I am a reasonable man. I give you exactly two weeks from today for our meeting to take place. Leave the details and location in a message on your voice mailbox. A final warning."

"Yes?"

"If you involve law enforcement in any way, I will kill your friends immediately.

"Understood." Sole had expected nothing less. "Now I have a question?"

"Yes?"

"Your name?"

"Ah, that. Your sense of honor and fair play always reveal themselves. Enemies should face each other and know each other. Is that it?" The voice gave a small laugh. "You have yet to understand there are no rules. I will remain anonymous to you. Goodbye, Detective Sole."

The call ended. John Sole stared at the wall behind Gurney's bar.

He had never held illusions about his personal survival, had always imagined his life would come to an end alone, facing the killer who took his family from him. Once more, others' lives were in peril because of his carelessness.

"Another?" The bartender asked.

"No." He placed a twenty on the bar and stood. "Keep it."

The man on the phone—the enemy—had set the rules of engagement. John Sole had to devise a battle plan.

SIXTY

Always

First things first. The old cold war adage in dealing with an enemy was to trust but verify. Verification was necessary before any plan could be prepared.

Sole drove slowly down a residential street in Dahlonega. As he neared the stone house where Billy Siever maintained his office, he slowed. Ahead, the lights of emergency vehicles, police, and paramedics, sent blue and red beams reflecting off the surrounding houses. Three black hearses sat ominously at the end of the driveway.

An officer stood at the driveway entrance as Sole cruised slowly by. He stepped into the road, waving a flashlight, signaling Sole to stop.

"License and registration, please." The officer shined the flashlight into Sole's face.

"Sure." Sole reached for his wallet slowly and retrieved his driver's license. "Registration is in the glove box."

"Get it." The officer took the license and kept the flashlight pointed at Sole as he leaned over toward the glove box.

"Right. Here you go." He handed over the registration. "Lot of lights here, officer. What's the problem?"

"William Myers," the officer said, ignoring the question. "From Tennessee."

"Yep." Sole smiled.

"What are you doing here in Dahlonega?"

"Just passing through. Stopped to look around the courthouse square" Sole grinned. "They used to mine gold around here ... right?"

Again, the officer ignored him and took out his notepad to write down the information from the driver's license and registration slip. Then he spoke into the radio mic hanging from his lapel. "Dispatch, 10-27, 10-28, 10-29 ..."

He read out the driver's license number, name, and vehicle information to the dispatcher. Sole recognized the ten-codes as a request to check the driver's license status, vehicle registration, and any wants on the subject of the request. Sole relaxed and waited.

A minute later, the dispatcher was back on the radio and confirmed, "Valid Tennessee license and registration. No wants."

"10-4," the officer said and looked at Sole, still undeterred from checking out the stranger. "And how did you happen to be on this street, Mr. Myers?"

"Just driving around the town. Left the square and was trying to find the highway, the one south toward Lake Lanier. Supposed to meet some buddies there and fish."

"Tonight?"

"Well, tonight will be more about drinking beer on my friend's boat." Sole grinned again. "You know how that is. Can't let fishing to get in the way of cold beer. Right?"

"Who's your friend with the boat?"

"Bob Sims," Sole said without a pause. "Has a house on

the lake outside Gainesville. Keeps the damn boat tied up at a dock right at his house." Sole shook his head, grinning a good old boy grin. "Damn, if Bob didn't make it big, not like the rest of us hillbillies he left behind in Tennessee."

There were thousands of boats on Lake Lanier. One of them might even be owned by a Bob Sims. It didn't matter. Sole would be long gone if the officer even bothered to verify his story.

"That boy can drink some beer. I swear he could drink three of us under the table when we were in school," Sole chattered on. "That's why we're drinking on the boat … you know, legal and all … tied up at that dock of his. Don't worry we'll be sober by morning when we head for some bass, but tonight we …"

"Move on, Mr. Myers." The officer handed back the license and registration. Go straight ahead for two blocks, then turn right until you hit Highway 19. Take it south to Highway 53, then left to Lake Lanier. Follow the signs. Good night."

"Thanks, officer," Sole said, taking the license from his hand and craning his neck to see around the officer up the driveway. "Holy shit!" he exclaimed. "Are those bodies?"

Sole had seen body bags before. There was no doubt what the attendants were rolling down the driveway to the waiting hearses.

"Move on," the officer barked.

Sole nodded and accelerated slowly away from the scene. Fear clenched his gut. Three bodies. Was one Billy? Did the enemy on the phone lie? Or had three more people paid with their lives for his mistakes. This had to end.

He drove to the outskirts of Dahlonega and pulled into the old motel parking lot. Inside the room, Monty heard three taps on the door and rose from the bed. He opened the door to find his son standing there, started to smile and stopped. The look on John's face made it plain that there was a problem, a big one.

"What's the matter?" Monty stepped aside to allow John to enter.

"Do you still want to help?"

"Always," his father replied.

SIXTY-ONE

Blood and Fresh Meat

"We will leave tonight."

Alejandro Garza spoke slowly, reviewing in his mind the myriad details of his plan. Bebé would want all the specifics along with a promise that it would be done quickly.

"You spoke with your North American?" Bebé Elizondo asked mildly.

"Yes."

"And he agreed to the exchange?"

"He did, but it is not as simple as that."

"Explain, please Alejandro," Elizondo sighed. "I thought I made it clear that it is time to bring this matter to a conclusion."

"I understand, and the end is now in sight."

Garza outlined the plan. Speaking in his usual calm, deliberate manner, unruffled by Elizondo's impatience, he promised the total elimination of their adversary.

"Very well," Elizondo said as the briefing ended. "Carry out your plans quickly, Alejandro."

"I promise to return soon," Garza said. "Two more weeks and this is finished."

In the SUV's rear cargo area, Isabella had emerged far enough from her drug-induced coma to follow the conversation in Spanish between the tall man in the front seat and someone on the phone. She listened to the plan as Garza explained it to Bebé.

John had warned them about these people. They would stop at nothing, never forget, and never stop trying to find a way to get to him, to eliminate him. Now, despite their new identities and everything he had done to lead them away, they found what made him vulnerable—his friends.

"Where are we going," She said, shaking her head to clear away the cobwebs inside.

Billy Siever stirred in the middle passenger seat and sat up. Isabella's eyes opened wide.

"Billy! I didn't know they … how …"

Beside her, a man she had never seen rolled over and sat up. Like her, he was bound hand and foot with duct tape.

"Who are you?" she asked.

Luis Acero, eyes wide with terror, shook his head. Of the three captives, he alone had the clearest understanding of who their captors were and what was going to happen to them.

A man in the middle seat beside Billy turned and pointed a pistol over the seat at her face.

"Sit back and shut up. You will see soon enough." He grinned. "I don't think you will want to rush things."

"Leave them alone," the tall man in front said.

The man with the gun grunted and turned back, giving Billy a push that forced him down to the floorboards and out of sight from Isabella. Isabella's mind was whirling with questions. Were Sandy or Jacinta harmed? Were they aware of what had happened? Had the kidnappers harmed Sam? What would John want them to do?

She knew he would want them to not lose hope, keep fighting, and trust that he was coming to find them. Until then, find a way to stay alive.

The SUV sped along a country road. The night rushed by in the wind, dark and forboding. After what seemed an eternity, but probably was only a couple of hours, the vehicle slowed, and the driver pulled down a lane running through a grove of trees.

Isabella's heart beat rapidly in her chest. Was this the place they would take their revenge? Leave their bodies in the woods?

The drive through the woods only lasted a few minutes. The SUV emerged into a wide-open area that looked like pasture land. A wide path was cut and graded through the pasture. Isabella's head swiveled, trying to take everything in.

A plane sat at one end of the graded path. Its marker lights were off, but the interior lights showed it to be a small jet, like the ones business executives used. Two men stood on the ground by the plane's open door, chatting. Another sat in the cockpit, his headset on, eyes focused on the control panel as he prepared the aircraft for flight.

The two men by the door were smiling. One was dressed in blue jeans and a denim work shirt. To Isabella, he looked like a local farmer. The other wore slacks and a white shirt with epaulets on the shoulders, denoting his status as one of the aircraft's pilots.

The SUV pulled up beside the jet. The driver and front passenger, the tall man, got out and came around to pull

Isabella and the man with her from the cargo space. The one who had pointed the gun at her dragged Billy out.

One by one, the men lifted their captives and dragged them up the steps into the plane, forcing them into seats and belting them in. When they were all on board, the tall man went back outside where the pilot was joking with the farmer.

"Everything okay?" the farmer asked.

His name was Silas Brandt. The Brandt family had been farming the land fifty miles north of Greensboro, North Carolina since before the Civil War and had always found a way to remain profitable, even as the days of slavery and sharecroppers faded away. Today, Silas was going to make a quick ten thousand dollars by allowing the unknown but friendly strangers the use of his private airstrip.

"Everything is as we directed," the tall man, Garza, said.

"Good. Then that's another five thousand in payment. That was the deal. Five up front and five when you got loaded."

Brandt smiled, waiting for the cash to be placed into his outstretched hand. Garza nodded and reached into his pocket.

There was only a moment of surprise on Brandt's face before it exploded in a cloud of red. The pilot had already turned and started up the stairs into the cockpit as the shot rang out. Garza followed and secured the door behind him.

The engines spooled up. The runway was barely long enough for the jet's takeoff, but the pilots were skilled. The cartel only paid for the best. As they climbed, Isabella saw the tops of trees passing a few feet below the plane, then they were gone and everything below was black.

In the field below, Silas Brandt lay on his back in a pool of blood, the surprise frozen on his face. A family of raccoons emerged from the woods, attracted by the scent of blood and fresh meat.

SIXTY-TWO

Getting Started

"You." Sandy opened the door wide and stared in surprise at the man on the porch.

"Hello, Sandy," Sole said.

"Where's ..." Sandy leaned to the side to see the man behind John. "Who is this?"

"A friend. Can we come in?"

Jacinta came up behind Sandy, looked over his shoulder, and grinned. "John! Yes, please come in. Sandy move and let them in."

Sandy stepped aside. Sole entered the small but tidy living room, followed by Monty. He had been there once before, the day they arrived in Georgia. When he left that same day, he'd had no intention of returning.

That was before. Things had changed. His plans had come apart.

"Mom's not here," Sandy said.

A round-faced man with a worried look on his face came out of the kitchen. He frowned when he saw the two men.

"What is it, Chris?" he asked.

"Friends," Sandy said, turning. "This is John and …"

"Monty," the older man said with a smile.

"Oh. I thought it might be your mother." The concern on his face deepened.

Sandy turned back to Sole. "Mom is missing. Sam came back from an appointment and found the office empty. We called the police a few hours ago and reported her missing. They took the report but said there was no evidence of a crime and sometimes people just decide to disappear so there wasn't much to do except put out an alert on the police radio in case anyone spotted her." His eyes narrowed. "You know my mom. She would never just disappear."

"Yes," Sole agreed. "We need to talk."

"What's going on?" Sam Goodwin stepped forward to face Sole. His eyes narrowed. "You're the one from her past. She never talks about you, but I know there was someone."

Sole nodded. "I suppose I am. Isabella and I …"

"Isabella?" Sam's brow furrowed. "Who the hell is Isabella?"

"Sorry. I mean, Abby." Sole shook his head. It was a stupid blunder. Goodwin only knew her as Abigail Banks. No matter, he decided. He was about to learn more than he probably wanted about the woman he planned to marry.

Sam looked at Sandy. "I suppose you aren't actually Chris Banks, and …" He nodded at Jacinta. "She's not Margarita."

"Sorry, we lied to you, Sam. We had to." Sandy grimaced, nodded, and touched his chest. "Sandy Palmeras. My mom is Isabella Palmeras, and this is Jacinta Martinez."

"What the hell is going on?" Sam slumped into a chair and shook his head. "I thought … I mean we were going to be married, and now this." He looked up at Sandy. "Was everything a lie?"

"No. Mom cares for you ... loves you. That wasn't a lie."

Sole watched the shock spread across the man's face and couldn't help but feel sympathy for him. He was in love with a woman and didn't even know her true name.

"Can we talk?" Sole asked. "I can explain everything."

"Talk," Sam said, looking up from the chair, his face a mask of confusion and pain.

Sole gave an abridged version of his past and how Isabella became a target of the *Los Salvajes* cartel. Out of respect for Sam's feelings, he omitted details about the intimacy that he had shared with Isabella and his personal feelings for her.

He concluded by saying, "I came here because I need your help."

"We have to call the police ... the FBI ... somebody," Sam said, rising from the chair.

"No." Sole stepped in front of him. "If they even suspect that law enforcement is involved, they will kill her immediately along with the others. These people won't negotiate. The bodies won't be found. The killers will disappear and never be tracked down."

"Seems like you've dragged a lot of innocent people into your shit storm," Sam snapped.

"I have." The words stung but they were true and Sole could only nod and agree. "I'm sorry for that."

"So the only way to get them back is for you to turn yourself over to the cartel in exchange for their release." Sam stared at Sole. "And you are willing to do this?"

"I am willing to do whatever is necessary to get Isabella and the others out safely."

"Isabella." Sam shook his head. "Every time you say that I have to remind myself you are talking about Abby, the woman I love and intend to marry."

"Sorry," Sole said. "I'll try to remember to call her by her new name."

"No." Sam shook his head. "No more lies … not to me … not if I am going to be involved in this. Isabella, Sandy, and Jacinta." He said the names slowly, nodding as he said each. "These are the people I have come to care about. I can't do this for strangers."

"Alright." Sole nodded.

Billy Siever was right. Sam Goodwin was a good man.

"What do we do?" Sam asked.

"We make a plan and try to survive."

Sam nodded. "Let's get started."

SIXTY-THREE

Reinforcements

They made the trip to Albuquerque, driving all night and the following day. Sole drove his pickup, alternating Monty. Sandy and Jacinta rode in Sam's car, taking turns at the wheel when fatigue overcame the driver. The only stops were for gas, restrooms, and fast food to eat as they drove.

When they pulled off I-40, Sole led them to an alley behind a store on a small inner-city street. He got out and walked to the back door. The others watched from the vehicles.

The store was closed. Sole used the key Edgar Dupart had given him and went up the stairs to the apartment.

"Bill?" Edgar looked up from the sofa as he walked in.

"Edgar," Sole smiled. "Good to see you."

"And you." Edgar's brow furrowed. "But I did not expect to see you again so soon."

"I didn't expect to be here again so soon, but I could use a favor."

"What is that?"

"A place to stay."

"Of course, you can stay with us. You are always welcome. Magdalena and Ben will be happy to see you back so soon."

"There are five of us, Edgar," Sole added. "We need a place for a week or two … a place out of sight."

"I see." Edgar nodded, lowering his head to look at him over the top of his glasses. "Are you in trouble?"

"Some. I won't lie, but we need a place to stay, and you are the only people I can trust."

"Such mystery. You are still on your mission." It was a statement of fact. There was no point in asking questions about his plans. "Where are your friends?"

"In the alley."

"Bring them in. I'll tell Maggie." He smiled. "Lucky for them it's her night to prepare dinner."

Sole led the procession up the back stairs. Maggie greeted him warmly with a hug. Ben stepped forward to shake his hand. Sole turned to make introductions without going into detail about why they were there.

There was a moment of awkward silence when he finished. Maggie stepped forward, put an arm around Jacinta.

"Come with me. You look like you could use a warm bath."

"I could. Thank you."

The women moved down the hall. Edgar looked at the men. "Sleeping arrangements may be a little cramped, but I think we can fit you all in."

"I was going to suggest that Sam and Sandy take the extra room that I used. Monty and I will sleep in here on the sofa and chair."

"I call the sofa," Monty said with a grin.

"You got it. I didn't figure your old-man back could handle the chair."

That got a chuckle from everyone. It was nothing, just a brief laugh, but it was a relief from the stress of the last few days.

Edgar went into the kitchen and returned with beers. He passed them around and sat in his chair. After a brief silence, he spoke.

"You won't tell me what this is about, but I would like to ask if you are in danger?"

"Not now." Sole shook his head. "No one knows we are here. We'll stay out of sight and keep a low profile so we don't attract attention."

"I understand." Edgar nodded. "I'll speak with Magdalena and Ben. They won't say anything."

"I know," Sole said, then added, "This is an imposition, and you are concerned for your family. I'm sorry about that, but there is no one else I can trust. I wouldn't be here if there were."

"Bah! You are a friend. Friends trust each other and help each other" Edgar smiled and looked at the others. "And now we have four more friends.

When Maggie returned from showing Jacinta the tub, she began preparing dinner. Sole rose, put the empty beer bottle on the counter, and turned for the front door.

"Where are you going, big brother?" Maggie asked.

"To see some people." He nodded at Monty. "You should come with me."

Monty sighed and stood, gulping down the last of his beer. "Duty calls."

The clomped down the stairs to the alley and climbed into Sole's pickup. He pulled out onto the street and passed in front of Dupart's Market. Monty studied the name on the sign.

"Nice people," he said.

"They are," Sole agreed.

"How did you meet them?"

Sole turned his head and gave a slight smile without responding.

"Okay. Fair enough." Monty chuckled. "I get it. Just glad you managed to make a few friends you can count on." He looked at his son. "You can count on me too, you know."

"I know that. If I didn't, you wouldn't be here."

"Alright then. Now that the tender father-son moment is out of the way, maybe you'll tell me where we're headed."

"To find reinforcements," Sole said seriously.

"Good. I like reinforcements. The more reinforcements, the better." Monty said, leaning back in the seat and folding his arms over his chest. "Just gonna take a short, old-man nap now. Let me know when we're there."

SIXTY-FOUR

Purgatory

They were all awake and fully conscious when the jet touched down. They were also terrified.

Seated across the aisle from each other, Billy and Isabella exchanged apprehensive looks. Luis Acero sat in a seat facing Billy. The look on his face was more than apprehensive. He trembled uncontrollably, a leaf clinging to a tree in the midst of a gale.

"Who are you?" Isabella asked him.

"Shut up!" one of their kidnappers called out from behind. It was Chico Saludo.

"It is no matter," another voice said. It was the tall man, the one who seemed to be in charge. "Let them speak if they want. It will change nothing."

Isabella turned back to the man cowering in the seat across from Billy Siever. "Who are you? Why did they bring you here?"

Luis stared wide-eyed at the woman for several seconds before he managed to force his mouth open and say in a croaking whisper, "Luis."

"Why are you here, Luis?" Isabella asked. "What do you have to do with this?"

"Nothing." He shook his head, and tears began to stream down his face. "Nothing. I swear it."

"Stop your blubbering, Rat," Chico Saludo cackled from behind.

"You know John?" Isabella asked.

"I don't know nothin'," Luis said, but there wasn't much conviction behind the words.

He knew that the tall man, Alejandro Garza, had already decided his fate. Unlike the others, he had no illusions about what would happen to them. The moments he had been clinging to were dwindling.

Billy Siever leaned over in his seat and spoke softly. "A friend of John's. He helped arrange your new identities." He motioned with his head to the men seated behind them. "That's probably how they found him."

Isabella nodded. And through him, they had found her and Billy. Everything John had worked for, all of his efforts to protect them, had been for nothing. She thanked God they had not taken Sandy and Jacinta as well, or even Sam Goodwin.

Her heart ached for them, and she wondered what they were all doing now. Sandy would be desperate, as would Jacinta. Sam would be trying to understand what had happened and why. No doubt he notified the police, and by now there would be a search for them.

She remembered John's warning about that. There was no place they could go, he said, where the cartel could not find them, reach them, do what they wanted to them. She looked out the window as the jet turned and taxied along a narrow concrete strip of runway to a small block building in the middle of a barren desert, landscape.

There were no trees or shrubbery, not even a cactus. Just barren, rocky plain extending to the surrounding mountains several miles away.

"Where are we?" she whispered to Billy.

"No, idea. Can't say how long we were drugged." He gazed around at their surroundings. "Someplace out west in the desert."

"You are correct." Garza stood as the plane rocked to a stop in front of the block building. "Someplace in the desert ... in Mexico."

"Mexico?" Isabella opened her eyes in surprise. "Is that legal ... crossing the border without going through ..."

Her mouth clamped shut at the absurdity of her question. Legality meant nothing to these men. The tall man's expression displayed a trace of humor at her comment.

"I see you understand that legality is not an issue for us." A thin, mean smile spread briefly across his face, and he turned to the front where one of the pilots opened the door. "Bring them inside," he called to his two assistants.

"Up! Let's go," the one who liked to do the talking said.

Chico jerked Isabella up by the arm. Roman motioned to Billy Siever to stand and then leaned over and grabbed Luis by the shirt to drag him to his feet.

"Go," he said. "Down the stairs and outside."

They moved to the front of the plane. The pilot had returned to the cockpit, going through the post-flight checklist with his copilot. They made a point of ignoring the three passengers whose hands were still bound with duct tape.

Billy, followed by Isabella, led the way down the short stairs to the desert floor. Luis came down in front of their guards, his knees barely able to support him. He stumbled on the last step and fell face first in the dust.

"Get up, rat!" Chico ordered and gave him a kick in the ribs.

Luis groaned and struggled to his feet. "Please," he whimpered. "I swear I don't ..."

His plea was cut short by a sharp slap to the face. "Shut up, rat! Move!" Chico motioned to Isabella and Billy. "You too. Get inside."

They plodded through the dust to the block building. Isabella noted a larger adobe-style building to the side, farther away from the runway. A windmill to bring water up from a well stood to one side. Two small palm trees stood in front of the adobe's entry stoop, out of place in the barren landscape. The attempt to beautify the desolate homestead seemed ludicrous.

She wondered who would have picked a place like this to live, and then realized the answer. Drug runners, of course.

They walked through the door into the block building. The air was stale and musty, not from humidity, but from the dust and odor of assorted reptiles that sought shelter in the building to escape the blistering sun.

No doubt, some made their nests there, birthed their young, deposited their droppings in the corners, and did their best to stay out of the heat. That was until the humans returned. Isabella noticed small shadows skittering away in the corners, as they walked in.

The square block building held four rooms, each about ten feet by ten feet. The room they entered had connecting doors to two of the others and they had doors into the fourth room. That last room held the toilet and a small sink and water tap.

The only way in or out was through the door they entered. The windows were high on the wall and not much more than slits, covered with steel bars. To say it was an uninviting place would have been an understatement. To Isabella, it looked like purgatory, a place where lost souls paid the price for their sins.

Garza waited for them inside. "You will stay here."

That was it. He said nothing more and turned to leave them.

"Wait!" Billy Siever looked around the room and then to Garza, the person they referred to as the tall man.

"What is your name?" he asked. "We have a right to know that."

"A lawyer's question," Garza said, smirking. "You have no rights here. You have what I allow you. Nothing more."

"Then why are we here?" Billy persisted. "At least you can tell us that."

"I think you know," Garza replied. "If not, you are a stupid lawyer." He looked at the others. "Think about it for a moment and you will see. You have one thing in common, one person, John Sole." His cold eyes bored into them. "Your fate rests in his hands."

Garza turned and stepped outside followed by Chico and Roman. The door closed. The sound of the locking bolt being thrown echoed inside the bare walls.

Only one thought held Isabella's attention as the door to their prison closed. *That was his name.*

After everything they had been through, she finally knew his full name—*John Sole*. She whispered it, her mouth forming the sounds, testing the two syllables carefully, as if tasting a new food. She didn't know whether to laugh or cry.

SIXTY-FIVE

All Our Asses

"What you doin' here? You ain't 'sposed to be back."

Monty Sole woke from his doze and blinked his eyes to clear away the cobwebs. He had just intended it to be a little power nap, but he didn't feel very powerful. After the nonstop journey from Georgia to Albuquerque, he was exhausted.

"You're an old man," he muttered to himself and sat up in the seat.

Three men surrounded the pickup. One stood in front, his hand resting ominously on the butt of a pistol only partially concealed in his waistband. The others, their shirts pulled up enough at the waist to reveal the guns they carried, stood on each side of the truck. The one at the passenger window glared in at Monty. John Sole spoke to the one on the driver's side.

"Here to see Big-C," Sole said calmly.

"You ain't 'sposed to be back," The hooded man repeated, his hand moving to the butt of his pistol as a warning to get the fuck out of the area.

Monty looked around. They were stopped in front of the bay door at an old gas station. It looked to have been abandoned for decades. The pumps had old-style rotary dial gauges. Monty sat up a little straighter in the seat, wishing he had armed himself before heading out with his son on whatever mission he had in mind.

There were supposed to be reinforcements here. That's what John said. Where were they? These three gangbangers did not appear ready to enlist in their little army.

"True." Sole nodded, maintaining his calm demeanor, unintimidated by the three threatening figures. "You remember me ... what I did for you?"

"Yeah, I remember."

"Good. I want to see Big-C," he repeated and added firmly, "Now."

The three men looked at each other for a few seconds. The one standing in front nodded, and they stepped away from the truck doors.

"Ar'right," the man on the driver's side said. "Inside."

"Come on." Sole exited the pickup and turned to look at his father. "It's alright. They're friends."

"That's not very comforting," Monty said stepping from the pickup, his eyes riveted on the man standing a few feet away with his hand on his semi-concealed pistol. "They don't seem to be the friendly sort."

"Friendly enough," Sole said and walked through the door into the old garage.

Inside, the three men led them to a small back office. It once belonged to the station owner and even after years of abandonment still smelled of grease, gasoline, dirty rags, and body sweat.

A large man sat behind a small desk, his feet propped up, swaying to the rhythm of the Latin tune he was listening to on his ear buds. He seemed relaxed and unconcerned about the unexpected visitors. Monty noted two monitors on a wall shelf showing high definition infrared views of the front and rear of the location. Their arrival had been observed.

The big man repeated the same admonition given by the men outside. "You ain't supposed to be back."

"Things changed. I have another arrangement for you. A profitable one." Sole returned the man's steely gaze and added, "And you owe me."

"That a fact?" The big man took his three hundred dollar sneakers off the desk and sat up straight in the old chair. "We paid up after what we did to them *Demonios de la Muerte*."

"That was for you," Sole shook his head and insisted. And for your sister."

"We been keepin' things quiet like we promised," Carlos —Big-C said.

"That is also good for you, isn't it? Good for your business."

"Hmmm." Carlos' eyes turned to Monty, standing quietly beside his son. "Who's this old fuck?"

"He's with me. We'll need him."

"He some kind of guru or somethin'?"

"He has skills."

"Really?" Carlos cast a doubtful glance toward Sole's companion. "What's your name, old man?"

"Monty. What's yours?"

There was movement behind as the three men crowded closer. Asking direct questions of their leader without an invitation to do so strained the protocols of gangbanger interactions. His dignity and stature as the one in the room with the biggest set of balls, or gun, or both, must be protected. Carlos shook his head, and they stepped back.

"Call me Carlos." The big man grinned and looked at Sole. "At least, he don't scare easy."

"Like I said. He has skills and we will need him."

"Alright," Carlos said, resting his forearms on the desk like a businessman about to negotiate a deal. "You saved my sister and helped us get rid of the DMs. I'll listen to what you got to say, but it better be good."

Sole spent an hour reviewing his plan. Carlos' skepticism transformed into acute interest. He listened attentively, asked a few questions, like a good businessman would, then sat back to think things over.

"This some serious shit. Lot of risk in doing something like this."

"Think of the return. It will be worthwhile, and like I said." Sole nodded. "You owe me this ... for your sister and for that little ambush we set up to eliminate your competition."

"Told you then we was paid up."

"Paid up for your sister?" Sole shook his head. "Really? Seems like a cheap price to pay for your own sister."

"That was the deal." Carlos paused and nodded. "But I suppose I do owe you something more. Juanita probably be dead if you didn't show up." Carlos leaned forward resting his elbows on the battered desk. "But after this, though, we paid up for sure ... in full. We walk away and no one owes anyone anything."

"Fair enough." Sole put out a hand.

Carlos rose from his chair and gave it one firm pump, then looked at Monty. "And you, old man. You up for this?"

"I reckon I am." Monty nodded.

"You reckon?" Carlos scowled and turned to Sole. "You really think this old man can do what it takes."

"He'll handle his end."

"He best do like you say," Carlos said, eying the white haired old man who would hold their lives in his hands when the shit hit the fan. "He don't, and all our asses be hangin' in the wind."

SIXTY-SIX

Preparations

"I'm going," Jacinta said firmly.

"No," Sandy replied more firmly.

"He's right Jacinta." Sole spoke softly, knowing she was as invested as anyone in the success of their plan to free the hostages. "Not because you are weak, but because there are special skills required, skills that you don't have."

"Teach me the skills!"

"There isn't time for that. No offense, but your presence would be a distraction that could cause someone to hesitate to look the wrong way. It could cost someone their life."

"And Sandy and Sam? They have the special skills you need?"

"Sandy and Sam have limited experience, but hunting they've picked up some familiarity with operating in the wild, and they know how to shoot. Even so, we will be asking a lot of them." He looked at Monty and nodded. "The two of us have had our share of this sort of thing ... understand what to expect. If something happens, if things go wrong, there won't be time to think or worry about another person. We will have to act quickly, instinctively. With you there, everyone will be worried about you."

"Still, I can help somehow."

"You can, but not at the exchange point. You will be waiting to help the hostages. They will be disoriented, confused. They will need someone to help them through the shock. That's as important as the rest of the plan." Sole leaned toward Jacinta. "Fact is, if we manage to get them out alive, it will be more important."

They sat in the Dupart's living room over the store. Maggie put an arm around Jacinta. "He's right."

Jacinta nodded without speaking, accepting the decision without liking it.

Sole looked at Sam and Sandy. "We start tomorrow."

The next week passed in a flurry of preparation. Carlos and the Cent Killers worked at procuring the weapons and ordinance Sole and Monty requested. It was a long list with some specialized items that Carlos warned would be pricey. Sole reminded him of the increased profits the Cent Killers would see when the operation was successfully completed. They agreed to split the expense and Sole handed over the bulk of his remaining cash from the sale of his home in Georgia.

Sam and Sandy spent time out in the backcountry around Albuquerque, acclimating to the desert and shooting at targets. It wasn't the same as pulling the trigger on a living person, but it was the best they could do with the time available to them.

Sole knew that there was really no way to prepare for the first time you fired a live round at another human being.

If all went as planned, that would never be necessary, and Sam and Sandy would be safely back across the border with the hostages without firing a shot. If not, Sole figured it wouldn't matter.

While Sam and Sandy honed their shooting skills, Sole and Monty crossed the border in his pickup, posing as a couple of hell-raising gringo tourists headed to Juarez for some R-and-R and female companionship. Once in Mexico, they drove through Juarez, picked up Highway 2, and disappeared into the desert.

A week had already passed and there wasn't much time to select the exchange point. He did not doubt that the man on the phone would keep his promise to execute the hostages if he did not contact him with the details of the exchange.

In a remote dry wash that formed a broad plain between two long ridges, he looked at Monty and nodded. "What do you think?"

Monty scanned the surrounding heights. "Wish we could get higher ... better field of vision that way but ..." He turned and eyed the walls of the cliffs along the wash and the narrow canyon road they had followed into the wash. He nodded. "We can make it work."

"Good."

Sole took out his phone and opened a mapping app, noting his location in the wash and the GPS longitude and latitude coordinates.

"Let's go."

They crossed back into the states from the small Mexican town of Puerto Palomas. There were a few questions from the Customs and Border agents, but they carried no contraband in the pickup. Sole's customary arsenal of weapons was stashed with Edgar Dupart.

As they drove back to Albuquerque, he made the call to the voice mailbox and read out the GPS coordinates for the exchange point. He ended the brief call and looked at Monty.

"Gonna have to turn you around quick. You'll have to be in position."

"Don't worry." Their eyes met and Monty nodded. "I'll be there this time. I promise."

SIXTY-SEVEN

This Ends

"Where are you going, Papi?"

Rosa Elizondo came into her father's bedroom where he sat on a chair putting on his shoes. Without invitation, she climbed up into his lap, seating herself there with authority, like a queen on a throne.

"To visit *Tío* Alejandro," he said, then opened his arms to wrap his daughter in a hug.

"I want to go!" Rosa exclaimed. "He has been gone for so long. I miss him."

"We all miss him, little one, but he will be home soon. He spoke to me just last night and promised." He leaned close and whispered in her ear. "And he said to give you something."

"What?" Rosa's eyes opened wide in excitement.

"This." Bebé Elizondo leaned down and kissed her forehead.

"Oh." Rosa's smile faded. "That's not the same."

"It will have to do for now." Elizondo lifted her from his

lap and stood. "I have to go now, but I promise I will come back soon with *Tio* Alejandro."

His wife Sofia and oldest daughter, Juana, stood by the door waiting. He kissed each on the cheek.

"When will you return?" Sofia asked.

"In a day or so. Not long. Alejandro has everything arranged."

"Then why must you go?" she persisted. "This is his sort of work, not yours."

"You forget my roots," Elizondo laughed. "I was once young and not fat like this." He patted his round belly. "Alejandro and I have faced many enemies together. This one has caught his attention in a way I have not seen before. I should be there. Besides, I will only be an observer. It is my way of supporting Alejandro. We owe him that."

"I suppose," Sofia said, doubt in her eyes. "It's only that I have a bad feeling about this one."

"A bad feeling!" Bebé Elizondo threw his head back and laughed. "Now you are becoming a superstitious old woman."

"I am not old," Juana said softly. "And I also have a bad feeling. I have never seen *Tio* Alejandro consumed like this."

"All the more reason for me to go," Bebé said firmly. "Stop your worrying. I will be surrounded by our men, and will stay far away from the action, only close enough to see Alejandro put an end to our enemy."

With that, he turned and walked into the hacienda's broad yard. The green grass was covered with fine dew from a morning mist that had climbed up over the hillside earlier, rising from the ocean below. A helicopter waited on the far side of the green expanse. Flanked by two of Garza's security men, Elizondo strode across the grass, his steps leaving dark impressions in the dew. Watching from the door, Sofia crossed herself and whispered a prayer for his protection.

The helicopter ride was brief, only to the airport in Lázaro Cárdenas. From there, Elizondo transferred to a waiting plane that would carry him to the desert airstrip. It was a small jet, capable of landing on the desert airstrip the cartel used for smuggling operations and which now served as the prison for Garza's captives.

They had spoken at length the night before, and Garza explained how the exchange would work. When it was completed, John Sole would be dead, along with the hostages. Garza assured him he was prepared for any eventuality. The problems with the detective would cease and their operations could return to normal.

Elizondo wasn't so sure. The North American had led them on a chase for more than two years now, always one step ahead of the cartel. If Garza's plan did not succeed, Elizondo wanted to be there to insist that this fruitless game of cat-and-mouse end.

The twelve hundred mile flight to the deserts of northern Mexico lasted three hours. Garza was waiting on the airstrip as Elizondo stepped from the jet. He nodded formally as Bebé strode forward to embrace him.

"Alejandro! It is good to see you." Bebé stepped back from the embrace, beaming at his deputy. "All things considered, you look well."

"All things considered I am well." Garza nodded.

"So, this is where the trap will be sprung." Elizondo looked around at the surrounding hills excitedly.

"Not here, but near enough that we can go by car."

"Good. I have had enough of flying for today."

"You are going with us?" Garza's eyes flickered for an instant in surprise.

It was not easy to surprise his deputy, and Elizondo smiled. "Yes, of course. This affair has taken you away from us for too long. Surely, you didn't think I would miss the conclusion, did you?"

"I don't think you should be there," Garza began.

"Enough." Bebé lifted a hand to cut him off. "This is not up for debate. I will be there, and after you will return to Lázaro Cárdenas with me."

The message was clear. Bebé had reached the end of his patience in the matter of the American. He was there in person to emphasize that point, and if necessary force Garza to return with him.

"Come, show me your hostages," Elizondo chirped like a boy on a school outing. "I want to see everything you have done to prepare for this moment."

They seemed remarkably calm, Elizondo thought, except for the rat. The man and woman looked up with interest as he was escorted into the building that served as their prison. Neither spoke. The rat trembled, his eyes wet with tears of dread. Elizondo grinned at him and nodded. The rat had good reason to tremble, and no doubt understood better what was going to happen to them.

Afterward, they retired to the nearby adobe house for refreshments. The security team surrounded the house as Bebé and Garza sat on the porch sipping wine and smoking cigars.

"You have prepared your trap well, Alejandro."

"Thank you."

"You understand why I am here?" Elizondo put his cigar in the oversized ashtray and looked at his deputy.

"I do," Garza replied, meeting his gaze.

"This ends," Elizondo added for emphasis. "One way or another, it is over."

Smiling, round-faced Bebé was the head of the most vicious cartel the world had ever known. There would be no further discussion on the matter. Even Alejandro Garza acquiesced and nodded without speaking.

SIXTY-EIGHT

A Chance to Survive

The trek through the desert of northern Mexico was different in many ways, but also similar to Monty's service in Vietnam almost fifty years earlier. There were no jungles, or leeches crawling up his leg to find the tender spots near his groin, or Viet Cong hiding in the brush to ambush his ass. In that respect, this mission was easier on him.

The similarities, however, were taxing. Monty Sole was pushing seventy years of age, and although he was in good shape for a child of the fifties, he was no longer a young man of nineteen. The fifty-pound pack on his back seemed to weigh a hundred.

The load was mostly water, a necessity in the desert. The other necessity was ammunition for the Winchester 70 slung over his shoulder. For food, he carried a plastic bag filled with nuts and M&Ms. Food would not be a problem. If all went well, the mission would only require two days in the field. If things went to hell in a hand basket, as John had warned they might, food would be the least of his worries.

The rifle belonged to his son. Actually, it had been Monty's. John inherited it after Monty disappeared from his life. They considered having Carlos and the Cent Killers procure a more modern rifle, but Monty refused, telling his son he had grown up using the Winchester, learned his shooting skills hunting with it in the north Georgia mountains, and would not be comfortable trying to acclimate to another rifle on such short notice. John had agreed and handed over the Winchester along with as much ammunition as Monty could carry.

Carlos—Big-C personally ferried him across the border that morning and drove him within ten miles of the exchange point.

"You be careful out there, old man," he called out as Monty climbed down from the SUV and pulled the rifle from its place of concealment under the floorboards.

"You too," Monty said. "Watch out for the others. Get in and out fast when they make the exchange."

"Shit! You ain't got to worry about that." Carlos grinned. "Fucking *Salvajes* are fucking crazy. We gonna get as far away from them as we can as fast as we can. You best do the same."

"That's the plan." Monty nodded, shrugged at the pack straps, adjusted the rifle sling, gave a wave of his hand and strode off across the desert.

A dust cloud rose behind him as Carlos spun the SUV's wheel and headed back toward the border to cross at a different point from where they had entered Mexico.

He was ten miles from the dry wash they had selected for the exchange. In making their plans, Monty and John agreed that any closer would risk detection.

Monty walked a mile before he stopped and unslung the

rifle. He loaded three .30-06 rounds into the magazine and knelt, squinting through the scope at a creosote bush three hundred yards away. The first round sailed high. Two clicks on the scope and he fired again. The second round kicked up dust a yard to the right of the creosote. One more click on the scope. The third round passed through the center of the bush, sending a spray of dust into the air ten feet behind it.

Satisfied, he slung the rifle over his shoulder again and continued the trek. They had calculated an average speed of a mile and a half an hour for the hike to the place they had selected on their scouting trip. With rest and water breaks included, they figured a conservative total of seven hours transit time. Monty was motivated and made it in five, maintaining a blistering two-mile-an-hour pace with the pack and rifle.

His early arrival was fortunate. Concealing himself in a crevice on a small ledge in the wash's cliff wall, he ducked low at the sound of an approaching vehicle. A minute later, a flatbed truck pulled into the desert clearing below. Three men climbed down from the bed, each carrying a rifle and small pack.

Their arrival was not unexpected, but the timing was. Monty realized they had underestimated their adversary. He was taking nothing for granted and was as diligent in his preparations as John had been.

Pushing his back into the shadows of the crevice, he pulled a pair of binoculars from his pack and scanned the scene below. One of the men was pointing and giving directions to the others, indicating places in the rocks along the cliff-like bluffs that formed the walls of the wash. Rifles slung over their shoulders, each made his way up the canyon side to their designated spot.

Monty realized there was little chance of being discovered. The attention of the men below was focused entirely on the area designated for the exchange. Still, he took no chances and stayed well back in his hiding place.

From his vantage point, he could see that each carried a hunting rifle similar to his but in .308 caliber. The rifles were fairly equally matched. The .308 was preferred these days by many shooters who felt the trajectory was flatter and more accurate.

Monty had to agree. The Winchester's .30-06 round had a trajectory more like a rainbow than a line, but he knew from his Vietnam experience that the real difference was in the shooter. He was supremely familiar with his weapon and confidant in his abilities.

The movements of the men below and the noise they made indicated that, however vicious they might be at killing in the streets and barrios, they were not as proficient in this type of shooting. That was understandable. Firing at a target, undetected from concealment, was a skill that had to be learned. In Mexico, on their home turf, concealment was not a major issue for *Los Salvajes*.

He was outnumbered, but in his mind, the advantage was his. He could see them. They had not seen him. If all went according to plan, he would make sure they never did.

Monty put the binoculars down, crossed his arms over his chest, and closed his eyes. In a few moments, he drifted into sleep. The men below continued their noisy preparations for the meeting that would take place in the wash below.

Sam Goodwin leaned forward, peering through the coating of dust on the windshield. He drove the pickup with Sandy riding shotgun and Sole in the crew cab rear seat.

"Not too close," Sole cautioned.

"Right." Sam eased off the accelerator.

Ahead, the two lead vehicles left a plume of dust hovering over the road. The first vehicle, the SUV driven by the Cent Killers' leader, Carlos, was invisible in the dust cloud. The second was a van, the same van that they had used the day Sole guided them in the ambush and slaughter of the *Demonios de la Muerte*. Including the drivers, there were four heavily armed gang members in each.

Their role would be crucial in the exchange of hostages. They were to make the initial contact with the cartel and the mystery man who had spoken to Sole on the phone, calling himself the enemy.

Fair enough. An enemy he was, and John Sole had no intention of underestimating him. He had taken every precaution he could think of to give the hostages at least a fighting chance at survival.

He harbored no illusions about their chances. Despite the promises to the contrary from his enemy, Sole knew that once he was in the cartel's grasp, they intended to kill Isabella, Billy, and Luis Acero.

"Stop here," he said.

Sam let the pickup roll to a stop while the two lead vehicles proceeded another half mile to a point where the canyon road they followed came out into the broad wash and open desert. Sole exited the pickup and turned to Sam and Sandy.

"You know what to do. Get them out of here fast. Don't stop. Don't come back."

"What if there's trouble?" Sandy asked. "If they start shooting?"

"Then shoot back, but do not stop the pickup. Get back across the border. Carlos and his men will be behind to cover you."

"And you?" Sam asked.

"I'll be alright. I have a plan to end this once and for all." It was a lie. Sole knew that his plan was thin at best, but he nodded reassuringly. "Your job is to get them back across the border. Now turn the pickup around and be ready to get the hell out of here when Carlos comes back with the hostages."

"Right." Sam put the truck in gear and backed around in the dirt so that the truck pointed in the direction they had come.

"Good luck, John." Sandy had been through a confrontation with men sent from the cartel once before in Texas and understood better than Sam what they faced.

"See you on the other side." Sole tried to give a reassuring smile. Sandy was not reassured.

He began trotting along the canyon road toward the opening into the wash. Ahead, the Cent Killers' two vehicles inched forward slowly, checking things out. When he reached the point where he could see beyond the canyon into the wash, Sole crouched near a jumble of rock and dirt that had fallen from the canyon wall during one of the infrequent rains that hit the region.

He watched Carlos' SUV slow to a stop a hundred yards from four vehicles, positioned in an arc facing them. Sole counted fifteen men, armed with automatic rifles, pistols tucked in their belts. A tall man stood in the center, and Sole knew he was the man who had taken the hostages, who had killed his family and partner. Fists clenched, he waited for the show to start.

Alejandro Garza had his binoculars out, spinning the focus ring as the vehicles approached. He nodded, satisfied. Soon, now. Very soon. The sooner the better.

He glanced over his shoulder at Bebé Elizondo watching from one of the vehicles. He had overruled Garza's protestations and insisted on being present for the final confrontation with the American. Garza understood that it was Elizondo's way of emphasizing that this quest to destroy their enemy ended today.

Fair enough. Garza turned back to the approaching vehicles. The next few minutes would bring everything to a conclusion.

Carlos guided the SUV closer, now just fifty yards from the cartel's waiting vehicles. Dust swirled around them as he braked to a stop and the van pulled up alongside. Making the initial contact with *Los Salvajes* was risky, but not as risky as what was to come.

The gringo had demonstrated his prowess in arranging the military-style ambush that eliminated the *Demonios de la Muerte*. Besides, participating in the exchange was a good business decision. The promise of ending the cartel's domination of the drug market in Albuquerque, and the chance to eliminate a good portion of Cent Killers' competition would boost their profits enormously.

The dust swirled away, and he exited the SUV. Five

other armed Cent Killers got out of the van and formed a protective arc around Big-C. They were outnumbered and outgunned and they knew it, but if all went according to plan they would be gone long before gunfire was exchanged.

"You the man in charge?" Carlos called across the open space to the tall man standing in the center of the cartel's circle of vehicles.

"Where is he?" Garza called back without answering the question.

"Watching." Carlos smiled. "He has a plan."

Garza nodded, his eyes briefly scanning the cliffs along the wash and the canyon opening. He had known the detective would be too clever to expose himself without the release of the hostages. It didn't matter. The result would be the same.

He shrugged and called back. "What is his plan?"

Carlos turned and nodded to the van. Two more Cent Killers came out and walked forward to place three bundles in the sand between the two groups.

"What is this?" Garza asked.

"He said you would know," Carlos replied and motioned for his people to retreat to the van.

Garza regarded the bundles and nodded. This man, John Sole, was an adversary worthy of respect. Still, he doubted that he would have the fortitude to go through with what he was proposing.

Garza motioned to one of his men who stepped forward and gingerly examined the three bundles. After a minute, he returned to Garza and verified that they were three bomb vests, the sort of suicide vests worn by terrorists. Each was packed with Semtex plastic explosives and a detonator that could be activated by a cell phone or radio transmitted signal.

"Now what?" Garza called out.

"First thing, he said to remind you no cell phones or radios. We wouldn't want to set them off by accident."

Garza eyed the gang leader, wondering why they had never recruited someone like this into the cartel operations. He had balls, and no doubt was planning to cash in on whatever Sole was planning.

"I can make you a better deal than he can," Garza said quietly, doubting that the Cent Killers leader would be swayed but figuring it was worth a try. As he expected, the gang leader shook his head.

"Already have a deal. Besides, I owe him."

"Then you will die with him," Garza said and shrugged. "So what do we do now?"

"Have them put the vests on," Carlos answered and repeated the instructions he had rehearsed with Sole word by word. "He is watching. When he sees that they are wearing the vests, and they are safely away, he will show himself. If you try to stop them, he will detonate the vests and you will never find him or be able to use the hostages against him in the future. He said to say, he will hunt you down and kill everyone and everything you care about."

"I see, but I doubt that he has the capacity for that. Still, it is an interesting proposition. I have a question, though."

"What?" Carlos watched the cartel man closely, expecting some attempt to thwart their plans. There wasn't any though, only a simple question.

"Does he honestly expect me to believe that he would kill his friends in this manner?" Garza shook his head. "I don't think so."

Carlos was ready for that question.

"He said to tell you he knows you will kill them anyway. This way they may die, but they have at least a chance to survive. He also said to remind you that you said their chance of survival was fifty-fifty. Now he figures it is sixty-forty. These are acceptable odds to him. If you want him, this is how you get him."

Garza had to admit the American was clever. He correctly deduced that his friends would be killed in any event and devised a plan that gave them at least a chance of survival. Let them leave safely, or he uses the bomb vests to kill them with his own hands, and the war between them continues.

But would he really do it? It was clever, but it was also a desperate proposal. Garza could not repress a smile. It didn't matter. Despite all of John Sole's planning and precautions, Garza knew the end would be the same

"One more question," he called out. "How do I know he will reveal himself and come forward?"

Carlos turned and lifted a hand. A half-mile away, a form rose and stood on a boulder at the mouth of the canyon.

"He says you will be able to identify him, and he is close enough for you to follow and catch him if he tries to get away."

Garza lifted the binoculars and studied the face he recognized from the newspaper stories. It was true. At that distance, he could not escape Garza's men, but it would also have been almost impossible for them to get off an aimed shot before he disappeared behind the boulder. Once again, the former detective had demonstrated his cunning, choosing a position that would not afford a clear field of vision into the canyon's mouth for any of the snipers Garza had positioned along the adjacent cliffs.

It didn't matter. Garza had also planned and was just as cunning. More importantly, in his mind, he was ruthless.

"Alright." Garza lowered the binoculars. "Signal him that we will comply."

Carlos raised his right arm and gave a circular wave toward the canyon mouth, then stepped back to the SUV and got behind the wheel.

Garza turned and nodded to one of the vans that had accompanied him. The side door slid open, and a terrified Luis Acero tumbled out, falling to his knees. Isabella and Billy followed, equally terrified but managing to remain on their feet.

"Each of you put one of those on."

The three hostages froze, eying the explosive vests from a distance of several feet. Billy Siever knew immediately what they were.

"If you are going to kill us, just do it," he snapped at the tall man standing in front of the circle of cartel vehicles.

"Not me." Garza shook his head and smiled. "Your friend. He said he would rather kill you himself than let me do it. He seems very stubborn on this point." He motioned to the vests on the ground. "Put them on if you want a chance to survive."

Without a word, Isabella stepped forward and picked up the nearest vest, held it up, inspecting it for a moment and then threw it over her shoulders and slid her arms in like she was donning a sweater on a chilly day. Billy watched and followed suit.

One of Garza's guards prodded Luis Acero forward with the muzzle of an AK-47. Hands trembling so badly that Isabella had to help him get his arms into the vest, Luis looked like he might pass out at any moment.

Watching from the canyon mouth, Sole climbed back up on the boulder, waving them forward and exposing himself to the cartel's men. He saw the man motion to the others to lower their weapons.

Isabella, Billy, and Luis shuffled to the Cent Killers' van and disappeared inside. Carlos gunned the SUV's engine and made a fishtailing circle, leading them away from the cartel vehicles and back into the canyon. The van followed.

Sole waited until they passed him at the canyon's mouth, then climbed down from the boulder and stepped into the open. He had given them a chance to survive. Now, he had to increase their odds of survival.

SIXTY-NINE

It was Enough

A half-mile up the canyon, Carlos slid the SUV to a stop. The van halted behind them in a cloud of dust.

Sandy, followed by Sam, ran to the van, and helped the hostages out. They stood under the canyon walls, bewildered and confused.

"What are …" Isabella began, then sobbed and threw her arms around Sandy and Sam. "I thought I'd never see you again."

Billy took a deep breath and offered a teary-eyed prayer of thanks. Luis' wobbly legs were unable to support him any longer, and he toppled to the ground, sobbing, the dust coating his wet face.

"There's no time for this shit!" Carlos and two Cent Killers ran up and began pulling the explosive vests from the hostages. He yelled at Sam and Sandy, "You know what to do! Do it!"

"Right." Sam nodded. "Come with us."

They pulled Isabella and Sam to the pickup while one of the gang members dragged Luis. Isabella recognized it as

John Sole's truck. The three hostages were crammed into the rear crew cab seat. Sam climbed behind the wheel. Sandy sat in the front passenger seat, a rifle over his knees with the muzzle out the window.

Sam revved the engine and raced along the canyon road away from the wash and toward the border.

On foot, Sole approached the waiting cartel vehicles. He forced himself not to scan for Monty's position in the nearby cliffs along the wash.

The tall man who seemed to be in charge gave a nod. Ten men armed with automatic rifles jumped into two of the vans and went roaring across the open space toward the canyon mouth.

Sole held the remote detonator up high for them to see as they passed, but they ignored him and raced into the canyon. He turned toward the tall man, blinking the dust out of his eyes. He had to trust the plan. Everything was in Carlos' hands now.

He came closer, and for the first time, saw his face clearly. Had his wife and children seen that face before they died? The children were murdered in their sleep, but Shaye had gone into the hallway, no doubt to confront the killer. She was a light sleeper. A small noise, a creak of a floorboard, might have alerted her that there was an intruder in the house. She must have seen that face before.

Teeth clenched, Sole drew nearer, fighting down the rage inside. Uncontrolled emotion would get everyone killed. The next few minutes would be critical. He focused on the tall man.

The face was calm, patrician even, descended from

some Spanish conquistador no doubt who had come to the new world seeking his fortune. Sole watched the man's eyes. The irises were dark brown, almost black and as devoid of feeling as a shark's.

As he stopped in front of the tall man, another, shorter and rounder, exited one of the vehicles and came to stand beside him.

"So this is the great enemy of *Los Salvajes*," the short round man said.

He spoke first, and Sole knew by the deference the tall man exhibited toward him that this round man was at least an equal to the tall man, perhaps even his boss, or even the boss of cartel bosses.

The round man's face was smooth and unmarred with worry. He looked more like a barber than a drug lord and murderer. Sole knew that killers, like everyone else, come in all shapes and sizes.

"You have what you wanted," Sole said. "Give me one thing in return."

"What?" the tall man asked.

"Your name." Sole blinked hard and swallowed down the lump of rage in his throat.

The tall man nodded and cast a glance at the short round man at his side. A second passed before he returned the nod, and just like that, they confirmed for Sole who was the boss of bosses.

"Call me Garza," the tall man said.

"And he is?" Sole stared at the round man at Garza's side.

"That is not important," Garza replied. "Enough questions."

"Alejandro," Elizondo said, throwing a beaming smile at Sole. "Our adversary should understand who has taken everything from him … his wife, his children, and now his life." He met Sole's stare with a coldly curious gaze, a cat examining a mouse he was toying with. "I am Juan Manuel Elizondo. They call me Bebé."

Finally, he could put faces and names to the phantoms that had haunted him. It was enough.

SEVENTY

It was Over

"They cannot escape. Surely, you understand this," Garza said, gazing at the point where the canyon road opened into the wash. "I admit to a certain respect for the effort you made to save them and to adhere to the code you have chosen."

"More of your code bullshit." Sole shook his head in disgust.

"Call it what you will," Garza said calmly. "But my code, my ruthlessness, has brought you here. Your friends will die in a few moments and you will follow. There was no way for you to prevail."

"We'll see."

The first reports of gunfire drifted over them. All eyes turned toward the canyon.

The lead cartel van careened down the canyon in pursuit of the vehicles that had escaped with the hostages. The driver never saw the small dusty hump in the middle of the road, or if he did, he did not recognize it as a threat. The van accelerated, tires spinning in the gravel, the driver intent on overtaking the Cent Killers' vehicles. Their mission ordered by Garza was simple—kill everyone.

The van entered a bend in the road. Concealed in the rocks along the side, Carlos lifted an arm high in the air and depressed the button on the remote transmitter Sole had provided. Covered with dust and gravel in the road, the three explosive vests worn by the hostages exploded simultaneously as the first van passed over them.

The van and its occupants disintegrated in a fireball that sent a plume of black smoke into the morning sky. The second van slid in the gravel, the driver desperately trying to avoid the debris and crater where the first van disappeared. He managed to veer to the right and slide to a stop against the canyon wall. This only simplified the work for Carlos and his Cent Killers.

Wedged tight against the canyon's perpendicular rock face, the cartel's killers could only exit the van on one side. From the rocks on the far side of the road, the Cent Killers took full advantage of their predicament, pouring round after round into and through the cartel van. Only a few wild, desperate shots were fired in return before all movement and life within the van ended.

Carlos left his place of concealment and approached the bullet-riddled hunk of metal and flesh. The five occupants were dead. He raised the Tech-9 machine pistol and put a round through the head of each for good measure then, turned and nodded at the other Cent Killers.

"Let's get the fuck out of here."

There was no argument. The SUV and van sped away,

following the pickup Sam had driven with Sandy and the hostages.

"You are right about one thing. They didn't escape." Sole turned to face Garza, a glimmer of victory in his eyes. "Your men are dead."

The thick column of black smoke boiling over the canyon ridge told the story. A few seconds later, the booming report of the explosion followed by the unmistakable thuds of distant gunfire echoed down the canyon and out into the open.

Chico Saludo, standing a few feet from his boss, muttered, "*Mierda*." Shit.

In the next instant, his head exploded in a red blossom of blood and skull fragments.

"Target down," Monty Sole whispered to himself, concealed in his crevice high on the cliff wall. He slid the .30-06's bolt smoothly back and forward, loading another 165 grain round into the chamber and centered the scope on his next target.

The plan his son had devised was not complicated. The explosion and gunfire down the canyon were his cues.

Monty's role was to eliminate as many threats as possible at long range while Sole dealt with the cartel leader at close quarters. There were no mothers holding babies here to shield the targets. These were the people responsible for the murders of his daughter-in-law and grandchildren. Monty would see that they paid for that.

He went to work. A squeeze on the trigger and a moment later, another of Garza's men crumpled to the ground just as he swung his rifle up to search for a target.

"Target down," Monty repeated as he would have for his platoon leader in the jungles of Vietnam. Another cartel man fell.

Sole had emphasized to his father that he would deal personally with whoever seemed in charge. That appeared to be the tall man facing him. Only if his son went down was Monty to take out the leader.

Until then, he was to focus on the other cartel men and prevent them from interfering. Monty fulfilled his role with methodical efficiency, using skills honed fifty years earlier.

Two cartel men were down in a matter of seconds. With two van loads gone and eliminated down the canyon road, only two armed security men remained alive with the tall man. Another man, short, chubby, and round-faced, had come from one of the vehicles, but he was unarmed and did not seem to be an immediate threat.

The two remaining armed guards fired their AK-47s wildly at the walls of the wash, spraying bullets with no effect. One dropped as he pulled the trigger on his rifle, a dark red stain spreading across the center of his chest.

Roman Madera paused, loaded another magazine into the AK-47, and aimed at a spot he thought might be the source of the gunfire. He sent a spray of .762 rounds into the cliff wall a hundred yards from Monty's position. He never fired again. Monty sent a round through his skull, and he toppled forward into the dust.

Less than thirty seconds had elapsed. Four cartel men were down.

There was only one target remaining. The short, round-faced man turned and began running toward one of the vehicles. Monty prepared to send one more round downrange, sighting at the center of the man's back. As he squeezed the trigger, a roar, followed by a spray of dirt that stung his eyes, startled him. It had taken nearly a minute, but the three cartel snipers who had been in hiding as a backup measure finally located him in the crevice on the cliff above.

His bullet struck the round-faced man low and off-target, entering through a kidney and exiting through his lower abdomen. Bebé Elizondo fell to the ground screaming in anguish, hands clutching at his intestines to keep them from spilling out of the fist-sized exit wound.

More explosions from gunfire below forced Monty back into his crevice. They had him zeroed in now. Round after round chattered and skittered around him. One ricocheted off the rock and opened a gash under his left eye. It was only a matter of time before they worked their way up the cliffs to a point where they could get a clear shot at him.

Monty Sole had no intention of waiting for that to happen. His son was engaged in a life and death struggle below. His promise to be there this time rang in his ears and pounded in his heart.

He leaned from his crevice in search of a target. One of the cartel snipers had climbed to a point fifty yards away. Monty sent a quick round through his chest and sank back into the crevice as more shots were fired in his direction from the other snipers.

The gunfire subsided. Monty inched around the crevice opening to try and spot his adversaries. Two shots rang out, both fired by the cartel snipers.

Monty fell back into his hiding place. Only one of the bullets found its target, but it was enough, tearing a hole in his neck and cutting the carotid artery. Monty lay back, his hand holding his throat, head resting against the rock wall. His chest rose high in deep breaths at first. Within seconds, they became more shallow, fading until they were just short panting gasps.

The remaining cartel snipers turned their attention to the struggle in the wash below. The two men writhing and wrapped together in the dust were indistinguishable. There was no way to identify a target from that range.

With Monty's first shot, Sole lunged at the tall man who had called himself Garza. They fell to the ground with Sole on top while Monty did his work, taking out the armed men. They fought like animals in the dirt, rolling over, looking for an advantage, gouging at eyes, clawing at exposed flesh.

Surrounded by his men and superior force, Garza's arrogant confidence and disdain for what he called Sole's code became his weakness. Sole waited for a chance, and when it came, he took full advantage.

Physically, they were equally matched, both lean, strong, and well-muscled. Garza found that the ruthlessness he believed gave him an edge over Sole's moral code meant nothing now. Reduced to this final animal struggle in the dirt, Sole was free to act as ruthlessly as Garza, and he did.

They squirmed in the dirt, panting and sweating as Garza's men went down one by one. Sole heard more shots and knew that Garza's men were trying to find Monty. He had to end this struggle quickly and help his father.

Rolling onto his back, he seemed about to give up and submit to Garza. Hands clenched at his throat, and Sole sputtered, gasping for air. He relaxed his body as Garza leaned forward, knees pressing into his chest, ignoring everything except his hands around his adversary's throat.

Sole's arm was free enough now to reach for the hunting

knife in the sheath at his side. Like the Winchester, it had been his father's.

He plunged the blade deep into the lower side of Alejandro Garza's abdomen until the point pierced through his back. The man's eyes opened wide in surprise. For a moment, his grip tightened on Sole's throat. Sole withdrew the blade and stabbed again, and again, thrusting the blade into the body of the man until the hands around his throat loosened.

He rolled out, pushing himself to his knees, blood dripping from his arm and the knife in his hand. Garza toppled over, and Sole gazed down at the man who had murdered his family.

There was no begging for mercy, no pleading look in the killer's eyes. Both knew that begging was pointless. Eyes wide open, he waited for the justice the North American held in his hand.

Sole obliged him. He passed the blade over Garza's throat, severing flesh, arteries, and cartilage in one motion. Alejandro Garza was dead.

Sole rose to examine the scene. The four, armed cartel men lay dead, looks of surprise and confusion still on their faces. He lifted an AK-47 from the ground beside one of the bodies. The round-faced man who had grinned and identified himself as Bebé Elizondo still lived, clutching at his spilling guts and moaning in the dirt near one of the vehicles.

"I can make you a rich man," Elizondo gasped at the man standing over him. "Richer than you can imagine. You can replace the man you killed. I can use someone like you. I can …"

Elizondo's negotiation ended. Sole fired a single round through his head, then turned his attention to the cliffs where the sniper firing had subsided. He scanned the rock walls, searching for the crevice where Monty had hidden, there was no movement.

Lower down, he could make out two forms clambering over the boulders until they came out to stand in the wash two hundred yards away. Sole checked the AK's magazine. Only three rounds had been fired from it, including the one that ended Bebé Elizondo's life. He readied himself to end the fight.

The two men exchanged words that Sole could not hear, then turned and began trotting along the cliffs at the edge of the wash away from the scene of the carnage. Sole understood.

They might be killers, but they were *paid* killers. They did not risk themselves without the promise of compensation. With their source of income lying dead in the dust, they took the reasonable business approach to the situation and called it a day.

Another cartel might be willing to pay for their skills, but that wasn't Sole's problem. He watched until they dwindled out of sight, lost against the background of the cliffs.

Then he sank to his knees in exhaustion. It was over.

SEVENTY-ONE

Life

"Where is John?" Isabella sat on the Dupart's sofa sandwiched protectively between Jacinta and Maggie Dupart.

"He said to say you won't see him again … that he is sorry for all the trouble he brought to you." Sam Goodwin sat in a chair facing her, their knees touching, her hands clenched in his.

"Did they kill him? Did he survive?" Isabella's red-rimmed eyes were damp with tears.

"Maybe. We're not sure," Sam said softly. "He had a plan … he and Monty."

"Who is Monty?"

"Someone from his past. John didn't go into details about him, just that he had some skills that they needed to help get you away." Sam shrugged. "There's a chance that they survived, but we aren't sure. Our job was to get you out. He said no matter what, drive and keep driving until we were over the border and back here."

"But how will we know?" Isabella looked up.

"We won't," Sandy said and knelt in front of his mother. "John wanted it that way. He said to move on. He wanted you and Sam to build a life together."

"Sounds like John," Billy Siever said from a chair in the corner of the room. "Always taking the fall for things."

"He said it was his fault that all of this happened to you." Sandy nodded. "His way of making up for things, I guess."

"He didn't create the cartel ... sell drugs ... murder people for money," Billy said. "They did all of that. If we are victims, he is too."

"Anyway, he said we wouldn't see him again, whatever happened." Sandy shrugged. "I believe him."

"So what's next?" Edgar Dupart stood in the kitchen doorway, arms folded, looking over the somber gathering of survivors.

"We go home, I suppose." Billy had been on the phone almost non-stop with his panic-stricken wife from the moment he found a phone to use. "Can't see that there is anything else to do."

"And John?" Isabella looked up. "We just leave him?"

"It does seem wrong," Sam agreed. "Just go on about our lives like nothing happened while John faces God knows what. I'm no hero, but it seems wrong to just turn away."

"It was what John wanted ... why he did what he did to get us free. I don't have any answers, and it's not the first time John has saved my ass, but I believe in my heart of hearts he would want us to move on." Billy shrugged. "I'm going home to Vera."

Luis Acero watched and listened from a dark corner of the room. The only thing he had in common with these people was the time spent imprisoned with them. They came from a different world, from different lives where people didn't sell drugs on street corners or make side money by snitching to police detectives. They were John Sole's people, and he was not one of them.

"And you?" Edgar Dupart watched Luis eying the others uncertainly, not sure of his place among them. "You will go home as well?"

"Don't have no home," Luis whispered through lips still swollen from the beating Garza and Roman Madera had administered.

"Your friend was our friend. He saved Ben from the gangs. You are welcome to stay here for as long as you like." Edgar's eyes narrowed. "But no selling drugs while you're here. You can help out in the store, look after things until you're ready to move on."

It was like peeking through a window into another world, the world John Sole had inhabited before Garza took his family from him. It opened his eyes to another facet of the detective who had saved his life twice now. These were good people; the type of people Sole once went home to at the end of the day, and Luis knew he was not one of them.

"No." He shook his head. "I better go too."

"Where?" Billy asked. "There's nothing for you back east."

"Then not east." Luis shrugged. "Somewhere else. It doesn't matter where. I'll find someplace."

They spent two more days with the Duparts, recovering from their ordeal and waiting things out to make sure the cartel was not looking for them. Carlos stopped by once to assure them that everything was quiet. The *Los Salvajes* cartel was eerily silent, and the gangs who worked with them were looking for partners. He told them it was a good sign, that Sole had accomplished what he set out to do.

The next day they left. Sam drove Isabella and Sandy

back to Georgia. Billy took a flight to Atlanta, where Vera waited at the airport. Luis Acero took a bus to an unknown location.

Each was headed to a life given back to them by John Sole. None had any idea where John was or if he even lived.

Except for her mother's sobs, the hacienda overlooking the Pacific was quiet. Juana Elizondo had received the news of her father's death from one of Alejandro Garza's men as she stood on the porch beside her mother. Her younger sister and mother had been sobbing and wailing non-stop since then.

Juana wept her tears with the brief efficiency her father always commended her for and then went to work. There was an empire to run.

She sat at her father's desk in his study. A folder lay open before her. It contained the information compiled by Alejandro Garza on the American, John Sole. She turned to a man standing unobtrusively in a dark corner of the room.

"Come here, Reynaldo."

"Yes, *señorita*."

He was one of the men assigned by Alejandro Garza to ensure the security of the Elizondo family. Juana had known him since she was ten and he a nineteen-year old recruit from the Cuban *Commando Tropas Especiales*.

At first Reynaldo had merely been a guard, walking the perimeter of the estate or watching the banks of video surveillance monitors at night while the family slept. As the years passed and his face became more familiar, he rose to head the house security team, reporting directly to Garza himself.

Now, rocked by the deaths of Garza and Bebé Elizondo, he stayed near the family, unsure what to do next, but reluctant to leave the post that had taken him out of the squalor of a *Centro Habana barrio*. He was also reluctant to leave Juana.

Their nine year age difference seemed to shrink as she matured into a young woman. Reynaldo Gutierrez began to look for assignments from Garza that would bring him into contact with Juana. A trip to Mexico City to shop. A concert in Morelia. A visit with friends to Paris. Their interactions were always proper, platonic, and well-chaperoned by her mother, Sofia.

Juana knew that he was smitten with her, even if others did not, and even if he could not have put his feelings into words. While she did not overtly encourage his feelings, she did not discourage them either. In her heart, she knew that Reynaldo and his hidden affection for her might be helpful at some point. Just as Bebé hid his cold, calculating ways beneath a soft, round face, Juana concealed hers beneath her pretty exterior.

"I will require your assistance, Reynaldo," she said, smiling. "Will you help me."

"*Sí, señorita*. Always."

Reynaldo stood before her, his eyes intent, anticipating her next words the way a faithful dog waits for the command to fetch. Yes, he would help her. He would die for her if she would only say the word.

"Good. Thank you for that. I knew you would be here when I needed you most, and I will need you a great deal in the next few months."

"I will always be here, *señorita*."

"*Jefa*. From now on you may address me as *jefa*. I will be taking my father's place."

"*Sí, jefa.*" Reynaldo said the words solemnly and nodded.

"Now leave me. I must think. Close the door, but stay close. I may need you."

"*Sí, jefa.*"

Reynaldo bowed his head, turned, and nearly floated to the door. When it closed behind him, Juana lifted a wrinkled newspaper clipping and studied the anguished face in the picture.

"I know your pain, John Sole." she whispered, staring at the image. "There will be more. I promise you that."

She replaced the clipping in the folder and closed it. There would be time for that later. There was work to do now.

Los Salvajes must survive. Her father would have wanted it that way.

It was impossible to bring the dead back, but one could learn from their mistakes. Her father and Alejandro Garza were excellent teachers. She would not repeat their mistakes.

It took an hour to climb to the top of the cliff walls and then descend to Monty's sniper nest in the rock crevice. Sole knew what he would find. That didn't make it any easier. The father he had known only for two short weeks lay still and silent in the bloodstained rocks.

Sole sat with him for a long while, leaning against the rock wall, gazing out through the opening to the blue desert sky and wash below. Side by side, shoulders touching, they sat together, father and son, one alive and feeling the pain of loss once more, the other finally beyond feeling and pain.

The sun was setting as he pulled himself from the crevice cave. Rose-colored shafts of light sprang into the darkening sky from behind the opposite ridge. Sole turned and began pulling rocks from the cliff to pile in front of the opening. It was the only tomb he could provide his father. He wished there was a way to bury him in Cassit Pass beside his mother. Clara would have liked that—Monty too, he thought.

But it was impossible. They would rest apart from each other in death as they had spent much of their lives. Both would have understood.

The first stars were beginning to show in the evening sky as he began the trek back toward the border. He had twenty miles to cover before daybreak. From there, he would cross back into the States, make his way to Albuquerque, pick up his truck, and once again say goodbye to the Duparts.

And after that, what? He had no idea. For now, it was enough to walk across the desert under the stars and remember those who gave him life.

Clara brought him into the world. Monty died protecting the life Clara had given him. In time, John Sole might be able to work out exactly what he would do with that life.

Next in the Sole Justice series

vinci-books.com/theghost

In a battle between small-time miners and a ruthless global conglomerate, a lone drifter becomes the only hope for a kidnapped girl and her desperate family.

John Sole finds himself caught in the crosshairs of a bitter conflict between independent mine operators and a powerful corporation determined to seize control. Despite his best efforts to remain uninvolved, Sole makes a promise to rescue the abducted daughter of a mine operator, thrusting him into the heart of the struggle.

Turn the page for a free preview…

The Ghost: Chapter One

DAMNED IF I KNOW

"There she is."

"You sure it's her?"

"Goddammit, Chester. You always askin' questions like you think I'm some kind of fool?"

"Sorry, Cope. I didn't mean nothing by it. Just wanted to be sure." Chester nodded. "You're right. You been doing this sorta thing a lot longer than me. I guess that's why I'm nervous about getting it right. Never done anything like this before."

"Here." Cope held out the binoculars. "See for yourself."

"Thanks." Chester took the binoculars, leaned against the truck bed's side to steady himself, and peered through the lenses. After a minute, he nodded. "Yeah, it's her Jeep. Gotta be her."

"It is," Cope snapped and snatched the binoculars back to give the pickup on the road below a last look. "I'd say she's doing about twenty, maybe twenty-five miles an hour. That gives us plenty of time."

Copeland Plunkett and Chester Welch leaned against the rusty fenders of a nondescript, beat-up four-wheel-drive pickup on a rocky promontory overlooking the canyon road. A winding switchback dirt trail climbed the mountainside to their observation point. It would take at least ten minutes to ease the pickup down the trail, over boulders and ruts.

That was no worry. From their vantage point, they could see the Jeep still had a good five miles of twisting turns and creek beds to navigate before it reached the bottom of their mountain. They had more than enough time to descend and set up before the Jeep rounded the last bend and found them waiting.

Cope pulled a ski mask from his back pocket. "Put your mask on and let's go."

Amelia Downes took the turns on the winding canyon road cautiously but with confidence. She'd driven it a thousand times before, had learned to drive long before the legal driving age on this very road in her father's old truck, him seated at her side, clutching the handhold on the doorframe when she took a turn too fast, but generally letting her figure things out without saying too much.

She rounded a bend and swerved expertly thirty yards up the mountainside to the right to detour around a boulder in the road. As big as a house, the boulder had been there as long as she could remember. For all she knew, it could have been deposited there ten thousand years ago, or a million. It didn't matter. The people who used the road accepted the boulder's presence the way they accepted the surrounding mountains, a permanent part of their landscape. The boulder belonged there as much as the mountains, so they detoured around it and kept going.

The first two hours of the trip to Elko to pick up supplies wound through the northern Nevada mountains, across creek fords, and around more boulders even larger than the one at the bend. It was a desolate country, and the isolated stretch of road could have been the model for all the lonesome roads sung about by everyone from Sinatra to Yoakam.

Amelia loved the desolation and loneliness of it. Hours, and sometimes days, could go by without ever seeing another vehicle. That suited her. She was at peace with the solitude.

Nestled along a small river in the northern Nevada mountains, the tiny town of Turnbridge was home. She had no desire to leave for the big city like most of the young people had. Still, she looked forward to the monthly run for supplies and made a day of each visit, picking up essentials and socializing for a few hours.

She spent her days helping her father and Uncle Ron Benson run the D&B Mine operation, which meant she spent most her of time with older men, some very old. The visits to Elko gave her a chance to catch up on news, chat with friends her own age, flirt with the taphouse bartender, sip a beer, and down a burger she hadn't cooked herself. Cal Jackson should be working the bar today, and Cal filled out those Wranglers just right.

She smiled and settled back. The day was dry and clear, the gravel road in reasonably good condition. What the hell. She knew this road like the back of her hand. Her foot pressed harder on the accelerator.

The old pickup made the final switchback turn a couple of hundred feet above the canyon road. Below them, the Jeep was in sight, much closer than they expected.

"Shit!" Cope sat in the passenger seat, pistol in hand, ready to carry out their orders. "We're gonna miss her. Step on it!"

"Step on it?" Wide-eyed, Chester turned his head.

"Faster! Gotta get there before her!"

Chester jerked his head back around to focus on the dirt trail, his knuckles turning white as he gripped the wheel and his foot stomped on the accelerator. The canyon road rose to meet them like a concrete wall. The pickup hit a dirt mound at the point where the mountain trail came out onto the road. The front end lifted a couple of feet and the truck's underframe bellied out as it came back down before sliding into the roadway without slowing.

"Nooo!" Chester yelled and closed his eyes.

Amelia looked up to the right in time to see the pickup come flying at her over the dirt mound. Then the world went dark.

Amazingly, the old truck's suspension held. The Jeep wasn't so fortunate. The cattle pusher mounted over the truck's grille cut a deep jagged V in the passenger side and pushed the Jeep across the road, slamming it into a rock wall.

Cope and Chester sat stunned for nearly a minute as the dust settled. The only sound was the popping and creaking of cooling metal.

Then Cope looked at Chester. "What in the fuck did you do!"

"You said go faster," Chester mumbled, still dazed.

"I didn't say kill her!"

"Kill her?" Chester's eyes were wider than ever now. "Did I ... You don't think she's ... Do you?"

"How the fuck do I know?" Cope pushed his door open and stepped out, rubbing his right knee. "You busted my knee up, dammit!" He limped around, working the knee up and down and wincing with the pain.

"I didn't mean to, Cope. Really, I didn't" Chester got out of the driver's side patting himself up and down to make sure he was all in one piece. "That's alright, Cope. I ain't hurt,"

"Well, that's just fucking great for you, ain't it."

"All I mean is, I can do what you want," Chester said meekly. "Just tell me what and you set back and rest up some. Only ..." A worried look came across his face. "Only don't tell me to ... you know ..."

"What? Don't kill her?" Cope sneered. "It's likely you already done that."

"Don't say that, Cope." Chester followed his partner to the Jeep.

Peering through the Jeep's caved in passenger side, they could see Amelia Downes laying against the driver's door, her head against the cracked window, bleeding. She wasn't moving, and the driver's side was lodged against the rocks.

"Shit," Cope muttered and walked around to the front of the Jeep. He turned, surveyed the ground around the rock wall, and pointed. "There, pick up that rock."

Chester paled. "Wh-what you want me to do with it?"

"Pick up the damned rock!" Cope's voice echoed off the mountain slope and rock wall.

"No." Chester shook his head solemnly, terrified that Cope's next order would be to smash the girl's skull with the rock. "Not 'til you tell me what for."

"So's we can break out the damned windshield and pull

her out." Cope shook his head in disgust. "You really are a moron, aren't you?"

"Don't say that," Chester said and bent over. "See I'm getting the rock."

It weighed about twenty-five pounds. Chester lifted it and banged it against the windshield. Nothing happened.

"Harder," Cope said.

Chester lifted the rock and hit the windshield harder. A spider web crack opened up in the glass.

"Again!" Cope shouted.

Chester repeated the process, and the safety glass shattered into thousands of pieces.

It took fifteen minutes to cut the seat belt off and work Amelia away from the door, over the steering wheel, and out through the shattered windshield. They laid her in the dirt beside the Jeep, catching their breath. She was alive but bleeding from the wound in her scalp and unconscious.

Chester said nothing and stood gawking at her. Cope rubbed his sore knee, thinking.

"What now?" Chester finally asked.

"Damned if I know."

The Ghost: Chapter Two

WHERE TO NOW?

Where to now? It was the question he asked himself a thousand times a day.

Sole gave himself the usual answer. I have no idea.

It had become his routine. Each day, he pointed the old pickup toward the sun, or away from it, randomly moving from state to state, from coast to coast, guided by instinct, or by chance. He wasn't really sure which.

He hoped the winding path he'd followed would be impossible to track. In the last year, he'd put ten thousand miles between himself and the confrontation in the Mexican desert with the *Los Salvajes* cartel.

On the surface, there seemed to be no reason to continue running. *Los Salvajes* had gone silent after he eliminated their leader, Bebé Elizondo, along with Alejandro Garza, the man who murdered his wife and children. John Sole had hoped that would be enough to kill the pain and fill the black hole sucking away his reason to exist.

It was not. The pain remained, just under the surface, a

wound scabbed over but not fully healed. The slightest thought, a brief memory of a smile or laugh ripped the scab away, and the wound bled.

Part of him was grateful for that. Healing and deliverance meant that the memories would fade away, that he would forget. He couldn't allow himself to do that.

So now what? The answer was simple—now nothing. Nothing was easy. Nothing was safer for everyone. There were no commitments, no attachments, no responsibilities. Without commitment, there could be no guilt. Without attachment there could be no loss. And without responsibility, he could not hurt others.

So, he kept moving, remaining anonymous. He stopped here and there to work some odd job and put a few dollars away in his pack. Then he moved on again.

He was moving now along a two-lane highway in northern Nevada, generally pointed toward Idaho but with no particular destination in mind. He'd driven all night and a couple of hundred more miles since daybreak. It was time to rest.

A sign up ahead hanging at an intersection with a gravel road read,

Turnbridge - 22 miles. Riddled with bullet holes, the sign hung precariously from a rusted metal pole.

He slowed, yawned, and stretched in the seat, then nodded and turned the pickup off the asphalt onto the gravel. "Looks like you're not going to make Idaho today, John-boy," he muttered.

The first few miles ran through ranch land, and he considered pulling off into one of the pasture entrances and sleeping in the pickup, but he'd done that three nights in a row, and besides the ache in his back, he was bone tired. Just twenty miles or so, and there will be some sort of bed and maybe something to eat besides convenience store snacks.

The ranch country disappeared. Mountains closed in around the road, in places rising vertically from the shoulder for thousands of feet.

After a few miles, he came to a stream crossing the road. Another sign warned, *Dickinson Ford—Danger—Do Not Cross During High Water.* He slowed and poked his head out the driver's window. The stream trickle pleasantly enough and he could see the gravel bottom. To be safe, he engaged the pickup's four-wheel-drive and rolled slowly into the water. He could hear a waterfall somewhere up the canyon. No doubt the spring melt would turn the stream into a torrent.

He crossed without a problem and accelerated as much as he dared in the dwindling light on an unfamiliar road. Ahead there was a fork, one branch taking a sharp bend to the right and the other heading off straight ahead, up a mountain ravine.

Which way now. Straight ahead or to the right. He looked around for another sign to guide him to Turnbridge, but whoever was in charge of signs must have figured that if you made it this far, you knew where Turnbridge was. If not, you were on your own.

The road heading up the mountain ravine seemed an unlikely place for a town to be situated. He opted for the bend to the right.

Fifteen miles more to Turnbridge, he reckoned. The thought occurred to him that the town might be nothing more than one of the old mining ghost towns scattered around the Nevada backcountry.

"Well, you're committed now," he whispered.

Sleeping with ghosts didn't seem so bad. Ghosts were quiet and didn't shoot at you.

No, but they haunt. They bring back memories and that's not good. He shook his head. Stop thinking and drive. Hunched over the wheel, he focused on the road to Turnbridge.

Grab your copy...
vinci-books.com/theghost

About the Author

Glenn Trust is the author of the bestselling *Hunters, Sole Justice, and Journey Series* of mystery/thriller/suspense novels. He has also written standalone works, including *Dying Embers, Mojave Sun,* and short stories.

There are no superheroes or knights in shining armor in his stories. According to Trust, knights are for fairy tales. His books are gritty and based in the real world, with characters who face their frailties while dealing with their roles in the story. The heroes are average people doing the best they can.

The villains, as real villains often do, look like us. Trust's monsters hide behind the smiling faces that pass us on the street. They look like us, and this makes them more frightening.

He is a Georgia native but has lived in most regions of the country at one time or another. Varied experiences, from construction worker to police officer, corporate executive to city manager, color and provide insight into the characters he creates. His stories are known for detailed plots, solid research, and realism.

Today, he writes full-time and lives quietly with his wife and two dogs, Gunner and Charlie.